RAVEN

TIMBER-GHOST, MONTANA CHAPTER

DEVIL'S HANDMAIDENS MC
BOOK 6

D.M. EARL

© Copyright 2023 D.M. Earl
All rights reserved.
Cover by Drue Hoffman, Buoni Amici Press
Editing by Karen Hrdlicka
Proofread by Joanne Thompson

All rights reserved. No part of this book may be reproduced in any form or by any electronic or mechanical means, including information storage and retrieval systems—except in the case of brief quotations embodied in critical articles or reviews—without permission in writing from the author.

This book is a work of fiction. The names, characters, and places portrayed in this book are entirely products of the author's imagination or used fictitiously. Any resemblance to actual events, locales, or persons, living or dead, is entirely coincidental and not intended by the author.

The unauthorized reproduction or distribution of this copyrighted work is illegal. Criminal copyright infringement, including infringement without monetary gain, is investigated by the FBI and is punishable by up to five years in federal prison and a fine of $250,000.

If you find any eBooks being sold or shared illegally, please contact the author at dm@dmearl.com.

ACKNOWLEDGMENTS

Karen Hrdlicka and **Joanne Thompson** my editing and proofreading team. I'm totally blessed to be working with these two ladies. Between them Karen and Joanne polish my stories so they shine. With their eyes on my stories I feel y'all are getting the best book possible due to their experience and knowledge of how I write.

Debra Presley and **Drue Hoffman** @ **Buoni Amici Press**. These two women are the BOMB. My two publicists work endlessly to handle the social media aspect, formatting, publishing and so much more which then allows me to concentrate on my writing. With them as part of the team I know everything is getting done and correctly and timely.

Enticing Journey Promotions. Ena and Amanda help me with every new release and are very professional and always on top of everything.

Bloggers. To every single one of you. What you do for each and every one of my releases and stories is something that I can never repay. Please know how much I appreciate each share, mention, post, and video.

My **DM's Babes** (ARC Team) and **DM's Horde** (Reader's group). These women in these two groups have become part of my family. I'm thrilled to spend time and engage with each and every one of them.

READERS without each of Y'all I'd not be able to live out my life's dream of writing books that make people tingle and just feel deep in their souls. Your support fills my heart and feeds my soul.

Chuck. Without you and your support not sure I'd have written as much as I have. Thank you for always having my back and supporting me. Means the world babe. Luv ya.

ONE
'RAVEN'
BRENNA

It's been almost two weeks since I saw Ash's dumb-as-fuck brother, Reed, at the hospital. Well, not actually that stupid 'cause he's one of Tank's doctors, but still my body trembles just thinking about his name. Ash. Since then, I can't get him outta my mind, which isn't good for me because the last time he just up and disappeared on me. It nearly broke me and if not for my brothers, sisters, and parents I'd probably have ended it all. Actually, Mom made me go speak to that therapist in Bozeman, which in the long run helped.

What hurts the most are the memories on video running through my mind day and night. I thought I'd finally put it all to rest, then I see Reed out of the clear blue sky. Knowing sleep will not happen tonight, I get up and throw on my ratty-ass sweatshirt from my community college time. Well, it hits me, not community college and it's Ash's sweatshirt, but I can't part with it.

Everything else I got rid of, except for a few boxes still in my parents' basement. I make my way to the kitchen, grab a coffee pod, and start my Keurig up.

While I wait, I go to the fridge, grab my oats creamer, and smile. God, would he love this creamer. Milk never agreed with him so he started drinking his coffee black, which he hated, especially since his family has one of the largest dairy farms in Montana. It was his dream to take over the family business after his dad retired. None of his brothers wanted it and he loved the land. Reed obviously became a doctor; Rue is on the rodeo circuit. Alder is working as a ranger for the state of Montana. Rowan, the baby, is still at home from what I hear. And the little I know from my mom, Ash is still on the farm doing what he does best, following his daddy's orders. Though I hear he built his own ranch home on some of the property.

Grabbing my coffee, I put in my creamer then head to the front porch of my cabin. Tink was gracious enough to make sure all of the Devil's Handmaidens officers had the opportunity of having their own home. It also makes it easier for us to be close by if needed. Over the last few years, it's been the best idea she ever came up with. For Christ's sake, my club sisters really can find them: the men in their lives along with total drama.

Pushing back and forth on my porch swing, I think back on our dramas from Tink to, holy shit, Shadow, didn't know that sister had an emotion in her entire tattooed body. Well, until Panther came along. Damn, she hit the jackpot, though Tink's Noodles is no slouch. Biggest surprise was my hippy sister, Taz, putting her star on an Intruder and that brother being Enforcer. Talk about badass though, all I ever see when he looks at Taz is true love shining from his eyes. Vixen I relate to, as she found her one and only when she wrestled with her past. Ironside, the ex-FBI agent, had a rough go, not only with Vixen but all of us because we all knew how badly she was hurt when he all but disappeared on her. Finally, Glory and another Intruder, this time a prospect, Yoggie. Damn, I moved too slow on that one. My mind draws up that memory of walking into Glory's room to find that fine as fuck specimen of a man lying in her bed. In the end though, each one of my sisters is finally enjoying life and that makes me happy. I'm still lonely and alone and that doesn't make me content.

Trying to blank my mind of everything, I still, swing, and watch the sun start to rise. It surprises me that, even being a night person, I love watching the sun come up. Especially like today when the ranch is quiet since everyone is probably still asleep. I can barely hear the horses whinny and some moos from our cows. Someone has let one of the dogs out 'cause I can hear them barking. Ranch life is truly the best. And being a Devil's Handmaiden sister comes in a close second.

Seeing a truck make its way up the long-ass driveway has the hair on the back of my neck go up. At this time in the morning, who the hell could this be? I know between Tank and Tink the gate is guarded at all times, so whoever it is had to pass through that checkpoint. I see the truck pass the main house and swing around to the cabins. Well, which sister is expecting an early morning guest or maybe a booty call? Can't wait to see where the pickup stops so I can have some juicy news. I can then make one of my sisters crazy as I think up all kinds of funny shit.

So stuck in my own thoughts of fucking with a sister, it takes me a second or two to notice the truck stops in front of my cabin. Who the hell is it? *One of my brothers*, I think, though I don't recognize the brand-new Chevy Silverado parked in front of me. Trying to squint to see who it is, the sun isn't helping, so I lean forward and wait. Apparently, whoever is in the truck is doing the exact same thing.

When the door opens, I've convinced myself it has to be one of my brothers because who else would come out this early. Unless maybe it's Onyx. Now that she's part of the Blue Sky Sanctuary, I've seen her around a lot. She's trying to repair our relationship, and so am I. I miss my sister.

Hearing the door slam, I look and I sympathize with Tank as I feel like I'm having a goddamn heart attack. Never in a million years would I think it was him. Gave up on that when he dumped me during our engagement party at my folks' house. Yeah, we were young as shit. I was what—seventeen, no, maybe eighteen—and madly in love with this asinine jerk. Never taking my eyes from him, he makes his way to and up the stairs. When he's in front of me, the cowboy hat comes off and he hangs on to it with his fingers, which are turning white. This is his rodeo not mine, so I sit back and wait.

"Morning, Darlin'. Ya ain't gonna make this easy on me, are ya? Told Reed nothin' had changed but he swore you were different. Guess he's an idiot wearing a doctor's coat. I came here to try and make peace, Brenna. Is that even possible? Can you give me a chance to explain?"

Taking time, I try to keep my temper in. First, I try to count to ten, then twenty, and finally fifty. No, it isn't working, damn it. Closing my eyes, I take in a couple of deep breaths like Taz is always telling us to do when stressed out. Now that worked, so I do it again. Okay, I can do this. Until I opened my eyes and Ash is standing right in front of me. Dang it, he can still move like a bobcat. He almost scared the crap out of me.

"Still move like a wild bobcat, don't you? What do you want, Ash, I got shit to do?"

"Told you, want to make peace between us. Since that day our families are torn apart and it's our fault. My mom misses your parents, and I'm sure they miss her too. My brothers haven't been hunting with your brothers since then. We need to fix this, Darlin'. So I'm being a gentleman, coming to you to try and figure out how to do it."

Feeling my head getting ready to blow off my shoulders, I stand up so fast the swing moves back and then hits me in the ass and upper thighs, sending me straight into Ash's arms. For Christ's sake, I can't make this shit up. He grabs my upper arms, holding me until I catch my balance.

"Get your hands off me, Ash, you lost that privilege a long time ago. And as far as making peace, a good way to start said peace is to tell me why you dumped me in the middle of our GODDAMN ENGAGEMENT PARTY, you asshole. Then you took off with Patsy Woods. How do you think that made me feel, you dickless jerk?"

He has the decency to drop his head down, but as usual says nothing. I'm done, so I move past him, going to the door. Before I can push it open, he's in front of me, blocking my way. Oh no, not playing any games. I shift and when I lift my leg to knee him in the groin; he moves faster than me. In the next minute, I'm up against the cabin and his entire body is plastered behind me. I can feel how huge he's gotten, and I mean huge everywhere. His breath is on my neck before I feel his lips there. Holy shit, no. I don't want this, swore to never forgive him for what he did and put me through. He annihilated my heart.

I try to push him off but he's too strong. Then I throw my head back and hear an 'oof' but he doesn't let go. When he leans into me again, I can feel something wet dripping on my neck, so I must have gotten him in the nose. Good for me.

"Darlin', enough of this bullshit. We need to have a grown-up conversation. Yeah, I know, Brenna, something you're not used to, but ya need to hear me out. So is that gonna happen today or do I need to keep coming here 'cause I don't have a problem with that.

One way or another we are gonna talk, you tell me when."

Before I can say a word, I hear a growl right before Ash is yanked away. When I turn, I see Avalanche whaling on him. Fuck, Shadow's Big Bird is going to kill my Ash. Wait, he isn't mine anymore.

"Avalanche, no, please let him up. Shit, brother, you're going to kill him and he isn't worth it. Avalanche, please."

He looks up at me then down at Ash, whose face is already swelling. Avalanche drops his head, all that long beautiful brown hair of his covering his face. Then he lets Ash go and stands up. When he offers Ash his hand, my heart wishes I could fall for Avalanche. He's one in a million.

"Raven, what the hell is going on? I come back here to do a walk by and see this asshole, well cowboy dude, has you pushed up against the cabin. Oh shit, did I interrupt a sexual moment? Are you into what do they call it, yeah, voyeurism? Oh fuck, didn't mean to intrude, you two. I can get outta your hair. Sorry, man, not my intention at all."

"Avalanche, shut the hell up. No, you didn't interrupt a tryst at all. And no, I don't like people to see me having sex, for Christ's sake. This is my ex, who suddenly decided we needed to make nice. Don't know why, but that's what he's trying to sell to me. As I told Ash, I'm not buying it, but he won't take no for an answer. As you can see by his bloody nose, I tried to explain it first vocally then physically. That's where we are right now."

Ash has been watching the interaction between Avalanche and me, and the look on his face shocks me. He actually looks hurt. What is that?

"Is he the reason we can't move on, Darlin'? Obviously, you did...uhm, moved on. Good for you. Sorry to bother ya. Hope you both have a nice day. No wait, I actually hope it totally sucks cow balls. You have no idea how hard this was for me to come here, Brenna, and you treat me like a piece of shit on your boot. Was gonna try to explain and hoped you at least would listen, but no, not you. Well, you are getting what you wished for, I'm gone."

With that he stomps to his truck, turns it on, shifts, pulling out, and leaves us in dust and smoke. I'm in total shock and just stand here watching his truck drive away. I actually jump when Avalanche whistles.

"That motherfucker has it bad, Raven. Whatcha do to him back in the day? Almost feel sorry for the son of a bitch. Come on, tell your big handsome brother, what's going on?"

Instead of speaking, I feel a breakdown coming. I try to make it up the porch and inside the cabin, but Avalanche grabs my arm and before he can pull me into him, the tears are already running down my face. Damn, there go my credentials as the clown. Nothing funny here, for sure.

"Come on, Raven, let's get inside and you can tell your strong studly brother all about it."

His words do exactly what he intended. I snort then giggle. We make it back into my cabin, with me still crying but also laughing. Damn, why doesn't fate work for me? I could be in bed with this stud instead of offering him some coffee. Oh well, welcome to my world.

TWO
'RAVEN'
BRENNA

Paybacks are a total bitch. After all the shit I've given my club sisters over the last couple of years, especially when they were lucky as fuck and found their 'one,' when Reed opened that door and mentioned Ash, all bets are now off. There's not a day that goes by when one or another of my club sisters ain't digging for info on the mysterious Ash. I'm so goddamn sick and tired of it all, but shit, what can I do…nothing. I guess being the club clown didn't help me at all, especially now.

And to top it up, Freak and I are still working on all the information that is being sent our way by Slick, or as everyone in our club but Taz calls him, the 'fuckin' loser.' Even though he's trying to make amends for what he did to Taz and Teddy, in my opinion, he's got a hell of a lot more to do. Though he's busting ass to put to paper and a USB stick all he can remember from his time with the Thunder Cloud Knuckle Brotherhood. Every other week, we get a certified delivery with yet another memory stick for the two of us to run through and try to find anything that might help us bring down the worst human trafficking group of total assholes. The Thunder Cloud Knuckle Brotherhood.

Now since the day Avalanche found Ash and me up against my cabin, he's been keeping an eye on me. And damn, it ain't no hardship. I wish with all my heart I could look at him as the devilish handsome man he is and not as one of my brothers. I don't even get a tingle or anything when he's around. I mean, yeah, he's always hawt and smells so good. And such a gentleman. I know my club sisters are wondering if something is going on between the two of us. Well, until that morning when Ash drove off like a maniac. Of course, Shadow was just pulling up and had just about all the prospects with her in Panther's huge-ass truck. So, Squirt, Kitty, Dottie, Dani, and the new one, shit, what the hell is her name? Some kind of candy, I don't personally give a fuck. She was a survivor from one of the circuits we busted up and she's afraid of her own shadow, but Tink thought it might build her confidence. Who knows?

When Ash blew past them that put up warning lights all over. Then they took a walk to my cabin and busted right in to see Avalanche with me crying in his arms, and all hell broke loose. Between Shadow screaming that he, or as she calls him Big Bird, better let her sister go and the prospects laughing like loons thinking maybe they busted up a booty call, I got an instant headache. No matter what Avalanche or I said, no one believed us until, of course, Shadow put two and two together.

"Raven, who the fuck was in the truck leaving here like their ass was on fire? No, don't try to lie, we saw him with our own eyes. So come on, sister, tell us who was behind the wheel looking like smoke was coming outta their ears? And, Big Bird, you got something to do with that anger? Remember, honesty is the best policy."

She ends with a shit-eating grin, enjoying this way too much. Finally, seeing my face, Avalanche literally pushes them out, turning to tell me he'd check on me later. Now that was four days ago and every morning he's here with coffee and a breakfast sandwich, and then again right before I settle in for the evening. He's quickly becoming my new best friend. Or new best guy friend.

Sitting on my front porch, finally alone and able to think for a second or two, it dawns on me what Shadow said a few days ago is true. Ash was beyond pissed. Or was he jealous? Really, how could he even think he has the right to be that after what he did? Since that happened, I've never opened up enough to let any man in. That doesn't mean I've not, ya know, had some fun here and there, but generally I've closed myself up. Can't handle that pain again.

Seeing dust coming up the road, I pray to God it's someone visiting someone else in these cabins. I've become like a drive-thru with visitors. But no, once again it's for me, though this time it's my sister, Onyx, which is a welcome surprise, I think. I sit, wait, and watch as she pulls in front and parks her kick-ass truck. She flings the door open and steps out with a bag of something. Then she reaches in and grabs a bottle too.

Uh oh, what's going on? Just as I'm about to ask, I see another vehicle on its way and I don't have a clue. As it gets closer, I see it's an Audi and damn fancy. Not one of my friends. We don't have that kind of bankroll, and if we did, would spend it on something much more important than a frigging car. When the door flies open my mouth drops. I know that hair anywhere 'cause it looks just like mine. When the rest of the body flows out, my eyes bug outta my head. No way, it can't be.

"Shut your mouth, lil' sister, gonna catch flies. And it hasn't been that long, has it?"

Onyx giggles then throws her arm around our sister, Bray. As they walk up to my tiny porch, they both look like models and, even more shocking, like best of friends. When did this shit happen? I didn't even think anyone in our family spoke to Bray. Not since her last get-rich scheme. I'm lost for words. Onyx comes right to me, putting her handful of shit down on the table, then pulls me up into one of her tight hugs. Damn, this feels like home. Being the youngest girl, if Mom wasn't around, my two older sisters would always know when my head was up my ass and I'd end up in one or the other's arms. Onyx doesn't rush, just holds me close. Then to my utter surprise Bray comes up, squeezing in behind me and smooshes me between the two of them. I try really hard but can't stop myself when I feel my eyes fill up. Fuck, come on, cut me some slack. When did I become such a wimp?

"Come on, little sister, let it all out. We're here for you, like always."

Bray gives me a squeeze then lets me go, looking around before going in my cabin and coming back out with one of my kitchen stools. Onyx lets me go but looks me in the eye. It's like she can read into my soul, which she always could. When she sees whatever it is, she nods then takes a seat in the rocker as Bray positions the stool in front of us.

"Okay, great way to start our first sister visit in forever and we start with drama. Really? What the hell? And what rock did you crawl out from under, Bray? I can't remember the last time I even saw you. Do you still even live in Montana?"

She laughs that deep husky one I remember, shifting her long-ass hair outta her face. She gives Onyx a quick look then glances back at me.

"Yeah, Brenna, I live in Montana, you smart-ass. See, you haven't changed, you silly clown. Actually, I'm not too far away, probably just between Oliver's and Bennett's ranches."

My eyes shoot to Onyx, who just raises that irritating eyebrow of hers. She's watching me like a hawk and it's starting to weigh on me.

"Okay, what gives? Why are you two here, did someone die? Oh my God, are Mom and Dad okay? Or is it one of the brothers? Shit, did Orin or Oliver have a heart attack or maybe something with either Bennett or Brooks?"

I hear Bray chuckle and Onyx smiles widely before she shocks the shit outta me.

"Wow, surprised you remember all your siblings'

names since Mom said you haven't been around hardly at all recently. So being the good daughters the two of us are, we decided to bring some of your favorite chow from the Wooden Spirits Bar and Grill. Kiwi said to tell your cook outdid herself today. Then I stopped at the Quick Stop and picked up some tequila. We are gonna figure out what's going on with you, lil' sister. And no, don't tell us nothing. I saw Reed at the hospital and he told me Ash is losing himself because you're fucking some huge Indian and wouldn't give him the time of day."

My mouth drops open and I can feel how shocked I am. Then to top it off, Bray jumps on the bandwagon.

"Yeah, Alder told me when he got home last night that Ash is a bear to be around. He asked me what my little sister did to his little brother. Since I wasn't in the know when Onyx called, I jumped right in."

Takes me a minute but then it hits me. Holy fuck.

"Are you two fucking Ash's older brothers?"

Bray's head drops and Onyx stares at me. Then she lets loose.

"Baby sister, just because you have no good sense when it comes to the Sterling brothers doesn't mean we don't. Now, Reed and I are just friends, though we've gotten a bit closer, but no, not like that; get your mind outta the gutter. Now that one over there, if you were paying attention, she said when Alder got home, so they obviously are playing house. I just found out myself. She's not telling me everything. Bottom line, we are here to help you get your head outta your ass yet again and figure out Ash is your one and only."

Shaking my head at both of them, I throw my hands in the air.

"Are you two lunatics? Do you remember what that dickless asshole did to me? How could you even think I'd want to give him a second chance?"

Bray leans toward me from her stool all serious.

"Brenna, since that day all you've done is mope around, and as far as I know, haven't given anyone else a chance. Then you up and joined the motorcycle club and almost broke Mom and Daddy's hearts. Finally, you've isolated yourself from the family and that has to stop now."

Jumping to my feet, I get in her face.

"You're one to talk, Bray, you left and never looked back. How dare you give me shit? Where the hell have you been the last couple of years? Did you check in with 'Mom and Daddy' like you're inferring I should. And for your information, I check in with Mom at least once every other week and we've met for dinner at the Wooden Spirit Bar and Grill at least once a month. Ask Mom, she'll tell you though, Dad is stubborn, he might come to every dinner."

Bray's head is down but when she lifts it, I see such deep pain, I'm shocked. Then my world falls apart.

"The reason I've not been around, little sister, is because I did something stupid. I trusted the wrong person, who sold me to some monster who lived in a cabin. So for the last couple of years, I've had no way to get ahold of any of you. If not for Alder, who found and saved me, I'd probably have died out there in the wilderness. Another reason I'm reaching out to you, need to talk to your club because Mom said that's what y'all do. Rescue victims and that motherfucker still has four other women up there somewhere."

Then she covers her face and starts to sob. Onyx looks stunned and I feel like a total asswipe. Then I hear the bellow before the bear. Looking up, I see Avalanche coming toward us, his face full of anger.

"Lil sister, what the ever-lovin' fuck is goin' on here? Who's this woman crying and why is she? Come on, pretty lady, it's okay."

When Avalanche reaches for Bray, she goes ape-shit wild. Nails come out while she growls at him. Onyx jumps up, grabbing her and putting her into a chokehold. Avalanche stares for just a second then kneels in front of Bray.

"Hey, look at me. I'm not gonna hurt you, I swear to Christ. My name is nitsaa yikah tsintah (arbre). Yeah, I know a mouthful, so my family and friends call me Avalanche. I'm friends with Raven, well, the entire Devil's Handmaidens Club, along with Tank's club the Intruders. You can trust me, ask my lil' sister, Raven."

"Looks like we have something in common. Raven is my, as you call her, 'lil' sister' and if she trusts you that means she's done a background search and knows just about everything about you. So as hard as it is, I'll try to trust you. I'm Bray, by the way, Brenna's older sister. Do you know Onyx already?"

I watch as Avalanche and Onyx look at each other, wait, what was that look? They both nod but don't say a word. Just as I'm about to ask what's going on between them, I see a truck coming down our way. Shit, just what I need at this moment. Ash fucking Sterling.

THREE
'ASH'
ASHTON

As I slowly make my way to Brenna's little cabin, I see there are a few folks on the front porch and stairs. Again, that dude with the long as fuck hair, what did she call him… Avalanche. And it looks like the women are, no way, it's her two older sisters, Onyx and Bray. I've seen Bray around in the last couple of weeks since Alder brought her down from the mountain and set her up in his home. Not sure what that's about, but I keep my nose outta other people's drama. Reed told me the other day when I saw him that he bumped into Onyx and they stopped to catch up. Shit, didn't want to do this in front of a crowd, but my brother, Reed, is right. I need to apologize not only to Brenna but also her 'friend,' Avalanche. I was a total dick, nope, a jealous asshole and I had no right to act like that. It's just when I see her and how gorgeous she is, I lose myself. It hits me all the time what we've missed together and it wasn't even my fault. When Momma finally told me to tell Brenna the truth, I almost passed the fuck out. I asked her what about *you know who*, and she told me direct she'd deal with any fallout. I wasted no time since Reed saw her at the hospital. Then I get here and she's all cozy with Avalanche. At first thought maybe they were together, like married and shit, but thank Christ not.

I pull next to the Audi, which I know is Alder's. Damn, he's letting Bray drive one of his babies, I'm shocked. Taking a deep breath, I grab the wildflower bouquet Momma helped me pull together from the field at my ranch. Then grabbing my cowboy hat, I get out of the truck and am faced with total silence. Not gonna make it easy. Brenna never did. When I fucked up, she made sure I groveled a bit before she'd listen. Well damn, here goes.

"Howdy, y'all. Avalanche, right? Came by hoping you'd be here. First off, I owe ya an apology, brother, for the way I acted last time I was here. No excuse, just being an asshole, which I've been told I can be from time to time. Hope we can start fresh?"

I walk to him so we are not too far from each other and put my hand out. He looks at it then me, just as Bray giggles a bit. He looks down at her, giving her a small grin. Then he reaches out, grabs my hand, and fuck, his paw is like a grizzly bear, for sure. He doesn't squeeze my hand like I know he could have if he was a jerk, he just gives me a good shake.

"Accepted and let's move on. I get it more than you can imagine. I hear through the grapevine you're a rancher. So are my brother and me. We have a stud farm about an hour away from here."

"Holy shit, no way. That huge stud farm? Wait, is your brother, Panther? Son of a bitch, can't believe it. We just finalized a deal to have Black Thunder impregnate our mare Morning's New Breeze. I'm not sure of the process but one of your guys, think his name was Dallas, he's going to walk me through it when I go out to the stud farm. Damn, can't believe it, small-ass world, brother."

Avalanche looks between me and Brenna then laughs.

"Good luck, brother. Come on, Bray and Onyx, let's go inside, give these kids a minute or two alone to talk. I could use whatever is in the bag. I'm starving."

The women laugh and get up, heading into the cabin, while Avalanche bends down and whispers in Brenna's ear. Her cheeks get pink as she pushes him away.

"Go eat my food before I kick your ass outta here. Now get."

I watch the interaction between them and my heart gets heavy. I screwed it all up and it's all on me. Well, me and my asshole father, but that's a story for another day. Or maybe today if Brenna even gives me a chance. I stand with my hat in one hand, the flowers in another, and wait. She turns to me and looks me up, then down, and up again.

"For fuck's sake, sit down. You look like the sad cowboy in a western coming for his woman. You want something to drink, Ash?"

I tell her a water or pop and she walks into the cabin. I'm sweating like crazy and not sure why. I'm so lost in my head not sure how, but I jump when I hear a throat clear. When I look in front of me, I almost shit myself. There are three women standing there. One I know as Maggie or Tink, president of the motorcycle club. The other, not sure, but she has rainbow hair and a calm around her. The third one is the one I almost shit my pants over. She's got long black hair, crystal-blue eyes, and a full-face skull tattoo. Her eyes are taking me in and I feel chills running up and down my spine.

"Um, hi, I guess."

"Who the fuck are you and why you sittin' on Raven's porch? Come on, cat got your tongue?"

I hear the screen door but can't turn fast enough before the woman with the skull face smirks at whomever is coming out.

"Big Bird, what's up and who is this tight-lipped dude? Is Raven okay? Are the two of you staying in for the night having a romantic dinner?"

I growl before I can control it and Avalanche's big hand lands on my shoulder, almost knocking me off the porch.

"Ash, ignore Shadow, she likes to stir the pot. Ladies, what can I do for y'all? Hang on, Raven will be right out. She's talking to her sisters."

"We're her sisters, you big dope. Move aside."

"Shadow, calm down. Lil' sister has enough to deal with, don't need any of your psychobabble on top of it all."

I watch those icy-blue eyes freeze up even more, but Maggie pushes her aside like nothing and looks up at the big man.

"Avalanche, everything okay? We just wanted to check on her, she has seemed off. Just tell her the three of us were here. Oh wait, Taz wanted to give her something, sorry, sister."

The rainbow-haired woman steps forward with a small pouch in her hand. When she reaches out to give it to Avalanche, I feel something in the air, not sure what. Her voice is peaceful and quiet.

"Avalanche, tell Raven both Teddy and I picked out these crystals just for her. Teddy wanted her to have clear quartz because it is the mother of healing and I added a blue lacy agate because it aids in peace and tranquility. The big purple one is for her cabin, it's amethyst. I wrote down all of the crystals and what they are used for. Tell her to call me if she has questions. Teddy told me to let his Auntie Raven know that she can come over anytime and help both Olivia and him plan their *wedding*."

As I listen to these folks talk, I realize Brenna made her own family, shit, what does my baby brother Rowan call it? Yeah, a chosen family. It sounds like my Brenna is loved by all. I mean, these three came to check on her and some kid named Teddy is sending shit and telling her to visit.

The screen door opens and Brenna steps out, sees the women, and her head falls down with hair covering her face. I can feel her anxiety from where I'm sitting with a bouquet of flowers in my hands. With that thought, the rainbow-haired woman looks at me with such a beautiful smile, I smile back. Then the angry one with the skull opens her mouth.

"Don't know who ya are, but better watch smiling at that one. Enforcer won't like it, that's for sure. Who the hell are you anyway?"

"He's a friend, Shadow, why do you care and why are you here?"

Maggie looks at me, then Brenna, and me again. Then she smiles and her face lights up. She puts her hand up and looks into my eyes.

"Hey, Ash, nice to see you again, been awhile. Hope the family is good. Nice touch, I mean the flowers."

I take her tiny hand in mine, but she's strong when she shakes. Shadow is watching our interaction and I can feel it coming. Her eyes literally shine when her head goes between Brenna and me. Then she grins like a lunatic.

"Is this the Ash that doctor was speaking about, Raven? Hum, funny we never heard about him then that doc says something and now he's here. What's going on, sister?"

Feeling protective of Brenna, even though I got no right, I jump right in headfirst.

"Yeah, I'm Ash Sterling and that doctor is my big brother, Reed. We all go way back, in fact, our families do. Just stopping by to catch up, that's all. Nice to meet y'all."

I reach over, offering my hand to Taz then Shadow.

She glares at it then me before she shakes it and lets it go. The door creaks open and Onyx and Bray step out. I can tell immediately Bray has been crying. So can everyone else. Taz steps up and for some reason grabs Bray's hands. We all quietly watch the interaction when she leans over and whispers into Brenna's sister's ear. I hear Taz tell her to take a few deep breaths and Bray does. I can actually see when Bray feels better, her head is up, shoulders back. Not sure how but Taz knows what she's doing. Maggie steps up and grabs Bray.

"Not sure where you been but welcome back, Bray. Stop by my ranch anytime. You passed it on the way to Brenna's cabin. Would love to catch up with you."

With that Bray's face falls, but to give her credit she looks Maggie in the eye.

"Yeah, Tink, right, not Maggie any more, I need to speak to you and the entire club. If not for Ash's brother, Alder, I'd still be stuck in a rundown cabin in the forest held by a crazy as shit madman. No, not now, let's set something up. Need to get going, not used to being around so many folks. Thanks though, nice to see ya too."

I watch as first Bray, then Onyx, gives Brenna a hug. Avalanche is next. Taz steps up, grabbing the pouch from the big man and handing it to Brenna, telling her to call if she has questions. Maggie is next and finally Shadow. She glares again at me then at Brenna.

"Just say the word and we'll throw him in my wet room. I can feel the anxiety, Raven. I got your back."

Brenna giggles, looks my way, and smiles at Shadow.

"I'll keep that in mind while we talk. Keep your phone on, just in case."

When the three women turn and walk away it's so quiet, I swear my heart is beating so loud Brenna should be able to hear it. I sit back down, then stand and push the flowers at her.

"Not sure, but you used to always love wildflowers back in the day. Mom helped me. I owe you an apology too, Brenna, for the other day and for what happened a long time ago. I never could tell you why or what happened until now. Mom gave me permission."

Her head flies up from looking at the bouquet. Her eyes are full of questions for a second or two then something comes over her face, not sure what.

"Come on in, Ash, while I find something to put these in. Thanks. I do still love wildflowers, always have, as you already know. That's why you took a chance and brought them, I'm guessing. I could be way off, but what did your asinine dad, who has no balls, get involved with that had you falling for his shit and dumping me at our engagement party?"

FOUR
'ASH'
ASHTON

Slowly moving into Brenna's cabin, I feel like a dead man walking. After all this time, this is the moment I've prayed, screamed, and hate to admit it, cried for late at night. I'll never forgive my father for his part in ruining the best thing in my life. Son of a bitch, my heart is racing, my palms are sweating, and I feel like I'm about to puke. So much for that Montana rugged cowboy bullshit they spout on television with all the new series about our state, people all over the country are now in love with it and want to come see. Experience the cowboy life. My father is making a living from it, thank God, as he owes everyone in our family and more.

Watching Brenna working on the flowers, I noticed she's gotten even more beautiful with age. Not that she's old, for Christ's sake. Shit, trying to think, she must be almost twenty-five as I'm just a bit older than her. Got held back in grade school. Yeah, my ADHD and just being a boy who clowned around all the time. Actually, that's how we became friends, fighting to be the class clown. Brenna won.

Once the flowers are done, she places them on the small dinette with a cloth already across it. She grabs two bottles of water and sits on the small love seat as I'm already on one of the two recliner rockers. Then she stares at me, no emotion in her eyes. Shit, if I didn't know any better, I'd say old badass skull face taught her to show nothing. Guess my time has come, but don't know how to start. She shocks me first.

"Ash, even though I want to know the truth, I have something to say to you also. First, how could you? After all we supposedly meant to each other, how could you so callously just up and leave with that skank on that night of all nights? I really don't give a flying fuck what your asshole father was into, we all know he's a pond sucker. No, let me get this out. Did you think I couldn't figure out it had something to do with him? It's no secret your older brothers dumped their girlfriends also within that month of our engagement party. You're so lucky my brothers didn't beat your ass."

I laugh loudly and her eyes pop.

"What makes you think they didn't? Brenna, I wasn't in school for two weeks after that rowdy bunch of O'Briens got done with me. Even your father, though he didn't put a hand on me, but he sure the hell kicked the shit outta my dad. If not for Ollie, Oliver, and Orin he might have killed him, and I'm not just saying that. Ask any of your brothers or even your father."

I watch as her head drops while she's shaking it. I

can see the pain is still there and for that I'll always be sorry and feel bad. I did that because I didn't have the balls to tell my old man to go fuck himself. And if it was just me, I would have, but I too have a family I was trying to protect. How Brenna knew Alder and Rue let their girls go too, as not many put two and two together, I have no idea. Taking a deep breath, I go to start but again she interrupts me.

"Before you start and I lose my courage, you need to know the consequences of that decision so long ago, Ash. You utterly obliterated my heart that night. I had planned to share something with you but then you embarrassed me and my family before topping it off with walking out arm in arm with Patsy Woods, swiping spit with her all the way out. Well, it's been what almost six years, so sorry it took so long, but my news was I was pregnant with your baby, Ash. After you decided you needed something and someone else, I went into a deep depression. No one knew about the baby but Onyx so when I got really bad cramps, I called her. She was on the verge of enrolling into the Navy but thank God she was home. Long story short, I lost our baby. Now tell me what was so fuckin' important that the life of our child was worth it."

The instant pain her words cause once I finally am able to understand them sends me to my knees. My chest hurts and it's hard to breathe. My hands are at my chest and I can feel my eyes fill up. Oh my God, what the fuck did I do? I can kinda hear Brenna screaming my name, but shit if I can make out any of what she's saying. Before I know it, I collapse on the rug under me and start to shiver. I had no idea Brenna was with child, as my mom would say. No, don't think of Mom right now. This is gonna break her heart.

I know I hear Brenna talking, to who, I have no idea, but I'm in my own world of pain right now. That is until four strong hands lift me up, which is not easy as I'm a big country boy. When I open my eyes, I'm looking into the greenest eyes I've ever seen in my life surrounded by straight, long black hair. Turning then, I see Avalanche whose face is filled with concern. Beside him is a huge dude who also seems worried.

"Lil' sister, what'd you do to him? I told you to talk to him, not kill him. Come on, man, let's get ya on the couch. Take a seat will ya? Raven, grab him a beer or shot of something, whatever shit you got. He's in shock. Panther, grab that throw, cover it over his ass."

I'm watching them all move around but nothing is penetrating. Once I have a cold beer in my hand, and I've taken a couple of pulls, the large man with the green eyes looks to Brenna.

"Raven, what did you say to him that set him off in a tailspin? No, you called us so better just suck it up and spill. We ain't leaving 'til you do. And just so you know, don't have much time because your club sisters are on the way. So either spill now or when they get here, and you know better than I do what they'll do to find out. Make a decision, lil' bird."

That endearment, as strange as it is, fits her with the name they all call her. Raven. Watching her as my body starts to warm as the fire is stoked up, I don't say a thing. Maybe I am in shock. Who the hell knows? How could this day go from unknown to the worst day of my life? Well, second worst day. The first was when I walked away from this woman, and I've never gotten over that. Over these years I've put everything into our ranch. Built it up so much more than my old man ever could have but that night still gives me chills, not to mention what happened to our family afterward.

So stuck in my own nightmare, I ignore what is being said until Maggie and Shadow show up. Knowing this is about to get out of hand, I carefully stand up, wiping my eyes before I clear my throat, causing all in the room to look my way. To my utter surprise, Brenna walks toward me, standing at my side though she doesn't touch me. Glancing at her, I can see she wants us to continue our conversation, which I do too. So I need to get this shit off my chest. Hoping I'm not stepping over anyone's feet, I look first at the men then at the women.

"I wish I was a speaker of words but I'm just an average rancher. To you guys, thanks so much for coming at the drop of a hat when Brenna called, but we have unfinished business and both of us want to get to that. Not that it's anyone's business, but she told me something I didn't know and it knocked the shit outta me. Saying that, can we please have some privacy to get through this finally? It's been years in the waiting and it's between us and our families. Yeah, don't, Shadow. Please, it's been a trying day and I get y'all are family now too. Not being a dick, we just need some time. I'd appreciate it."

Brenna leans into me slightly and, damn, that little movement makes my day. The man I now know as Panther grabs Shadow's hand and they leave together. Well, hello, that gentle man is with that devil of a woman. Opposites do attract. Maggie and Noodles leave next. Avalanche walks up to us silently.

"If either of you need anything, reach out. I mean that. And, Ash, if you hurt her again, I swear to all that I find sacred there won't be enough for your family to claim. I'll check in later, lil' sister."

When we are finally alone again Brenna takes a seat, this time on the couch, and pats the cushion next to her. She leans into the arm with one leg crossed under her. I can see all kinds of emotions running across her face. I'm not sure why I do it, but something drives me to place a soft chaste kiss on her beautiful lips. It's brief but by the time I look at her face, her mouth is open in a perfect 'O' and her eyes are twinkling. Good, something to put her at ease because this ain't gonna be easy at all. I take a deep breath and try to get the words together to explain to her why I did what I did that not only broke her heart but mine also.

"Okay, give me a minute or two, but to give you some background, my father is not who any of us thought. My mother was totally in the dark until the day before our engagement and she begged him to not ruin our day. Being the selfish bastard he was and still is, he didn't think twice. Let me back up. Mom had no idea everything he'd told her over the years was a lie. He didn't lose his entire family to a fire when he was a kid. His family is living and right here in Montana. Everyone knows what your club does, Brenna. Well, I do now too since Alder found Bray. Your momma told my momma that Bray desperately needs some kind of help with what she went through, and your momma said to take her to the Devil's Handmaidens because that's what they do. Sorry, going off track again. My mom found out the night before our engagement party that my dad has ties to a racist group who believes their kind is the only kind who should live in Montana. How she found out was in the worst way possible. Dad told her he was staying at the summer camp because of having to fix fences or shit like that. She felt bad so she told Rowan where she was going and went up there to surprise him with some things she thought he might need and a good meal.

"What she walked into was her worst nightmare. He wasn't fixin' fences, no him and a few of his boys were holding women up there against their will. Mom didn't know a bunkhouse was built and there were eight women being held up there. Women who didn't matter in their eyes. Some of color, some of Hispanic origin, and some they considered white trash. All in horrific shape. You could tell they had been mistreated by these men repeatedly.

"When Dad saw Mom, instead of getting her the hell outta there, he brought her in then taught her a lesson so he looked like a man in front of his friends. I didn't learn about this until recently because if I knew back then the outcome would have been different. When they got home, he was trying to act like everything was okay but Mom was in so much pain, though none of us knew why.

"The night of our party, Rowan was just a little kid, so when he walked into my parents' room asking Mom to help him with his little bow tie, he screamed when he saw her back. She'd been whipped, Brenna. Slashed to pieces. We all ran in and, fuck, didn't know what to do. Reed went to the barn and got the udder ointment we used on the cows. Gently he put it on her back and it must have helped after a bit because she let out a breath and just about collapsed. That's when he walked in and point-blank lied to us. Told us he was being blackmailed and they did that to our momma. Then he told me I had to call off our engagement because he owed them a ton of money and they wanted to take our ranch to use it for bad things. Mom's head jerked up and the look she gave him, I'll never forget. It was filled with hate and disgust. Dad said if I didn't let you go, they would attack Mom worse and then start on you and your sisters and momma. Brenna, fuck, I was a kid myself. Seeing my mom like that tore a part of my heart out. I couldn't live with you gettin' hurt. After he strutted out of the house, Mom came to my room. She sat down and told me what he said wasn't true but she couldn't tell me the truth, not yet. But what she did know was my father wasn't who she thought he was and she didn't want to put you in danger. She loves you too, I hope you know. We talked about it and decided to try and do it discreetly. Little did we know, my dad had planned it with his friends. That's how Patsy Woods got in the mix. Her father is one of his cronies. Ya know, she tried to kill herself like three months after we broke up. Sent me a note apologizing for what happened and told me to watch my back because those people are evil. Her words, not mine."

I take a few minutes to breathe and try to read Brenna. I can see the pain all over her face, and for that I'm so sorry. The situation sucked all around. And I've been fighting it now for years. My mom finally told me to tell Brenna everything and get her club to help before it's too late.

"So, Ash, you're telling me your daddy had some bad friends and because of that you broke up with me. He's been with you since then, living high on the hog at your ranch. Come on, I'm supposed to believe this story? Do you take me for a fool?"

Like I planned it, we hear a vehicle drive in. We both get up and step onto the porch, looking and waiting. I see the vehicle making its way down the road of cabins to park next to my truck. Reed, Rowan, Rue, and Momma step out. I know Alder wanted to be here but he's probably home waiting on Brenna's sister, Bray, to get back. Another fucked-up story that intermingles with mine. I watch as each of my brothers greet Brenna like long-lost family. Momma is last and she pulls her in for a kiss and a hug. Never realized how much she's aged. We need to stop this. Brenna opens the door and we all walk in, finding any seat available. I nod at

Momma when she looks into my eyes. Yeah, she figured Brenna wouldn't believe such an outrageous story.

Brenna is on one of the stools when Momma walks up to her, turning around. When she pulls her sweater off, I can hear the gasp from Brenna. Then Momma pulls the tank top off leaving her in a thinner racerback top. We watch as Brenna reaches out, placing a hand on the scars showing.

"Brenna, this happened a long time ago. My boys and I have been fighting to get that piece of crap off our land since then. He's invited that crowd of hooligans and they've taken up on the acreage farthest away from our homestead. Yeah, right next to the forest preserve. Yeah, that's where Alder found Bray, and I think it's his friends who took her and those other women. Reason we are coming out to you now is we heard your club has been having trouble and when we heard the name, we had to come clean."

Brenna is looking between all of us when something clicks and it's like watching a light bulb go on. Then she asks the million-dollar question.

"Mrs. Sterling, is the group your husband is hanging with and causing all this trouble for your family the Thunder Cloud Knuckle Brotherhood?"

Momma looks at her for a bit as tears start rolling down her face. Looking at her sons, my mom then glances at Brenna before she nods and softly says, "Yes, it is."

Watching Brenna's face go white, her eyes huge in her face as she turns to look at me, it hits me in the gut.

Yeah, my father is part of that fucked-up group that is doing horrific things, not only in Montana but in the entire country. My family needs help and fingers crossed Brenna and her club sisters will be able to get us out from under this shit.

FIVE
'RAVEN'
BRENNA

Ash stayed for a while after his family left, trying to explain how they have been living while hiding all that's going on at their ranch. He told me Alder had enough and almost got himself killed when he refused to let the band of morons stay right off of their property in the forest. That is how he came upon Bray. Well, Bray and other women. He could only grab one so he picked my sister because he recognized her and she was in pretty bad shape.

My head is pounding along with my heart. How did my sister get in that situation, and why didn't anyone in my family even think something bad could have happened to her? I mean, yeah, she's our wild child, but son of a bitch, did Mom or Dad even…no, I can't blame them for any of this. They've been suffering all this time, not knowing where Bray was. And to find out she was in our own backyard, so to speak. I thought she looked pale with Onyx tonight, but everything was happening so fast. Shame on me for not taking a minute to check in with my older sister.

Then a quick memory comes to my mind and I realize I'm all over the place. When I asked Ash why Patsy Woods, he explained her father is part of the brotherhood organization. His dad, along with Patsy's, figured a long time ago if the two of them hooked up, their kids would be the ultimate race. Patsy being the skank she is, went along with it, and even accused Ash of being her baby daddy. Well until, from what Ash said, she surprised everyone when the child was born and it came out much darker than he is. Her father was going to kill the baby, thank God Ash was there. He told them he'd take care of it then took the little one to his mom's house. His mom named the baby Joshua and he is still at the ranch under his momma's care. She dared his father to say or do anything. Yeah, she did, though she also had a gun in her hand pointed at his face.

The way Ash explained it, they are living in a war zone. Every one of them carry whenever on the property, even his mom. I can't even get that picture in my brain, Mrs. Sterling walking around with a gun on her side. They've been able to keep most of their ranch, but his dad has taken over just about a hundred acres closest to the forest preserve on the far northwest side. Ash says he's seen all kinds of traffic coming and going lately but doesn't dare go over there. The last time someone got nosy it was Rowan, and they almost killed his little brother. Surprisingly, his dad stepped up and sent him home, ordering—yeah that's what Rowan told them—

their dad demanded the brotherhood leave him alone, something about that was their deal. For being a nosy teenager, Rowan ended up with two black eyes, a broken nose and wrist, bruised ribs, and a few chipped teeth.

I asked him to give me a few hours. His family is waiting to hear from me so they can come over and explain what they know about this chapter of the Thunder Cloud Knuckle Brotherhood. Ash says they are particularly cruel, leaning on the side of sadists. I need to make some calls, but first I reach out to Onyx to check on Bray. What she tells me has me wanting to jump in my cage and go out there and kill each and every one of those motherfuckers who put their filthy hands on my big sister. Onyx said that Alder, along with two of his ranger friends who live on his property, are holding down the fort and protecting Bray. I'm not sure her being around a bunch of men is the right thing but until I hear differently, I'll let it stand for now.

After hanging up with Onyx, with a promise for us to get together and really talk, I get up and grab an ice-cold bottle of water. This next call I'm dreading. Gonna reach out to Tink to see if we can all get together on the ranch in our conference hall, so I can share what I just found out. Problem is, I'll have to share some very personal things that have been kept secret for years with my club sisters. Guess, as my mom would say, it's time to put on my big girl panties and face the music, whatever the hell that means. I hit Tink's number and sit on my front porch in my favorite rocker.

"Hey, Raven, what's up, sister?"

"Tink, is it possible, can we maybe call a meeting? I need to talk to the club about some things I just found out that have to do with the Thunder Cloud Knuckle Brotherhood and, unfortunately, my past too."

I hear silence then some whispering, which I make out is Tink telling Noodles she needs a minute or two. One thing I can say about our prez is she's always there for all of us, no matter if it's day or night. That's why she's perfect for that position.

"Raven, sure, I'll put out a text. Do you need me to come over so we can hash some of this shit out first, just the two of us? I can either come to you or you're more than welcome up here. It isn't like we're miles from each other. It's not a bother, really."

Feeling the insecurity rising up in me that always makes me want to crack jokes, I push it aside.

"Yeah, sure, if you don't mind walking down. Is Glory or Shadow around? If so, bring them along too, I guess. Get it out all at once so I don't have to keep repeating my life story."

"Hang tight, sister, we'll be there shortly. Hey, did you eat?"

Realizing I didn't eat because that big bear Avalanche ate my dinner, I tell Tink no. She laughs and says she'll bring some leftovers, which I pray Noodles or one of the other sisters made. Tink is getting better, but uh no, not tonight, don't think I can take another thing going wrong... like my gut. Not sure a night in the bathroom is something I'd be looking forward to like, ever.

As I wait for my club sisters to make their way here, I

sit on the rocker trying to get my thoughts together. For once in my life, I can't find anything to joke or laugh about. That thought scares the ever-lovin' crap outta me. I've always used jokes to not show my true emotions or to hide my past. Actually, anything that makes me dive into my emotions. Since I've never dealt with my feelings for Ash, he is on the top of that list. Not sure I want to deal with him now either.

My head goes to the kiss he pressed on my lips before he turned and got in his truck and took off. He's not the kid I fell in love with. I could tell by that quick, intense kiss. His firm lips wasted no time and when he bit my bottom lip, I couldn't stop the moan from coming out of my mouth. His hands ran up and down my sides, ghosting over the curves of my breasts, making me gasp deep in my throat. When he licked my lips, I couldn't resist, so I opened and he ate at me like a man starving. Right when my arms went around his neck and I gave him my weight, he pulled me so close I could feel how much he wanted me. Then he pressed a kiss on the tip of my nose before he left. It took me a while to catch my breath but when I did, it was with a huge smile across my face.

I'm so caught up in my own thoughts, I almost crap myself when I hear Shadow's cackling in front of me.

"Damn, Goldilocks, look at her face. We are about to enter another Devil's Handmaidens' drama that's for sure. The signs are written all over her face. Fuck, I haven't recovered from Glory's shit. Couldn't give us a little time off, Raven? Though if the drama is with that tall drink of cowboy, can't say I blame Raven at all. Damn, sister, you been holding out on us. Now let's get inside so you can fill us in on whatever the fuck is goin' on with ya. Never thought I'd say this, but I'm missing our easygoing, fun-lovin' prankster sister."

I feel my eyes start to itch but I push it back, now is not the time. First, I have to do something I should have done years ago when these three women gave me the chance that literally saved my life.

"Hey, before we get into all this bullshit, first, I want each of you to know how much you mean to me, all kidding and bullshitting aside. Back when I started in the Devil's Handmaidens, I kept my life separate from the club and y'all. Well, tried to, anyway. The thing none of you know is if not for the club, I might have done something really stupid and permanent. No, hang on, Shadow, let me talk. I'll explain in great detail, but to sum it up, Ash and I were engaged and the night of our engagement party—you know my mom—she always finds something to throw a party about. So she threw a huge barn get-together. Music, food and drinks. Seemed like everyone and everything was going great until Ash had a huge fight with his father. I mean, so bad my dad and brothers had to drag his father off of Ash. Next thing I know, he's calling off our engagement and walking out with a skank we went to high school with. And was known to put out on top of it."

Hearing Shadow literally growl, I giggle. Damn, I love this woman. Glory and Tink are watching me closely but don't say a word.

"Little did he know that I had a surprise for him that night. I'd just found out I was pregnant and was excited because we were starting our lives together. You know married, kids, ranch, horses, and some dogs and cats. Yeah, what a night. After he walked out, I kinda—just like those romance books are always spouting—let my life literally fall apart because of a man. I was so disgusted with myself. Then one day I didn't feel good. It got worse and before I knew it started hemorrhaging and, eventually, I lost our child. Spiraling is the only word that fits what was going on in my life. Then I fell into the Wooden Spirit Bar and Grill, which led me to the Devil's Handmaidens and the three of you. No one ever truly believed in me like the three of you did. My family kind of did but also humored me. We live in Timber-Ghost, Montana so my path was determined when I was born a female. I got flack for wanting to go to college but I ended up with my associate's degree from our community college. Y'all not only gave me a job but even a chance to prospect after. I never knew what folks meant when they said they had a given family and a chosen one. I can honestly say, right at this moment, my given and chosen family to me are all the same, and I love each and every one in my *family.*"

Wiping my face with my sleeve, I take a deep breath. Glory comes close, bumping shoulders with me but doesn't reach out. She's always been the one who was able to figure out what the best thing was for each of her club sisters. She knew if she hugged me, I'd break, but she didn't, so this was the second-best way to show me her support.

"When I was prospecting, you offered to let me go back to school. Yeah, I was already hacking shit. Been doing that since I was in high school, before I even met the club, but what I learned over the last couple of years I can't even comprehend. What I can do on a computer blows my mind, and that's because of you. Not to mention, Tink, your dad's computer dude, Freak, has helped me grow so much, and Karma with the Grimm Wolves too. They've had so much more experience than me it's crazy. When the three of us get together, it's nerd city for sure.

"So before we go into my cabin and I explain how badly this is fucked up, I wanted you to know how much I appreciate you. I just found out those jagoffs, the Thunder Cloud Knuckle Brotherhood, had been holding my older sister captive all this time. We thought she took off to follow her hippy heart, so yeah, I get it, Shadow. I hope you can feel how badly I want to take these motherfuckers down. Bray has to come first and if it's okay, I'm gonna try to talk her into coming to stay at the ranch for a bit, talk to our therapist, and get checked out by Dr. Cora. Now, sister, let me finish, almost there. I love you like my own blood sisters, sometimes even more because I chose you. I'm beyond thankful and hope to Christ I live and die a Devil's Handmaiden sister because what we do gives me solace and lets me know that evil will never win over good.

"Now get your fine asses in here so I can drop all my

family and love drama on you. Might even end up on the Hallmark Channel as a movie of the week, who knows, we are in books now."

Hearing them all laugh gives me the strength for what comes next. Me baring my soul without any jokes or laughs. Nothing to laugh about at the moment.

SIX
'TINK'
MAGGIE/GOLDILOCK

Damn, talk about a total shitshow of a night. Poor Raven, I had no idea she'd been through so much. Yeah, she's younger than me, but shit, how did I not know all of this? I kind of remember some party at her family's ranch, but we didn't run in the same circles back then.

Though with what she told us tonight, wish we had. I'd have kicked Ash's ass for sure. Surprised Ollie and her other brothers didn't kill him outright. This gives us some insight and explains where those assholes have been holed up. My heart breaks for the Sterling family. Well, everyone except Cliff, the father. I always had a bad feeling around him, even when I was a little girl. I think Mom felt it too because when there were county fairs and stuff she always told us kids to stay as far away as possible from Cliff Sterling. I'm sensing a conversation needs to be had with Mom in the very near future.

I just finished sending the text to every sister in the

club; members and prospects. Or as they say all-hands-on-deck. Dad usually says that, but since his heart attack he's not like he used to be. Maybe it scared him or maybe Mom scared him, don't know, but need to make time—just him and me. I miss my old man, even if he is kinda grumpy and old-fashioned. Especially when it comes to his daughters.

Knowing I should go to bed, or at least fill in Noodles, I just need some quiet time so I head down to the front porch. When I open the door, a huge smile hits my face when I see my man already out there with what looks to be hot chocolate and a heavy throw. *Damn, how did I get so lucky,* I think to myself.

"Sweet Pea, thought you'd make your way out here. Beautiful night to look at all the stars. Come on, Maggie, take a seat, two shoulders and ears, no waiting. And as you know, I can keep a secret."

Looking at Noodles my heart jumps in my chest. Even with all that we've been through and the drama all my club sisters have struggled with, this man never falters in his devotion and love. I thank God every day for him and even more today after hearing Raven's story.

"We are about to be hit by a shitstorm hurricane, and I don't know how to fix or stop it, soldier boy. This time it has to do with Raven. Noodles, the evil out there scares me more and more each and every day."

"So take a deep breath and tell me what's got you so worried and frightened. That's not like you, Maggie."

"It's that goddamn brotherhood that's scaring me,

Noodles. No matter how hard we work to save victims, there are always so many more out there. Tonight, I found out Raven's sister, Bray, is the newest victim. Shit, let me start from the beginning."

While I give Noodles all the information I have on the current situation, my mind is drowning in everything that is going through my head at the same time. Need to check on both Mom and Dad, see what new drama Hannah is up to. Figure out who keeps messing with our equipment at the trucking company. Working through our wedding planning. Last, but not least, my pregnancy situation or lack of it. Seems like any of my club sisters can get pregnant at the drop of a pair of jeans. Vixen is more than a little pregnant right now with her third child, though the other two she just got back during her drama. Fuck, we're a mess and getting so far from our original cause and purpose. With all of our attention narrowed on the Thunder Cloud Knuckle Brotherhood, we've started handing off some cases either to Panther and his guys or any chapters close enough to us for the time being. I've never had to do that before, so either we are lapsing in our purpose or the traffickers have upped their game. I pray to Christ it's on me and not the bad guys.

I'm not sure what the problem is, but it is starting to weigh on my mind and take up necessary space I need to run the club. I mean, I already have a grown child so we know I can get pregnant. One day at a time is what my mom's been telling me since this started. I can always depend on her. No matter what the subject is, she tries to be as open-minded as possible.

"Maggie, what's got you frowning like that? Don't shove me aside, I'm here, willing and able to give a helping hand if you only let me. So walk me through your plan for the morning? Do you know who's coming? Is Tank able to or are you not calling him? Fuck, I'm an asshole at times. Take a minute, Sweet Pea, drink your hot chocolate and chill. Enjoy the stars, relax your mind. Then we can talk. Make sure you've got an idea on how to keep this meeting under control. Am I allowed or is it a closed meeting, just for the Devil's Handmaidens club sisters?"

"Noodles, let me get through the beginning of the meeting with just my sisters. After that, all hell is going to break loose, so would rather have you close than far away. Only God knows the path He's chosen us to go on next. All I can do is pray He's taken in all the good we do. That way maybe He can overlook all that is Zoey."

Hearing him laugh gives me a moment of solace before once again my mind runs off in so many directions, it makes my head hurt. Though my heart is broken for my sister Raven, need to share some of it with my ol' man.

"Raven shared something tonight that tore me in two. I'm losing my mind trying to get pregnant. She not only was pregnant when all that shit went down, she had planned on telling Ash after the party. Once he left, with all the added stress, she lost the baby and almost died from hemorrhaging. She then went into a dark place and was considering doing something to end her pain. Then she walked into the Wooden Spirit Bar and Grill. She heard Zoey, Glory, and I talking about needing a technology person and she asked about it. The rest is, like they say, history. I thank God it fell the way it did because I can't imagine her doing something to end her life. Noodles, she has so much to offer. I mean, you know she's quick as a whip, funny as shit and, man, what she can do with a computer. She's saved our asses on numerous occasions, just sayin'."

He pulls me up after he grabs the throw, then puts me on his lap, covering us both up. Feeling his warmth, I lean into him, putting my head on his chest, listening to his heartbeat. We sit like this for I don't even know how long, but my body fully relaxes and I close my eyes and just be.

"Sweet Pea, what will be, will be. I mean that for every single thing you mentioned tonight, but mostly the worry you are carrying about getting pregnant. It will happen, just let it. You need to try and ease up on yourself, Maggie. Don't compare yourself to anyone else. Things happen when they should, not when we want them too. That I found you and we are planning our wedding is more than enough for me, and no, I'm not saying I don't want kids. Don't put words in my mouth. It's just that our world is spinning extremely fast. Maybe that's one of the reasons it's not happening. Let shit just happen and quit trying to control every goddamn thing, Maggie. You're driving yourself crazy. I love you and you love me, what else can we want?"

I feel it and try to stop it, but the sob comes out. Damn it, I've become a crybaby since he came into my life, for Christ's sake.

"Come on, Sweet Pea, let me take you to bed and take your mind off of everything for one night. Can you do that for me?"

Smiling, I lean back and look him in the eyes. His are sparkling with laughter.

"Sure can, soldier boy. Take me to bed and have your way with me. I dare you to."

Since my man never passes up a dare, both laughing we get off the rocker and, hand in hand, we go into the house, walk past our nightly guard, and head up to our bedroom, where Noodles removes all my worries as I concentrate on everything that is him.

SEVEN
'RAVEN'
BRENNA

I'm not hardly able to sleep at all, so I push myself up out of bed, take a shower, brush my teeth, wrap my hair in a towel, then throw on my fluffy robe. Then I head to my Keurig so I can juice up with some coffee. Sitting at my table, I try to prioritize how I'm going to explain to my club sisters everything I need to, while keeping as much of my private life just that… private.

I left a message last night for Bray but haven't heard anything back. Deep in my soul I feel so much pain for her, there are no words. We, her family, assumed she was out and about roaming the country, when, in fact, for almost two years she was at the sadistic mercy of that fucking brotherhood. I can't even imagine or want to think about what all they did to her.

I was there when Lilly, Glory's daughter, shared what she went through being held captive. What she did to protect her daughter from any abuse, damn, she's a strong as fuck woman. I'm surrounded by the best of the best as far as women. Glory was held captive by her brother-in-law until she was rescued. Fast forward and that same jagoff got his hands on Lilly, which led to her getting pregnant and having Angel. That circle of abuse ended though when Tank's friend, Nova, found both Lilly and Angel and brought them home to Glory. They are still trying to find their place together. Glory's man, Yoggie, is in the process of building an addition, which is going to equal another house attached for Lilly and Angel. Life with our club is never dull.

Hearing someone knocking at my door, it shocks me. Who the hell is up at the crack of dawn at my door? Opening my junk drawer, I grab my gun, holding it to my side. Looking through the peephole, I feel my body tense when I see my two sisters and from the looks of it most or all of my brothers. Fuck!!! Someone opened their mouth, for sure. I unlock the door, crack it open, and look out.

"Uh, morning. Why is the O'Brien clan standing at my door at the crack of dawn looking all serious?"

"You gonna ask us in, little sister, or is there a reason you don't want us to come into your home? Got something to hide?"

"Really, Bennett? Obviously, y'all know what happened yesterday so who the hell do you think I'm hiding from you? Get your asses in here, for Christ's sake."

I stand aside and let all five of my brothers and my two sisters in. When Bray goes to walk past me, head down, I gently tap her arm. She stops, lifts her hand, and

I motion I want to hug her. She nods and I pull her to me. My God, there's nothing left of her. I can feel her entire rib cage. My big sister used to be a brick house. She was one-hundred-percent woman but muscular. She lifted weights, hiked all over the mountains, and even knew how to box. She hangs on and so do I. I kiss her cheek and give her a squeeze.

She lifts her head and I smile. Then I lead her to the kitchen, right to the coffee machine, pushing Ollie, Orin, and Brooks out of the way. None of them say a word when they see I'm pushing Bray in front of them. Yeah, that's right, brothers, don't push me today. Feeling arms coming round me, I look over my shoulder to see Onyx, a worried look on her face. Goddamn, I've missed her. When she enlisted into the Navy it broke my heart. I idolized her. One minute she was there then the next she was gone. Mom and Dad never understood both Onyx and Ollie enlisting. I did though because if I'd thought it through, after Ash broke my heart, it might have done me some good to enlist too. Though I'll never regret my choice of the Devil's Handmaidens MC.

Feeling Onyx squeeze me around my middle, I turn and look up. She's watching me and not drawing attention from the others, she mouths, "I'm so sorry. Should have been here for you, baby sister."

Not wanting to talk about this shit, though it means the world to me she gave me that, I drop my head on her chest and hang on for dear life. No one interrupts us so we have our moment then turn to the others. Taking a deep breath, I let it out and ask the question of the day.

"Why y'all here? I've got to finish getting ready, got a meeting with my club shortly."

Ollie looks at me then steps directly in front of me.

"No, baby sister, we have a meeting with the Devil's Handmaidens Motorcycle Club. No, don't argue. We let you down once, it ain't ever gonna happen again. Oh shit, Oliver, go get that shit from my truck. Paisley sent some goodies for you. Said to tell you she loves you, and if you need her, call and she'll be here in no time at all. We've got two mares in labor, only reason she's not here."

Oliver comes back in with a huge shopping bag filled with Tupperware containers. As everyone gets their coffee and Ollie opens all the containers, I wrap my arms around myself, feeling so much love in my tiny cabin. I've always had this love though I fought it. In my youth, didn't realize that family love is just as special. It wasn't anyone's fault what happened except Cliff Sterling and the brotherhood.

"Oh, Brenna, Mom and Dad will be at the meeting too. Dad had to run into town so they told us they'll meet us there. No point in trying to argue, I'm talking about our parents. They don't take no for an answer, you should know that already, where do you think we all get it from?"

Hearing Bennett laughing at his own words, I grin at him. Well, if you can't fight it, might as well join them. Reaching, I grab a piece of frosted banana bread. The first bite and oh my God. Ollie is one lucky bastard, that's for sure, not sure how my big brother stays so fit with this kind of homemade heaven around all the time.

Looking at all my siblings, the love filling this room has me thanking God for giving me such a strong support system. Listening to them all goof around with each other, I glance at Bray, who's watching everything with huge eyes. She's standing off by the big chair in my reading nook. I walk over, grab her hand, and pull her until we're right in front of the chair. I sit and she kind of follows and falls into me since I still have her hand in mine. That brings a small giggle from her, which has everyone look her way. I watch her look at everyone then she shocks the shit out of all of us.

"What? Jesus Christ, guys, I'm still human and alive. Yeah, I giggled because of our little sister here. Like usual, she's always trying to make everyone laugh and feel better. Well, she did it again, 'kay?"

I turn and hug her to me. No matter what it takes, I promise myself I'll do whatever I have to do to help Bray. But right this moment got to get my ass in gear and get ready for what's to come next. Fuck, not ready to face the day but got no choice.

* * *

We walk to the conference hall/pole barn as one unit. When we get close, I can't believe the trucks and vehicles in front of our newly established pole barn that we use for meetings at the ranch. Looking through the trucks I see Dad's beast there too, both my parents sitting in the cab, obviously, waiting on us to arrive. As we make our way to their truck, we hear more traffic coming up the road. My heart stops when I see Ash's truck followed by three more behind him. In his cab, I can see his momma and baby brother. So, I'm going to assume the other trucks are his brothers. This is getting real about now. Shit, I can feel sweat running down my shoulder blades as my hands tremble. All of a sudden, I'm surrounded by my sisters and brothers. I hope to Christ this doesn't turn into a frigging barn fight.

Mom and Dad are getting out of their truck when Ash and his family pull in. I watch as he gets out, hat in hand, walks around, and opens the door for his momma. Once he gets her out, she turns and stops when she spots all of us. That's when my mom walks up to them and pulls Ash's mom into her arms. Neither says a word for a second then Mom, as always, saves the day.

"Gertie, my God, woman, why didn't you come to me? We were friends forever; we even went to school together. There is nothing I wouldn't do for you and the kids. Even after this dumbass dumped my girl over there. No, Ash, now's not the time. I've heard some of it and neither my husband nor I blame you at all. You were in a no-win situation, we get it. Gertie, promise me you'll never do this crap again. If trouble is knocking on your door, you pick up the darn phone and call me. Promise me, please."

Hearing the tremble in my mom's voice, I'm shocked. She's a tough bird, usually. I knew they were close; guess I didn't know how tight they were. Gertie promises. Seeing Dad, thought he was going to Mom but he doesn't stop, he walks directly to Alder and grabs him close. Again, I'm shocked to see his eyes getting wet. I feel Bray move up close to me, so I wrap my arms around her, feeling her tremble. Then Dad says his peace.

"Son, there are no words I can say to let you know what it means to us, what you did for my Bray. My family is in your debt, never doubt that. I can say thank you from the bottom of my heart but it just ain't enough, though I truly mean it. We got a lot of fences to mend now, but I'm grateful to you and God that we have this chance with her. Now, let's figure out how to get rid of these pain in the ass bastards for good."

Just as I'm about to try and get some control of this mishmash, I hear voices behind me. Turning, I see just about every sister from the Devil's Handmaidens walking toward the group of us. I'm so proud to be able to wear the kutte that identifies me as one of them. I make my way to the three women in front—Tink, Shadow, and Glory. Tink reaches up, grabbing my forearms, and giving them a squeeze.

"You ready for this, Raven? Remember, no matter what, we have your back, each and every one of us. I see your family and the Sterlings are here. As you can see, the misfits are trailing us."

I look around to see Noodles, Panther, and good old Avalanche messing around behind the last stragglers of club sisters. When I whistle, they all look up smiling and Avalanche even waves like the goof he is.

"Look at Big Bird trying to be cute, numbnuts that he is. Don't fall for his antics, Raven, he's trouble for sure."

I look at Shadow and her words bring a small grin to my face. Again, before I can open my mouth, Tink jumps right in.

"Really? Kettle meet pot, for Christ's sake. Let's get this shitshow going because from the looks of it this is going to be an all-day thing. Kiwi and Peanut, make sure we have lunch planned and some snacks too, will you, sisters? Call the Wooden Spirit, have the cook make something and maybe one of us can run in to pick it up. Now, Raven, let the club go in first and have a quick talk, then we can bring in Bray by herself, or if she needs it, I'm guessing Alder but not your parents, right?"

I nod because Bray just told me a bit ago, if possible, she doesn't want the family to know what was done to her. The only one besides me she's okay with is Onyx. I feel like she already shared a little with her.

Tink walks past me to the groups of folks waiting. She explains that as a club we have some business to discuss then she'll be calling folks in. As she's talking, I see Cynthia come out of the conference hall with a huge coffeepot in her arms. Hearing boots hitting the ground, I feel a whoosh as Avalanche, Panther, and Noodles go to help. Cynthia whispers to them. Two go inside as Noodles walks to the large table leaning against a tree. It takes him under two minutes to set it up. Once done, he helps Cynthia place the coffeepot in the middle, just as the other two men come out with bins in their hands. Between the four of them, they set up a coffee bar and baked goods. Cynthia waves to Tink when she's done and our prez tells everyone they can help themselves. It's then I truly notice that picnic benches and some chairs have been scattered around. Well, damn, someone has been busy.

Shadow whistles so all the Devil's Handmaidens start to enter the building. I can feel my heart racing just as I feel Onyx beside me.

"Don't worry, smart-ass, know I can't go in. Just wanted to let you know you have all of us out here to hold you up. If you need any one of us, just call out and we'll be there. Kick major ass, Brenna. You got this."

I smile her way then turn and walk right in, not looking left or right. When everyone is seated, Tink looks my way and nods. I stand and, without a second thought, I start with my story, hoping I can get through it without one tear.

EIGHT
'RAVEN'
BRENNA

Holy shit, I thought going through my story was going to tear me up. It went smoothly and when I was done, my chest felt lighter. Maybe it helped because not one of my club sisters treated me any different. Well, Taz came to me holding on tightly. Probably because of the baby I lost. She's our softhearted sister in the Devil's Handmaidens, unless you mess with those she loves then she's a momma grizzly, for sure.

After taking a quick potty break, we all take our seats. Tink looks to Wildcat and says, "Bray" and my stomach drops. Oh no! I wait and it doesn't take but a minute for my older sister to slowly walk in. Her eyes are shifting all over, and she's nervous with her back to the door. Of all people, Shadow stands up, walks to her, and gets close, then touches her arm, all the while watching her face. Bray doesn't do a thing, even I can tell she's fascinated with Shadow's skull-face tattoo.

When she looks around, her eyes find mine and she shocks the shit out of me.

"Hey, Brenna, think Mom and Dad would freak if I did something like that on my face?"

Shadow looks to me and grins, then back at Bray.

"Think twice before you do it. I don't regret it but there are days it would make life easier if this wasn't here. Even though my ol' man loves me, no matter what."

We all laugh because before Panther, Shadow was just tough and mean. She'd never kid around. Tink hits the table with her hand and everyone settles. Then our prez addresses my sister.

"Bray, I know this is going to be really hard. I can't imagine, so take your time. Hey, come on, sit down. Pick a seat that you're comfortable in first. We'll wait."

Thought she might come by me but she walked over and took the empty chair next to Shadow. Well, fuck me, my timid sister and my club enforcer. That's one for the books. They look so funny next to each other.

Over the next couple of hours we listen as Bray explains in great detail what she'd been through in the last two years. How she was moved all around this area. She recognized some of the Thunder Club Knuckle Brotherhood members, and she named them off while I took notes on my laptop. Also had my iPad open as I researched some of the names, and damn, was I shocked. Some were businessmen while others were politicians, cops, and rangers. What a clusterfuck.

Bray is struggling right now with what actually

happened to her. She's hanging on to Shadow, who has no expression on her face at all. We all hate this brotherhood and human trafficking, but to Shadow it's personal. She's been through it, so if anyone has an understanding, it's her. When Bray starts to cry, Tink calls for a break. Both Shadow and Tink are quietly talking to Bray, so I step outside and walk to where Onyx is drinking coffee. Damn, she is going to be wired, which isn't good 'cause she can get a bit crazy.

"Hey, she's having a hard time. Which is better, you or Alder stepping in to help her?"

"Not sure, baby sister, she's been struggling telling me what happened. Hey, Alder, come over here, will you, please?"

We both watch as Ash's brother walks over. Damn, he should be a model with that swagger walk. But he's oblivious to it. Just how the Sterling boys are. When he reaches us, he nods my way and greets Onyx. She winks at him, which makes him blush. Come on, really?

"Brenna just asked who would be better to support Bray. She's trying to get through what actually happened to her and she's struggling. Whatcha think, me or you, Alder? I know some but not all. Did she tell you?"

He looks to both of us and nods. The look on his face is murderous so I'm thinking the worst.

"Why does she have to relive those nightmares? Can't she give a brief kind of summary?"

Onyx looks to me and since this is our area, I explain why it's necessary.

"Alder, it's more for her than us, though the more

details the better it will be to bring them down. When we bust up a human trafficking circuit, it takes many hours to go through an intake form. It asks everything we can think of. There's a reason because when we ask about the people involved, if they have any kind of distinguishing marks like tattoos, scars, birthmarks, that makes it easier when the busts go down. Each section helps to establish who did what, and then when we go to court we have—as Glory says—'our ducks in a row.' Believe me, I don't want to sit in there and listen to what those sorry fucking perverted bastards did to my sister, but for her it's the first step to recovery. Getting it out of her head. No, it won't 'cure' her, but once she realizes as we talk to her that she's not the only victim to go through this, it helps her to accept and try to move forward. So which one of you is it going to be? I got to get back inside."

Two minutes later we walk in and everyone turns, and mouths drop open. Leave it to Shadow to blow the hell up.

"Raven, what the fuck is he doing in here? This is our Church and none but Devil's Handmaidens are allowed. No, Bray, you are allowed because you're a survivor telling us your story."

Tink pulls on Shadow's arm to bring her to her level. Then she whispers in her ear. Not sure what she says but Shadow looks at Bray out of the corner of her eye. Then back at Tink and nods. Tink waves us both in and I take my seat as Alder strolls around the table, grabs a chair, and sits directly next to my sister. Bray's sides are covered as she is surrounded by Shadow and Alder. God help her.

Bray was quiet at first but the more she talked the madder she got. The O'Brien temper, we all have it. She had a moment that took her awhile, especially with what they did to her. I swear on anything sacred, if I have a chance at all, those motherfuckers are going to feel extreme pain. I'm nowhere near as good as Shadow, but I have something she doesn't have. Bray's my sister and that love of family goes deep.

By the time Bray is finishing up, Peanut's phone vibrates. Only reason she even had a phone on her was she ordered food and two of my brothers offered to pick it up. Must be here. When I look to Bray, Alder has her in his arms. And the look on his face, oh my God, that man is in love with her. If not, he's a damn good actor. Part of me feels sorry for him because I know from past survivors, Bray has a long way to go before she can even think about a real relationship. Hope Alder knows that.

"Let's take a break, get some lunch. After lunch, let's bring in everyone else so Wildfire, Heartbreaker, and Duchess, after you eat can you open up the walls and get it ready for the crowd we have outside? I'd appreciate it."

I wait for everyone to clear the room. Bray is sitting back down with Alder kneeling before her. Surprisingly, Shadow is still sitting next to my sister. Bray is clinging to Shadow's hand, which totally bewilders me. I didn't think they had met until this morning.

"Bray, hey, sis, let's get you something to eat. I can

take you to my cabin so you can have some privacy, if you want."

She flips her head up and she looks pissed while she looks at me.

"Why, Brenna, are you now embarrassed by what I just said, don't want anyone to associate you with me? Don't worry, little sister, you're safe, doubt anyone will do that. I'm the dirty whore, not you."

Besides shocking the shit out of me, her words piss me off and that is saying a lot. Usually, I use my humor but not this time, instead I use my voice.

"What the fuck, Bray? You idiot, I'm not embarrassed by you or what happened. I'm worried about you; guess you forgot what my club does. I've seen hundreds of women just like you, no, let me finish. What comes next is one of the hardest things you'll ever go through, that's what I'm worried about. I thought maybe you'd need a quiet place for a second or two, not everyone up your ass and in your business, and not in that order. So do what you want, Bray, just trying to be your sister and friend."

I turn to walk out until I hear the first sob. It literally breaks my heart, but I keep walking. She's got to want me here for her, I can't force it. By the third sob I'm dragging my feet. Then I hear it.

"Please don't go, Brenna. I'm sorry, seems like I'm barking at all the wrong people. Don't go, little sister, I need you."

Turning, she's almost right in front of me and crushes me in her arms, silently sobbing. Wrapping my arms around her I hang on tightly, knowing there is nothing I can do to take her pain away except be here for her. Not sure how but, within minutes, the entire O'Brien clan is in the room, all surrounding Bray. Though we all lose it when our dad pushes to the front and gently lifts Bray's face.

"I'm proud of ya, lass. Now you hold that pretty head up high and tell them all to go fuck themselves."

Dad always gets a bit more Irish when he's pissed. I just knew Mom wasn't going to let him get away with what he said.

"Paddy, language please, you're talking to a lady. Bray, I agree with your daddy, just forget the filthy words he used to get his point across. Now let's suck it up, we're O'Briens. Tink and Mamma Diane tell me we need to get out there before the men eat everything and leave us crumbs."

With that my family breaks apart, though Dad holds on to Bray's hand as he starts to walk back out. Well, until Alder comes on the other side of my sister. So she walks out holding two men's hands and surrounded by my four brothers. She has her own security if needed. Feeling a hand land hard on my shoulder, I look to see Shadow glaring at me.

"Good job, Raven. There's hope for you yet. Let's eat, I'm starving, and we are only half through this shit. Up next is your ex, which should be fun. Hey, don't say a word. I won't put my hands on him unless the club says it's okay. I follow the rules at all times."

The serious look on her face and those words has me

cracking up. She watches for a few seconds then she too starts to laugh. Together we walk out with smiles on our faces to the amazement of everyone on the outside.

Once everyone is sitting again, I wait. When Glory clears her thoughts, she starts talking about what's going to happen next. When she calls our family name, every one of us—including Alder—up front stands and makes our way to the center of the circle of tables. Mom starts with what she had written down.

"Hi, y'all, I'm Gertie Sterling and these are my boys Reed, Rue, Alder, Asher, and Rowan. We've lived on our ranch in Timber-Ghost, Montana since before Asher was born. Now, before I begin, neither my boys nor I have anything good to say about Cliff Sterling. We don't claim him as part of our family, haven't for years. We will do everything we can to help you with bringing down that brotherhood of despicable men. Though there are some foul women included, just so you know. Now there is no question that we won't answer. So go ahead, start, we're ready, right, boys?"

We all start to shake our heads until my eyes are drawn to Shadow's dead icy-blue eyes. They are staring a hole into my chest. Glaring at me, she raises her eyebrows at Gertie's words. Oh shit, I have a feeling this one is going to be the monkey on my back. Like Gertie said, there is no question they won't answer. Lucky me.

NINE
'ASH'
ASHTON

Can't believe I was able to get some food down, but damn, it's from the Wooden Spirit Bar and Grill. I've never had a bad meal there. And after looking around, everyone in my family seems to be in agreement. As some of Brenna's, I guess I'd call them her club sisters, start to clean up, I see her prez, VP, and the skull face one coming our way. Mom stands right in front of me, though she wouldn't be able to do much. These women are trained in a way they could kill me before I would even know what hit me, I'm sure.

"Mrs. Sterling, my name is Tink. To my right is my Vice President Glory, and to my left is our Security President Shadow. Thank you for taking the time to come out to the ranch and try to help us with the Thunder Cloud Knuckle Brotherhood. They've been a pain in our butts and, hopefully, we might be able to work together to clear our town—no, our state—of those asinine bastards. Pardon my language, my mom would soap my mouth for talking so disrespectfully."

I watch Mom put her hand out to Tink, who grabs it. I'm close enough to hear their conversation, though barely.

"Tink, thank you for that. Glory, nice to mee you. Shadow, nice to meet you also, though I think Security President is stretching it a bit, don't you? I wasn't born yesterday, ladies. Now please, quit walking on eggshells. See these men around me, them there are my boys and not a one of them has ever apologized for cussing. Now I know we have some things to discuss, are you ready for us yet?"

I watch as the women seem to be bonding. Alder is still with Bray, so that leaves me with my three brothers, Reed, Rue, Rowan. Mom turns and starts to introduce us. Though when she says my name everything stops. Shadow growls low in her throat and everyone steps back, even Mom, with huge eyes. Before anyone can do or say a thing, Avalanche and another man with long black hair in a braid walk up behind her. I think I heard someone call him Panther. So the one I think is Panther puts his hand on Shadow's shoulder.

"Nizhoni, we spoke about this. Growling is not acceptable, you know this. Look, you scared everyone. She's okay, folks, just a bit protective over her sister, Raven."

Mom and my brothers look at me and I mouth, "Brenna" and they all nod. Tink pushes, yeah literally pushes, Shadow aside and holds on to my mom's hand.

"My real name is Maggie; you call me whichever you're comfortable with. May I ask your name, or do you prefer Mrs. Sterling?"

"Maggie, no, I hate that name. You can call me Gertrude or Gertie."

As the two women start talking and walking, we all slowly follow, though I'm nervous and don't want Shadow behind me. When one of my brothers puts a hand on my shoulder, I turn to see I'm surrounded by my brothers, with both Reed and Rue behind me and with my younger brother Rowan at my side. Well, that makes me feel more secure. I know Brenna is pissed at me, but for fuck's sake, we were both played as fools by my dad. We all take a seat as Tink walks to the head of the tables set in a circular design.

I hear someone bang on a table and the room goes quiet, until I turn to see the older couple walk through the doors surrounded by a bunch of mean as fuck men. Can't believe Momma Diane and Tank made it. I heard Tank had a heart attack not that long ago.

Suddenly, everyone is on their feet clapping and talking at once. I can see Tank getting a bit overwhelmed until Momma Diane puts her hands up.

"Come on, give Tank a break. He knows everyone is happy he's here. This is way too important for us to miss, on so many levels. So go on, get with it, we'll just mind our business over here. Oh wow. Hi, Gertie. Hey, boys. It's been a while. Paddy and Bronagh, good to see you both. And the whole O'Brien clan. Damn, good time to have a party, though with that thought not a good time. Sorry, Maggie, go on. Zipping it now."

That brings a grin to my face because that's how women are. All over the place. Feeling eyes on me, I look up and see both Brenna and Shadow watching my every move, though I think for different reasons.

"First off, I would like to thank everyone for coming together with a unified purpose: to help get rid of the Thunder Cloud Knuckle Brotherhood from our town and state. Now this next phase is going to be difficult for the Sterling family, so please hold your comments and tongues until they are done. Turning over the floor to the Sterlings. Please explain what has happened and what is still going on. I understand there is an entire section of land, approximately one hundred acres, that the brotherhood is now using as their own. Also, are we to understand that Cliff Sterling is a part of the brotherhood organization? The floor is yours."

Mom looks around the room then at all of us before she glances at Bray and Alder. I can tell she hates the defeated look on Bray's face and feels responsible because of our asshole father. She smiles at Bray, who gives her a small grin back.

"My name is Gertie Sterling. I hate that last name but it's mine. I had no idea about the man I married and it took years for his true colors to come out. Unfortunately for Brenna and Asher, it came out at their engagement party. For that I will be forever sorry because if two kids were ever supposed to be together, it was my Ash and Brenna.

"What Cliff did that night shocked our entire family. I thought he was messing around with some woman in another town. God, if only. There was no way that Thunder Cloud Knuckle Brotherhood would allow Asher to marry Brenna. They didn't consider her purebred enough. Not my way of thinking, O'Brien clan, swear to God. To me, people are people to be judged on their actions and how they treat folks.

"When we got back to the ranch after Cliff broke the kids up, when Ash got home after leaving with Patsy, Cliff took Ash and locked him in the root cellar on our ranch. And he beat him to an inch of his life because Asher would not marry Patsy Woods as Cliff was ordering him to. Then he just lost his mind. Started beating each boy because he was trying to get to me. My boys refused to let him put his hands on me so they all took a beating. Well, until Rue took a branding iron to the back of his head. Then together we packed his crap and the boys drove him to the edge of our property. That's when we found out what he'd been up to. There were cabins and tents along with campers. And a lot of folks we didn't know. Reed checked his father first 'cause he's softhearted, then the boys dumped him and his crap out of the truck and left.

"We've not seen or heard from Cliff since then. Until he drove right up to our ranch home and walked right in like it was his. Rowan was home with me and he grabbed the hunting rifle we keep in the living room. When Cliff challenged him, my boy Rowan lifted the rifle and pointed it right at his father. Cliff called him, excuse my language, 'a fruit cup pussy,' which pushed Rowan to pull the trigger. The bullet grazed his upper arm or shoulder. He looked at Rowan and told him to watch his back because no one shoots at him and gets away with it. Then he proceeded to tell me I had to sign the papers he brought with him that would sell over two hundred acres of our ranch to some corporation I've never heard of. Now let me tell ya, my boys and I have kept that ranch running all this time. Ash has just about died running it, and Alder, Rue and Reed are always there to lend a hand. Rowan is following in Ash's footsteps. I'm not letting anyone buy our land. And to make it worse, Cliff told me any money from the sale would be his since he was kicked outta his own home. That home belonged to my parents. We're here today because we need help. That brotherhood is trying to run us off our property. Stuff has been happening recently that has never happened before. We lost half of our chicken coop because someone opened the latched door and some predator walked right in, caught them, and tore them to pieces. One of the tractors was messed with to the point Ash can't even use it anymore. And we can't afford a new one."

I hear a voice clear in the back of the room. When I turn, Tank has got his hand up, well, two fingers. Tink nods so he jumps in.

"Mrs. Sterling, I mean, Gertie, I've got just about every kind of farming equipment a man can have. Tomorrow, Ash, you come by, tell me which tractor you need, and I'll have one of the Intruders bring it to your ranch. Also, if you're okay with it, I'll put a rotation in so there will always be a few Intruders around your homestead. Gertie, that's mainly for your protection as I don't trust Cliff or those bastards, pardon my language, he runs with. Zoey can get with her dad, Sheriff George, to make sure the county deputies drive by the house more too. It might let them sons of bitches know you're not alone or scared of them. I suggest everyone start carrying. And I mean on you, holster it up. Better to be safe than sorry. Sorry, Maggie, go on."

"Nope, Dad, thanks. Also, Gertie, the Devil's Handmaidens will also have a few of our sisters out to the ranch, so they see there are others who will protect you while having your backs. And if needed, we have other chapters all over the country who would be more than willing to pitch in."

Mom looks around and we can tell she's about to lose it. For so long we've tried to deal with this on our own. Until Alder found Bray. That's when I hear my brother's voice.

"It ain't my story to tell and no one's business if she don't want to share. I saw where they were keeping Bray and the other women. In my heart, I believe when we got away, they killed those poor women. It ain't right what they are doing. I aim to protect the forests and its population of wildlife being a LEO. Sorry, law enforcement officer. We've seen carcasses all over that area they are poaching for food but leaving most of the remains right where they dropped them. There is a circle of life out there and they are altering it. That circle is the way nature takes and gives back life to our earth. When that process is messed with, a lot of things fall off course. We Montanans are proud of our state and especially our forests. We need to get them and their filthy ways out of there and off our property. The problem is their numbers are growing quickly, so we need help."

The room goes eerily quiet. Glancing around, I can see everyone is trying to come up with a plan, but there is no quick fix. It's going to take some time and effort to rid these assholes from our town.

"Ash, what are your thoughts on all of this? We've heard from your momma and brother, now I want to hear from you, boy."

Knowing she's trying to rile me up, I look right at her and smirk. Her eyes turn ice-blue and she tilts her head at me. Everyone is watching our back-and-forth, kinda like a tennis match. I don't know or owe her anything. Though when Mom grabs my hand, I know I'm gonna have to play nice. At least for now.

"Shadow, I'm totally on board with my mom and brothers. We want them gone; however it happens. They are not only trouble, I'm afraid of what they are doing up there on public land. Lots of activity, which tells me they got nothing but bad intentions. I'm here for two reasons and I'll share them with the room. Our family needs help from our community. Now we could have gone to a town hall meeting but what are the hundreds of ranchers gonna do. We don't want to be responsible for anyone else getting hurt. From what I hear, the Devil's Handmaidens have dealt with similar situations.

Mom finally let loose on the keeping things close to the chest, as they say. Though my second reason for me being here is where my attention will be concentrated on."

I don't say another word. She glares at me then the room. Finally, she lets loose as I knew she would.

"Whatcha waiting for, boy? What's your second reason for being here today? I mean, I've been here for years and I might have seen you a couple times in the distance or when you came into the Wooden Spirit Bar and Grill with your momma or brothers. So you gonna share or are we playin' a guessing game, Ash? 'Cause we still have to come up with a plan, so time is wasting."

I look around the room, making eye contact with a few folks. Avalanche, who grins. I'm guessing he knows what my second reason is. Momma Diane and Tank, who nod my way. Tink, who is watching between Shadow and me. Finally, I lay eyes on her. Brenna. Her cheeks start to turn pink and when I see movement—it's two of her brothers—one being the ex-military beast from the Blue Sky Sanctuary. Can't remember his name. When he stands, along with his brothers, mine come up behind me just as Alder walks up to us. It's time, so I just say what's on my mind.

"My main reason for finally reaching out is because Mom let loose on the gag order. I'm here to get my fiancée back and start our lives together. So, Shadow, to be clear, my intentions are for Brenna. Not that it's any of your goddamn business, lady, but since you asked and I was raised by a woman who taught us to respect our elders, I'm trying to right now."

I hear the gasp go through the room. And if I'm right, Shadow's face turned a bit red under that tattoo.

"So, to finish this up so we can get onto what's important right now. I'm making it clear to the O'Briens, Devil's Handmaidens MC, Tank's club, and anyone else who wants to know. I'm staking my claim. Brenna O'Brien, you're mine, always have been and always will be. With Mr. O'Brien's permission, I'm gonna be courting you again, woman. Be ready. Now as much as I hate to bring them into anything that is close to Brenna, let's work on figuring out how to rid our town of the brotherhood."

With that I sit down as my legs are shaking. My brothers pound on my shoulders and back while Mom gives me one of her short smiles, the ones when we do something she's proud of. Not wanting to but I feel the need, I glance to Shadow to see she's looking right back at me. When she sees my eyes, she gives me a demented smile then claps a few times silently. Then she motions her fingers to her eyes then at me. Great, she's watching me.

When I can drag my eyes from hers, I look to where Brenna is. Her cute face is all pink and her head is down. Knowing I embarrassed her, it hurts to know she hates her business out there for all to see. At that moment, her dad makes it worse.

"Ash, son, listen up. Brenna's mom and I give you permission but this time if you hurt her again—I'm sorry, Gertie—but I'll bust your arse over my knees. Don't screw it up, Ash."

I hear the slight giggle and see Brenna looking at her dad with a cute little smile on her face. It's quiet for a few then Tink calls both Brenna and someone named Freak to come around with their computers. Then we all buckle down and concentrate on our main problem in Timber-Ghost, Montana. The assholes that go by the Thunder Cloud Knuckle Brotherhood.

TEN
'RAVEN'
BRENNA

The meeting ran on and on, seemed like forever. Freak and I ran the computer part of it. We hacked just about every government agency in Montana, trying to find out who's backing the brotherhood. We have some ideas but not enough proof. Tink finally called it at around six thirty in the evening.

Everyone starts to get up and leave. I grab my stuff, put it in my messenger bag, and quietly walk out of the barn, heading directly to my cabin. I need some solace to try and concentrate on all that happened today. Too much information, my brain actually hurts. I send a quick text to both Onyx and Ollie, letting them know I have a headache coming on. Tink already told me in the morning we would meet at the clubhouse and start the digging and pulling apart whatever documents we found. And I'm taking a deep look at Cliff Sterling and who he is. Something doesn't sit right, not sure why.

Just as I walk past the empty cabin next to me, I hear

footsteps. I ignore them and move a bit quicker to my own cabin.

"Brenna, wait a second, need to talk to you."

Shit, it's Ash. I don't have the energy or desire to have this conversation now, though don't think I'm going to have a choice.

"Come on in, Ash, I'll grab us some waters. Just letting you know, not sure how long I'll last, getting a migraine. So if at all possible, make it quick."

Not looking his way, I open the cabin up and walk right to the refrigerator, opening it and grabbing two bottles of water. When I go to turn, he is right there. So close I drop the waters on the floor. He leans in and only his mouth touches mine in a soft gentle kiss. That's it, then he's turning, walks to the sectional, and sits.

I pick up the waters and go to the chair, plopping down. I throw his water at him. We both drink down at least a quarter of the bottle.

"I know you're private, but I had to say what I did. And I mean it, Brenna. Regardless if you believe it or not, we belong together. I'm not going to lose this opportunity to be with you again. So warning, I'll be around, gonna have to get used to it. I'll let you get some rest tonight. See ya tomorrow."

With that he gets up, leans in front of me, gives me another kiss but this one is a bit more. His lips are firm and when he swipes the seam of my lips, I gasp, which gives him an in. When he starts to taste me, I can't stop the moan from escaping. His hands are in my hair and his fingers are applying pressure. As he moves his hands this way then that, I can feel the tension in my head becoming less. His mouth searches mine and his scent fills my nose. My arms are around his neck, holding him to me. Just as it starts to move in the right direction, I hear that familiar growl. Oh, come on, are you kidding me?

"Kids, time to break. Ash, if you're gonna court our girl, probably going to need a chaperone. Don't want no hanky-panky right off the bat. So say a quick goodnight now."

She turns around, facing the wall, but I can tell she's holding in her laughter as her shoulders are shaking. Right before Ash lets loose, Panther is at the door.

"Come on, Zoey, enough for tonight. They are adults, let them be. No, let's go home. Ma'iitsoh and Zhį́'ii need to be taken care of and need some attention. Ash, those are our wolves back at our ranch. Enjoy your evening. Raven, I'll see you tomorrow. George is also looking into some of the stuff we went over, so he'll come along tomorrow to share what he's found. Come on, Nizhoni, let's go home."

Watching them leave, I feel lonely and alone. Even Shadow found someone, actually her soulmate.

"What does nizhoni mean, Brenna? Never heard that word before."

"It's Navajo for beautiful, I believe. Now are you going, Ash?"

"Are you asking me to leave, or maybe you want me to stay?"

Looking at him, I cross my arms over my chest. His eyes go to my arms then to my body.

"You've changed, Brenna. When did you get so well ripped?"

"Part of the job, Ash. I'm tired and need to get some rest. I'm sorry you and your family have gone through what you have. I can't imagine that. My club sisters and I will help as much as possible."

He stares for a bit then nods, turning and walking out the door. I follow, close the heavy wooden door, and lock the deadbolt and handle lock. By the time I make it to my bedroom, my head is throbbing. Ripping my clothes off, I move to the shower, letting the cool water run through my thick hair. Quickly and efficiently, I wash my hair then condition. Next, I wash my body. Once done, I step out, dry off, and walk into my bedroom. Finding some sleep shorts and a long sleeve T-shirt, I put them on then walk directly to my bed, pulling the covers down and getting in. Already feeling better from the shower, I hit the button for my fan. Grabbing my lavender eye mask Taz gave me, which seems to help when a headache is coming on, I put it on and close my eyes. I start to take the deep breaths she's always talked to me about. Probably by breath ten I fall into a deep sleep.

Not sure what wakes me, but immediately I'm wide awake. Lying in my bed, I take a minute or two to try and fully wake up and figure out what the hell woke me from such a deep sleep. Then I hear it again, my phone is vibrating on my dresser. Jumping up, I grab it and see a bunch of missed calls. Going to my phone section there are calls from Onyx, Alder, and just now Orin. What the fuck?

I hit the last call, which is Orin, and wait impatiently. When he picks up, I immediately know something is wrong by the tone in his voice.

"Brenna, please tell me Bray is at your place? My God, we can't find her and Onyx and Alder are going to kill each other with blame. I don't know what to do. How could she just disappear into thin air? Brenna, what do I do?"

His panic actually puts me at ease. I always work best under pressure.

"Orin, chill. Did you reach out to anyone else? Like Ollie or Mom and Dad? Okay, let's split it up. I'll call Ollie and Bennett; you call Oliver and Brooks. You call the Sterling ranch and I'll reach out to the parents. I'll also reach out to Tink to see what she thinks. Make the calls, Orin, now, and then get back to me. Talk to you in a bit."

Without thought, I make my calls, taking notes, and telling everyone to keep their eyes open. Tink tells me she'll be right down and hangs up. Great, better put on some clothes. I grab some leggings and a heavy sweatshirt, pulling my hair into a ponytail. Finally, heavy wool socks since right now Montana weather is all over the place.

I just walk into the kitchen to start some tea when I hear a knock. Walking to the door, I look out the peephole and see not only Tink but also Noodles, Squirt,

Peanut, and Wildcat. I open the door and wave them in. Tink jumps right in.

"Anything, Raven? I put a shout-out to Zoey. She, Panther, and Avalanche are going to head over to Alder's as they are closer. Didn't want to but called my dad and he's putting out a call out to all Intruders to get their asses up and start looking for Bray. Zoey said she'd call Sheriff George to go over to the Sterling ranch and make sure those assholes didn't grab Bray again. I need you to stay chill, sister, we'll find her, promise."

I nod then ask if anyone wants some tea or coffee. As everyone sits around, I go back to the kitchen and start the kettle and get my Keurig ready to make a pot of coffee. I'm so in my head that when I look up at the window by the kitchen sink and see a face, I scream like crazy. The face ducks down and everyone runs to see what's wrong. I point to the window, unable to get a word out, and Noodles is the first out the door, followed by Wildcat.

By the time I get out the front door, I hear some scuffling and muffles in the back of the cabin.

"Calm down, woman. Come on, we need to get you inside, you're freezing. No, I'm not gonna let you go. Either walk or I'll pick you up, choice is yours."

Watching Wildcat come around the corner first, I can see Noodles dragging someone carefully. Don't recognize her at first but when she lifts her head, I see it's Bray.

"Bray, holy shit, you scared the ever-lovin' fuck outta me, sister. What the hell, why are you sneaking around at night by yourself? Come on, let's get inside. Noodles is right, you're freezing, let's get some dry clothes on you and some hot tea. No, don't argue, I've got tons of folks looking for you, Bray. Move your bony ass inside, now."

Slowly she walks in front of me toward the cabin. When inside, I can see her trembling badly. Very gently I put my hands on her upper arms and give her a push toward my bedroom. I can hear my club sisters following as Noodles is on his phone letting people know she's here.

"Bray, get out of those wet clothes. I'll get you something dry and warm. Come on, don't be shy now."

I don't see her face but when she takes off the flannel-lined shirt and pulls her T-shirt up and off, I hear a gasp. Turning from my dresser, I see Bray standing in the middle of my bedroom, hands covering her bra-clad body. Tink and Wildcat are in the hallway and both have horrified looks on their faces. I squint to see her body better and notice the lines across her stomach. Also see round red circles. Just as I'm about to ask her how she got them, Squirt and Peanut push past Tink and Wildcat and pull Bray into the bathroom, closing the door. *What the hell is going on*, I think to myself?

"I'm lost, why did Squirt and Peanut grab Bray and shove her into the bathroom? I'm confused as hell?"

Tink and Wildcat look at each other, then both walk toward me. Wildcat pushes me down onto the edge of the bed as they both kneel in front of me.

"Raven, not sure, but Tink and I've seen that kind of

abuse before. It's done over a long period of time and is the work of sadistic pricks. I think our younger sisters saw how upset and embarrassed Bray was. Especially with you seeing the damage done to her. We'll go sit with Noodles, try to get Bray alone. Then let her know how much you love her and are proud of her strength. Tell the young ones to come out so you two can have some private time."

Nodding, I wait 'til they leave then go and knock on the door softly.

"Bray, hey, it's just me. Come on, it's okay. There's nothing you can tell or show me that's going to make me not be proud of my big sister. You survived, don't forget that, so they didn't win. Please come out and talk to me. You came to me for a reason, don't let the fear push you back down. Bray, we're sisters, no matter what. Remember what you, Onyx, and I used to say? 'Sisters forever and always, no matter what comes our way. We'll always be honest and tell each other the worst first.' Please trust me."

I wait and finally I see the doorknob turning. Squirt comes out first, grabs me, and pulls me close.

"Raven, she's fucked up. Something wigged her out but she won't say what. Take it slow. I'll be out there if you need me."

Next is Peanut, who just gives me a tiny smile then walks out following Squirt. I wait, and after maybe five minutes Bray comes out in my robe. It hangs on her and it isn't until this minute I realize how skinny she is. I mean skeletal. I wait and don't rush her, just stand here.

She eventually walks toward me but stops within a foot or so from me. We look at each other and finally she drops her head.

"I can't stay with Alder anymore. He doesn't deserve to have to deal with my neuroses. He should be with someone who has their shit together. And if he knew what happened, he'd never even talk to me again. I know everyone wants to know every detail but, Brenna, all I want to do is forget. Why do I have to relive it? My mind is almost broken, don't want to take the chance and lose the little bit of myself left. Do you understand?"

I nod but still keep my tongue. I'm outta my element. I'm best behind a computer being the nerd I am. Or being the clown of the club. I don't know what to say or do and am afraid of doing more damage to my already severely damaged sister. Since I've not said a word, Bray turns around and drops my robe off her shoulders so it gathers at her waist. My mouth drops open and I can feel the tears rolling down my face. Her back is beyond a mess. I have no idea what they did or used, but her entire back is covered in scars on top of scars. Some look like old wounds while others look pretty recent. One even looks infected. *My poor sister,* I think as she pulls the robe back up.

"I can't show this to Mom and Dad. Definitely not our alpha brothers, they'll go to the Thunder Cloud Knuckle Brotherhood and get themselves killed. I don't belong here and I can't go back. Tonight, I was in the bathroom holding a razor blade, trying to get up the courage to just cut my wrists and end all this pain."

That right there brings me out of my lack of reaction. I grab Bray and pull her close. As soon as she hits my chest, she starts to wail loudly. When I see Squirt and Tink in the doorway, I tell them to call Dr. Cora and the therapist from Blue Sky Sanctuary. My sister is in a downward spiral and needs intervention right now. I can only pray it's not too late because my family will never be the same if she does something to hurt herself.

When Tink comes back, I quietly tell her to call my parents and tell them they are needed at my place. She nods and goes to do my bidding.

ELEVEN
'TINK'
MAGGIE/GOLDILOCK

After telling Squirt to make the calls, something pulls me back to where Raven and Bray are. Watching the two of them together, it's apparent something is going on with Bray. She's extremely pale and it looks like she's fighting to keep her eyes open. Not sure why, but I look down to her hands and when I see the red at her wrists, I go into reactive form.

"Raven, pull that robe off of her. Now, sister, something isn't right. She's got blood coming out from under the sleeve of that robe."

As soon as Bray feels Raven grabbing for the robe sleeve she starts to fight. Knowing time is of the essence, I grab Bray's arms and pull them back, which jerks her to me. I see Raven's eyes taking in every part of her sister. When her eyes get huge, I know she's seen what I just saw also. Bray goes limp in my arms. Even though she's taller, I manage to get her to a rocker and gently sit her down. I've let her arms go and I have one robe sleeve while Raven has the other. Slowly and carefully, one at a time, we remove Bray's arms out of the fluffy robe. Even though I suspected it, the sight before me tears my heart out, seeing the towels wrapped around Bray's wrists, which are now covered in blood.

"Motherfucker, Bray, what the hell are ya thinking? I put a shout-out to our family. Do you want them to see you like this? For Christ's sake. Holy shit, those are my washrags. You did this here in my home, like right now? What the fuck, Bray?"

Bray is softly crying as Raven rips into her. I'm totally surprised at my club sister's reaction, but I don't interrupt because I wouldn't like it if the roles were reversed. I walk into the kitchen, go through some cabinets, and come out with two baking bowls. I go to the freezer and grab ice, partially filling the bowls. I walk to Bray and lift her arms, placing each one in a bowl, then I cover her wrists with ice to slow down the bleeding. She isn't going to die; the cuts are horizontal and not too deep. Probably will need stitches, but Dr. Cora can do it here or at her clinic. If we take Bray to the hospital, they will put her into a seventy-two-hour psych lockdown, and that's something she doesn't need right now.

Hearing boots pounding up the front stairs, the door bursts open and the O'Briens rush in. As soon as Raven's mom, Bronagh, sees Bray and what she's done, she kneels in front of her, placing her head in her daughter's lap. Everyone is shocked, well, until Bray leans over her mom and starts to cry. Everyone is trying to give them some privacy so the O'Brien sons and dad step back out. Raven is standing right off to the side of her sister and mom, watching them both closely. I take a second to try and read what's going on, and it's typical victim/survivor mentality. One thing is for sure, Bray is going to need some deep intense therapy if she plans to try and move forward to find her place in this crazy as shit world we live in. Once trust is broken it never can be rebuilt one-hundred-percent. It's going to take a very special person for Bray to trust even a little bit.

Knowing I should get out and try and calm down the male O'Brien clan, I head toward the door. Just as I go to push open the door, I hear a soft, "Wait." Turning, I see Bray looking my way, face a mess. Something in her eyes stops me dead in my tracks.

"I'm afraid to even say these words, especially since Brenna already thinks even less of me. I'm in trouble, Tink, I need help. I was against it when Onyx brought it up, but do you by chance have any room so I can stay on your ranch? Maybe get some help with these issues that are bombarding me. Please?"

My heart breaks at how wounded and scared Bray sounds. I look to Raven to see she's shocked by her sister's words. Well, she was going at her pretty hard. Then Bray shocks the shit out of all of us in the room.

"Oh, Brenna, to answer your question, yes, I slit my wrists here in your cabin. Want to know why? Because I needed to feel some kind of release and doing it here, I knew I would be safe because you were also here. You stooge, I don't want to kill myself, I wanted to get some of the pressure off of me. That's all. Thanks though for your confidence in me. Means the world, lil' sister. Just sayin'."

I walk back over to Bray and lean down, though we're almost the same height with her sitting down. I gently put my hands on her shoulders and squeeze.

"Bray, you are welcome here any time. That's for you, not for Raven. Our doors are always open for someone who is trying to survive what they've been through. Now let me check on your family then make sure Dr. Cora is on her way. She'll take care of everything. In the meantime, I'll figure out where you can sleep tonight. Tomorrow we'll do a full intake then set you up. Do you have any digital footprints out there? You know, mobile phone, tablet, or social media? Need to know that before anything else."

Bray's eyes continue to look my way, except when I said digital footprint. Then she looks at her sister with confusion in her eyes. Raven explains as best she can.

"Bray, digital footprint means if you've been on electronics and they are registered in your name or you just post, stating who you are, then you can be traced, and maybe even found wherever you're hiding. That's why it so important for Tink to know this because if the Devil's Handmaidens club is taking you on, they have to make sure not only you are safe but also so is everyone else on the ranch in protective custody. Some of the survivors are planning on making the ranch their home, so we have to secure their safety. Just be honest, big sister, all we can ask of you."

Watching the two of them together, it's hard to believe Bray is the older one. She's way underweight and her skin color is off. She has barely any muscle tone while Raven is ripped. She's very dedicated to working out, though now I think some of it was her trying to keep her mind off her past and loss. I'm going to make Bray a top priority because she's my sister Raven's biological sister. Best I can do. Both Raven and I are looking at Bray, waiting on her answer to our question.

"Oh, sorry, had a brain fart. No, I've not been on any social media. Well, I looked through Alder's Facebook page but didn't post anything. Also, I don't have a cell phone, they took mine and stomped on it when they took me. They wanted me to know I had no way to reach out to anyone."

"Bray, honey, think about it right now. You did kind of reach out to Alder when he walked in and saw you there. The FBI is going to hike with Alder in the morning so they can try to help those other women up there. Now we are going to take care of you. So after the intake, I'll make sure our technology officer gives you a brand-new cell phone with all the contact numbers of each Devil's Handmaidens sister. Also, my parents, Tank and Momma Diane. Finally, the phone will have numbers for my man Noodles, Shadow's man, Panther, and our brother, Avalanche. That will give you options if you need to call for a hand with anything that comes up. Does that sound good to you?"

"Yeah, it does, Tink. I'll try my best to not upset your technology officer too much. Well, as long as she doesn't get all snippy with me. I appreciate all you're doing for me."

Mrs. O'Brien leans up, tears in her eyes, as she intensely looks my way. Knowing how my mom is, I see Mrs. O'Brien's gratitude and something I can't recognize in her eyes. I smile widely and she returns with one of her own.

Just as I'm about to go into more details of what Bray can expect, I see Squirt walking through the front door, leading Dr. Cora in.

"Prez, got Dr. Cora here. Might want to step outside and give them O'Brien men an update on what's going on in here. They are about to tear this cabin off its foundation and take it back to their ranch. Just a heads-up."

Smiling at Squirt, I nod at Dr. Cora.

"Doc, she needs a full assessment, if not tonight then tomorrow. She's going to be getting a full intake interview. Then we'll assess and figure the next steps. As of right now, no digital footprint or social media except through a friend's Facebook page, though no actual comments put out by Bray. She probably needs some stitches and something to cut the edge, don't think she's been sleeping too much. Definite PTSD and victim's remorse. Will need a full blood panel and also will probably need a full workup, including for sexually transmitted diseases. No, Bray, lift your head high, that's not on you, sweetie. Now I'm going to give you some privacy as I go talk to your dad and brothers. Don't worry, I'll only tell them that you're okay and talking to

Dr. Cora. Be back shortly. Tonight, you'll stay at the ranch with us. I already have one of our club sister's preparing a room for you. We got you, Bray, swear to God."

Before I even make it to the door, I feel very thin arms wrap around me from behind. Bray lays her head on my back and in a barely-there whisper takes my breath away.

"Tink, there are no words but let me try though, understand I've been out of the loop for a while. We didn't get to talk much up there in that cabin. I will forever be in your debt and the Devil's Handmaidens club. Between you, your club, and Alder, I have many folks to pay back. No, don't say it, I'll figure it out eventually with some help. For now, if whoever is setting up my room for the night, can they leave a pad of paper and pencils or pens? Before my brain goes to mush, I need to write down everything I can remember. I need to feel like I'm doing something to bring those jerks down, even if what I give you doesn't help. Again, they are only words but please know how much I appreciate what you're doing. I couldn't go to my parents' house right now. I wake up screaming, wanting to run out of the house. Yeah, poor Alder, don't think he's gotten much sleep either. Oh, guess it's good I'm telling you this now and not when I'm screaming in the middle of the night."

Turning slowly, I grab her hands and squeeze them lightly. Looking past her, I see Raven, head down, while her mom holds on to one of her hands. Yeah, lots of history here, this family is going to need to get some help. I knew Raven's parents weren't thrilled when she decided to join the Devil's Handmaidens but thought they got over it. We'll see. Then I glance down at Bray, who must have turned her head, because she also is watching her mom and sister. Then her eyes look to me.

"Bray, I'm glad you told me but you need to know a few things. First, the ranch house always has people on guard, in and outside of the house. It could be one of my club sisters or one of my dad's brothers from his club. Or my ol' man or Shadow's or even Avalanche. Once in a great while we have to call in the troops, and that's when Ollie's crew helps out. Before you ask the question in your eyes, we take in survivors who have been abused, beaten, raped, and even worse. To keep them here we have to make sure they understand they are safe. We also have to be safe and in the last couple of years that wasn't so. Bad people got on my ranch with devious intentions. So now we do what we must. Not to mention that Sheriff George has us on a rotation so his deputies will drive up to the ranch and make sure all looks good. If you scream, is it better to wake you or let you be? Hey, look at me, Bray, we've all been there in one capacity or another. Now, if you need someone to talk to about the nightmares and shit, go to either Shadow, Glory, Taz, or Vixen. Each one of those sisters will be able to help you with how to handle those nightmares. Also, once you've agreed to stay with us, we'll introduce you to the therapist who works with us and with Blue Sky Sanctuary. She's really good and never judges, just so you know. Now let me go have a word with your dad and brothers. Go be with your mom and sister; they probably are worried sick about you. Dr. Cora will take good care of you. Bray, welcome, sister, we got you."

After another brief hug she lets me go, and I walk out into a tornado of emotions coming off the men standing and sitting on the stairs of Raven's cabin. Damn, why didn't I bring Noodles with me, he could have defused this situation way quicker than I'm going to be able to. Oh well, will do my best, that's all I can do.

TWELVE
'ASH'
ASHTON

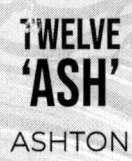

I hate calling for help. For fuck's sake, I've been ranching my entire life so why does this have to be so hard? Horses give birth all the time. I've watched and helped when needed, but this one we're gonna lose if I don't put in a call. Goddamn it, not what I want to do. Mom seems a bit out of it, so don't want to bother her if I don't have to. I texted Reed to see if he could come give me a hand but got nothing back. So, reaching for my phone again, I look up the number to Blue Sky Sanctuary. Well, it's Ollie's cell so I hit dial and wait. It doesn't take him long, wonder why he's not asleep.

"Ash, what ya need at this time of night? If it can wait, I'd appreciate it."

"Wish it could, Ollie. I need Paisley here, got a horse in distress and I can't seem to help her. I even put a call out to the doctor in our family but he's not getting back to me. From what I can tell the foal is breach and I can't turn it, though I've tried a few times. Mom's breathing is getting a bit rough so before I lose them both, if at all possible, do you think Paisley can come on by to give me a hand?"

I don't hear anything for a second or two then I hear him let out a huge breath. Oh shit, maybe he's involved with something himself. I didn't even think of that. That sanctuary takes in not only ex-military who need help physically, mentally, and emotionally but also animals who are either abused or abandoned. Damn, I'm sure he's got his hands full.

"Ollie, forget it, you sound like you have your hands full. Let me put out a call to my brothers, someone should be able to give me a hand. Sorry to bother ya."

Before I can hang up, I hear him yelling not to hang up so I don't.

"Fuck, Ash, it's not you. We're at Brenna's because Bray ran away from Alder's tonight and showed up here. Then she went into Brenna's bathroom and slit her wrists. Now she's on suicide watch and will be staying with the Devil's Handmaidens at the ranch so there are eyes on her all the time. Just another long night, brother, that's all. Let me see if Phantom or one of the other folks can drive Paisley to the ranch. Which barn are you set up in so I can let her know? Probably gonna have to give her around forty-five minutes before she can get there. Well, unless it's Phantom driving then she'll be there quicker. Does that work for ya?"

Grateful as fuck, I tell him yes just as the horse starts to have another contraction. I let Ollie know I need to get off the phone, throw it on the railing of the stall, and get back down with her, trying to keep her calm. I pray to Christ we have forty-five minutes to an hour before Paisley gets here. Otherwise, tonight I'm gonna lose not only a good quarter horse but also the foal.

Fuck, I'm tired of all this shit. It never ends and that's only half of it. Those jagoffs with my old man are amping up and trying to intimidate all of us. It ain't gonna work. If it gets too bad, I'll have Mom move either with Momma Diane or maybe even Maggie. She's got tons of room and that club seems to know what they're doing. I can't let anything happen to our mom because if it does, I'll personally drag my old man away from his demented friends and put a bullet right between his eyes.

Getting my head outta my own ass, I clean up the straw that's been messed up from the mare and her last two contractions. She let loose some soft manure so I grab a wheelbarrow and fill it up with clean straw so I can spread it around the horse's back end. Gotta try to keep it as clean as possible because don't want anything to get the little one sick before it gets some of momma's colostrum. That shit is rich in antibodies and is a must for any newborn animal on our ranch.

So deep in my own head, I just about jump outta my skin when someone clears their throat from behind me. When I turn, I let out a screech at what I see. Not sure how or why but Shadow, Panther, and Avalanche are standing in the barn watching me. Of course, Shadow has a smirk on her face while Panther comes up to me, pats me on the shoulder, then goes to the mare right away. Avalanche follows him. Immediately, they both start to, I don't know, chant or sing… maybe hum, can't figure it out. The sound seems to relax the mare as she lets out a huge breath, then another. Panther is speaking in his native language, I'm assuming, when Avalanche stands, gives me a chin lift, then walks outta the barn going who the fuck knows where. I feel like I'm watching a tennis match back and forth.

"Avalanche just went to the truck to bring some of their equipment they use when a horse starts foaling. Don't worry, Ash, they know what they're doing."

"How did you even know what was going on? I mean, you didn't just stop by, I'm sure."

She looks at me with her sky-blue eyes, with something in them I can't read. She leans and looks at what Panther is doing then looks back at me.

"Well, it's like this. Believe me or not, Ash, but Panther had a feeling all day something was going to happen tonight. So we've been ready and waiting on a call. Not sure who from and why, but when either Panther or Avalanche have a feeling, we now know to be ready. When Ollie called, Panther, Avalanche, and I packed the truck. We knew what the feeling was about so we headed here. Ollie just didn't want you by yourself with the mare in trouble."

Hearing the horse making some pretty loud noises of pain, I turn to see Panther is up to his shoulders inside the horse, still chanting to her. When Avalanche comes back in and sees Panther, he literally throws the shit in his arms down and runs, sliding in the hay to get next to the horse. He's speaking to Panther in that language so I have no idea what pissed him off. I watch as Avalanche starts pushing and manipulating the horse's stomach, while Panther tries to reach a leg or something.

"I've seen them do this before, it's like a choreographed dance. Damn, they are good, will say that. Don't panic, Ash, they got this and Paisley should be here shortly. Phantom was driving so I'm surprised they aren't showing up in a helicopter, for Christ's sake."

Then I hear it and, holy shit, Shadow is right, that's how they are getting here. Great, just what I need, those Thunder Cloud Knuckle Brotherhood assholes to hear and see a helicopter landing. And for sure this is going to wake up Mom and Rowan. Goddamn it, nothing ever goes right.

Feeling a small hand on my upper arm, I look down to see Shadow watching me. She leans in closer and gets up on her tippy-toes.

"You got this, Ash. Don't worry about those assholes in the woods. If they come down here, they are in for a big surprise. We didn't come alone, Panther brought three of his men, all ex-military special forces. And I'm sure Phantom has at least one other person with him. I hope the brotherhood makes an appearance because, personally, I'll take down as many as possible, swear to God. I'm sick and tired of their fucking shenanigans."

I can't help but smile at her words. The more I'm around her it makes me realize she puts up a front for most folks. Like she's that tattoo on her face. When in all reality she's got a heart bigger than Texas. She must see something in my face 'cause she puts her hands on her hips, throwing one out. Oh, that's not a good sign. Gotta stop her before she lets loose.

"Shadow, your secret is safe with me as long as you don't lose your cool right now. Too much is at stake, so please take a breath or a walk but don't throw a temper tantrum right now. I'm sure in the next minute or two my mom and little brother are gonna be out here, and I don't want them to witness anything that you might be doing."

Right before she can reply, I hear my mom screaming my name and Rowan screaming for her. She literally runs into the barn, still in her pajamas, with a coat on and her gun in her hand. She's waving it all over and when Shadow sees that, she walks right up to her and grabs the gun before Mom can even try to understand what's going on. Rowan sees Shadow approaching Mom and he goes to get between them. I don't have time to warn him, but Panther must have looked up because he screams to her from the stall.

"Nizhoni! Rowan is just protecting his mom. Don't do it, Zoey."

She stops immediately, just as Rowan is standing right in front of her. I don't know when it appeared, but she was holding a huge Bowie hunting knife in one hand and Mom's gun in the other. Mom looks down, sees the knife, and grabs Rowan, pulling him back and behind her. Then she looks at Shadow with fear on her face, but Mom has never taken the easy way out and she doesn't now.

"You plan on using that hunting knife, young lady? 'Cause if your plan is to use it on my boy, then we have a problem. I come out to my barn to see what in the ever-lovin' heck is going on and you attack me. Why? I wasn't going to shoot anyone, just needed to check that Ash was okay. Those jerks in the trees have had helicopters come and land, so I wanted to make sure if they had bad intentions or had come to start some stuff."

The barn is quiet for maybe ten seconds then I hear a whoop from Avalanche.

"Damn, brother, you did it. How the hell did you flip that foal without the mother losing her shit? I saw the entire body do a flip. The momma horse let out an actual cry then she seemed to relax. I bet she's not in half the pain she was. She's breathing easier too. Great job, Panther."

Panther is still chanting and has all but blanked us out. He speaks in a low voice to Avalanche then takes up the chanting again. I walk to the stall and when I get close, Panther looks up at me.

"As far as I can tell, everything is back to normal. Don't think anything happened to the foal, and this mare is actually a lot more relaxed since we flipped that big old foal in her. You might want to see if she'll eat or drink. Oh wait, look, her water just broke, it should move pretty quick now. Ash, might want to lay down an old blanket or something so when the foal comes out, we can place it on the blanket. That way if momma needs help, we can wipe her baby down. Remember the one-two-three rule of birthing for horses."

I look at him like he's a fucking loon. He's calm as can be and asking me, a rancher, if I know the rule of foaling. Fuck, I don't need this shit.

"Panther, first hour the foal should stand. The second hour it should nurse, and third hour the mare should pass the placenta."

He grins at me and it hits me he was just messing with me, trying to calm me down. I went in the opposite direction because I'm so thin-skinned lately, as Mom has told me.

Panther whistles and everyone walks to the stall, just as we see two hooves pushing out of the mare. This right here is a miracle few ever get to witness. I never get sick of it, even though tonight was a bit rough. People are whispering and Avalanche is back in the stall with Panther. I walk around everyone and into the stall. I head to the mare's head, kneel down, and start to stroke her, softly talking to her. Telling her it's gonna be okay and she's getting ready to be a momma. She neighs at me. I'm sure she knows we only want to help her. Animals aren't stupid.

When I raise my eyes, Panther is watching me with those green eyes of his. Something happens because all of my anxiety seems to vanish and I don't feel as wiped as I did just a minute or two ago. Hearing someone let a loud breath out, I look to see it's Panther. Avalanche leans into him, touching his shoulder, and for a second they just remain like that, connected by Avalanche's hand on Panther's shoulder as they chant. Looking around I can see everyone is enamored with the two men. Something about them pulls you to them and I know, not sure how, but it was Panther who made me feel better. When Shadow comes in and kneels next to me, I wait because I know she's got a reason for being here.

"Ash, you know what an empath is? Or in the native culture it might be called a shaman. Well, you are looking at two of the best from the Navajo tribe. It's fucking eerie they know what I'm thinking at times before I even have a moment to process my thoughts. So just be warned, if you are thinking negative or bad things about either, try and control it because they'll get into your head."

Just as she finishes, I glance down and see the foal is almost all the way out. Panther reaches for some kind of, I don't know, a bunch of weeds. Avalanche passes him an abalone shell and a lighter. Wait, is he gonna set shit on fire in a barn filled with straw and hay? Though before I say a word, Panther stands and walks out of the stall, down the middle of the barn, and out the doors. That's when he lights the shit. What did Shadow say it was...yeah, sage, and starts singing and waving the sage around. Not sure why but we all stand there and watch while listening. Whatever it is he's singing, it's beautiful and peaceful. When he comes back in, he takes the bundle and slowly swings it by the stall door, and when he blows on the sage, he goes from left to right. Avalanche is up on his feet and he's drawing in the smoke and almost giving the foal a smoke bath. Then he directs some of the smoke to the mare. By this time

Panther is back outside, and as I walk toward him, I can see he's putting out the bundle. Shadow is right behind me, probably to check and make sure I don't do anything stupid.

I walk directly to Panther, grab his hand, shaking it with my own.

"Panther, my God, thank you so much. This would have ended up in a bad way if you guys hadn't shown up. Appreciate the help, seriously. Between you and Paisley, damn, I'm just glad both the mare and foal are okay. Gotta get back in there, but I truly mean it, thanks a lot, man."

When I go back into the stable, Paisley is checking the foal out. She looks at me with a smile.

"You have a colt, Ash. And a big one at that. I'm going to give him some time but think he'll be up way before the hour. Mom seems infatuated with her baby already. She's licking and cleaning him, which is a good sign. All's good that ends well, right?"

And with that she goes back to checking the foal out as Mom rushes into my arms. Rowan stands to my side but says nothing. He's a quiet kid and a people watcher. Hugging Mom to me, I lift my head and say a quick prayer of thanks that the evening didn't end up down the shitter. I just hope everything that is happening at Brenna's turns out okay too.

THIRTEEN
'TAZ'
RAQUEL/QUE

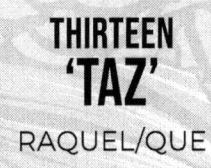

Lying in bed, not wanting to even get up. I'm dreading today, as it's my job—well, Vixen's and mine—to do the intake on Raven's sister, Bray. I'm not looking forward to it at all. To top it off I didn't get much sleep last night, this kid is going to be a kicker in the NFL, for sure. I don't remember Teddy being this crazy active.

Hearing something at the door, I turn and see Travis with a cup in his hand. When he sees me, a huge smile appears on his face. Then he reaches into his sleep pants, pulling out a sleeve of saltines. My hero for sure.

"Que, figured you'd need some herbal tea and crackers before you start your day. I know how much you ain't looking forward to today so take your time. If you're late, Vixen can start, don't make yourself sick."

I pat the bed down beside me. First he walks to my nightstand and puts down the tea on my coaster and the sleeve of crackers. Then he walks back to the door, closing and locking it, before he makes his way to his side of the bed. He gets in and moves right into my space, which is fine with me.

"Handsome, this baby of yours is kicking my kidneys and bladder to hell. Not sure I'm going to make it through this pregnancy without losing a kidney. Dang, I must have gotten up like three or four times to pee last night, when what I needed was a good night's sleep so I can get through this day. Not sure why Tink thought it would be a good idea to have me, of all the sisters, do the intake."

"Maybe, Que, she thought you'd be good for Bray's sensitive mind right now. Between you and Vixen, both of you will make this uncomfortable interview, or whatever it is, as easy as possible for Bray. That's what Tink is betting on. I mean, who else should she assign? Shadow, Raven, Squirt, or Heartbreaker to name a few. I mean, I can just see how it would go with Shadow and Raven. My God, Bray wouldn't last ten minutes. Now lay your head on my chest for five minutes while your tea steeps. Then you can start your day, maybe meditate for a bit to relax yourself. I'll get Teddy up and taken care of so all you have to worry about is yourself."

"I love you, Travis, so very much. Thank you for this, means the world to me. I want to do right by not only Bray, but my sister Raven too. She's getting hit from all sides right now. Where at one time Raven was all jokes and laughs, now I can't remember the last time she let a good one go. Since this started with her ex, Ash, then to add to it his brother finds Bray. Coincidence, don't you think?"

"What're you sayin', Que? You think the Sterlings were involved with Bray being taken? I find that hard to believe, especially after all they shared at the meeting. Though I never doubt your feelings, so keep an open mind and path, see what comes your way. Now chill for five minutes, I wanna feel my woman up."

Then he proceeds to run his rough hands up and down my body, which starts to relax me, until I hear the door handle move and Teddy hit the door when it doesn't open.

"Hey, Momma, I need to come in, whatcha doing?"

Travis looks at me then gets outta bed, walks to the door, unlocks it, and opens it. Teddy looks at him then rushes to the bed. I can tell he's been crying.

"Honey, what's wrong? Come on, crawl up. Talk to us, Son, what's bothering you?"

"It's Tuna, she's not feeling good. I tried to stay up all night but fell asleep. Before I did though, made sure her heating pad was on her back legs and the blanket was tucked around her. Also put her head on her pillow. She just woke me up and, oh my gosh, she crapped the room with running poo. It smells so bad and I know she feels bad. So I grabbed some paper towels and was able to clean most of it up, but then she started puking. I need some help."

Travis gets out of bed, grabs some gym shoes, and heads out of our room but not before telling me to stay put. I look at Teddy, who's watching where Travis went.

"Do you want to go with your dad?"

"Yeah, I need to check on Tuna. Momma, this cancer

treatment stuff doesn't seem to be working. I don't want her to be sick then have her, you know..."

My son whispers the end of that and my heart breaks. This poor kid is growing up way too quickly. First the crap with Slick, then the brotherhood and getting in the mess at the grocery store. I mean he shot some guy in his junk that day to protect Olivia. Now even though Paisley, our vet, and the veterinary hospital we are taking Tuna to for her chemotherapy told us it was a long shot, Teddy wanted to try. I think he's seeing why they said it would be a long shot. Why does this keep happening to us? The first time we get dogs, well three dogs, one has advanced cancer. Well, we will deal with it like we've dealt with everything thrown our way.

I sit on the edge of the bed and reach for my tea. Pulling my steeping container out, I place it on the coaster then take a sip. Yummy, Lemon Balm. One of my favorites and since I can't drink chamomile tea while pregnant, I'll settle for the Lemon Balm. I take maybe three sips and realize I have to pee. Dang this child. I slowly stand and make my way to our bathroom. First, I pee then I wash my hands and face and brush my teeth. Knowing I won't have time to fuck with my hair, I grab a scrunchie and put it in a messy knot. Then I close the door slightly, and after getting naked, I walk into our shower and take a quick one. By the time I dry off and grab my robe off the hook, I open the door to find Travis is leaning with his hands on the doorframe. Scaring me to death.

"Jesus, Handsome, give me a heart attack why don't

you? How's she doing? More importantly, how's Teddy holding up?"

"Que, she's not good, I'll put a call out to Paisley, maybe she can give us something for her upset tummy. Our boy is trying but it's tearing his heart out. He made me pick her up and put Tuna on his bed after he put a huge towel down for her to lie on. Then he grabbed her heating pad and put it on her hips before he got behind her and covered them both up. If this progresses, it's gonna kill him, Que. I can't bear to see him so upset. I want to take the pain from him but I can't, can I?"

"No, Travis, all we can do is support him and be by his side. If the treatments are making her worse, maybe we stop them now. Talk to Paisley, get her thoughts. I'm going to be tied up most of the day, can you maybe hang with Teddy here with Tuna and the other two pups at home, or do you have stuff to take care of?"

"Yeah, my kid, that's what I gotta take care of. I'll call Yoggie, tell him what's going on; he'll understand. And Tank's starting to get involved again, so should be no problem. You want some breakfast?"

"Maybe some toast and really hard scrambled eggs, if you don't mind? I'm going to get dressed and check on Tuna and Teddy. Where are the other two pups?"

"With Tuna and Teddy. They know something's wrong with her so they are sticking close. I'll get breakfast started, come down whenever."

I watch him walk out, thanking my lucky stars for bringing him into our lives. Everything can't always go wrong.

* * *

My God, how do they do this whenever we break up a human trafficking circuit? We just started going over the intake form and I feel horrible asking Bray these invasive questions, though she doesn't seem to mind. She's being brutally honest, which I think is easier since we forbade Raven from coming into the interview. She's pissed, I mean it took Glory and Shadow to keep her out. When I heard her call those two sisters 'bitches,' knew it was time to come in and lock the door. Before we even started, Bray apologized for her younger sister, stating she was always a bit hot-blooded.

Feeling the need to pee, I ask Bray if she could use a break and I'm grateful she says yes. Vixen offers to stay with her so I can go potty. Making my way out of the room, I see Raven sitting on the floor, knees bent, elbows to them, head held by her hands. Fuck.

"Raven, sister, come on, get up. I gotta pee so get up and go check on your sister, we're taking a break. Vixen is with her but remember this isn't about you, but her. Bray is doing remarkably well, but this isn't easy. I had no idea what an intake was and now that I do, man, these survivors are truly strong beyond words. Now I'm going to hit the bathroom."

I don't look back because I've wasted too much time and don't want to pee in my pants. By the time I take care of business, wash my hands, throw water on my face, and start to head back, I realize we've been at it for hours. I pull my phone out and see I have a few texts.

When I look at them my heart shatters. I hit dial and not even a full ring sounds before Travis picks up.

"Que, you okay?"

"No, how long did Paisley say she'd have?"

"Well, she wants to try something first. We have to wait five days then she's going to put her on steroids. She said sometimes it helps with lymphoma in animals. If it doesn't work, it won't hurt her. The side effects are eating and drinking a lot and restlessness. I already talked to Teddy and he wants to try the roids, his words. I'm going to pack up the tribe and we're going to drive over to Blue Sky Sanctuary to see Paisley. She's in the clinic today. How's shit there?"

I tell him about what we've covered so far and that this is a long-ass process. He told me he'll drop some food and drinks off on his way to the Sanctuary. Then we say our goodbyes and I head back to the meeting room. When I enter, I see Bray but no Raven or Vixen. What the hell?

"Bray, you okay? Where are Vixen and Raven?"

She lifts her head then looks around. Oh crap, she was sleeping. Damn, I'm an idiot.

"I'm sorry, sweetie, go ahead and put your head down, get a few more minutes of sleep. I'll be right back."

She nods then puts her head on her forearms and I hear a sigh. I turn and as soon as I hit the hallway, I see both of my club sisters making their way back to the room, arms full of stuff.

"Thought you could use a sugar-free lemon lime,

Taz. And we brought some crackers, bread, cheese cubes, and fruit, not sure what you'd want."

I can see Raven is trying really hard, so I smile her way and we walk back into the room. Bray is up and asks to use the bathroom. Vixen goes with her, saying she needs to go too, but I know it's to keep an eye on Bray. She's in a very sensitive way right now and the more we hear about her captivity, my worries for her escalate. While I have a minute, I send a quick text to Tink, letting her know where we are and my initial thoughts. Bray shouldn't be left alone. She's going to need guidance and companionship during these first few weeks. We talked and I think Tink is right, she should stay at the ranch house. There is always someone there and she won't be alone. Also, we can keep her on track with all of her therapies.

By the time I'm done, Bray and Vixen are back. We sit and snack on all the goodies that Raven and Vixen brought back. When we are ready to start up again, I look to Raven who stands up, kissed Bray's cheek, and starts to walk out.

"Brenna, you can stay if you want, just don't scream at me, please. If you don't think you can handle it, that's okay too."

Raven stops and I see it first. Her shoulders are shaking. Oh no, I get up and rush to her, grabbing her around the waist, trying to get as close as my pregnant tummy will allow me. She puts her hands on top of mine and we stay like this for a few, until both Vixen and Bray join us, wrapping Raven up. Well, until she starts laughing like a loon.

"What is so frigging funny, Raven?"

"You, Taz, your maniac kid just kicked me in my back three times, hard. Damn, that one will either be in football or soccer, for sure."

That helps break the mood and Vixen and I head back to the table. Raven turns to her sister, pulling her into her arms.

"Bray, I'm so sorry I yelled at you before. I'm so mad at all of us for not even looking for you. Just thought you were on your next adventure. It's not you I'm yelling at, well it is, but it's because I can't scream at myself or our family. If it's okay, I'll stay and be by your side and won't say anything. I promise. This is about you not me, so time for me to act like the Devil's Handmaidens sister I am. I've got your back."

Watching them together helps me to realize that this baby will be good for Teddy. He needs a sibling, even though he's going to be so much older. When I hear the chairs moving, I look and see both Bray and Raven sitting down, so I reach over, hit record, and we start back in. This time though with Bray having family to lean on. And man does it make a difference.

FOURTEEN
'ASH'
ASHTON

Not sure why I thought this was a good idea. I'm sitting on Brenna's steps, waiting for her to show up from wherever she's at. I didn't call or text either. Since last night with the birthing of the foal, I feel off. And no matter what everyone said to me it didn't matter, I needed to see and talk to Brenna. So here I am like a goof or lovesick idiot, waiting for the pretty girl to come home.

Hearing crunching in the distance, I look up to see Brenna making her way down the road to her cabin. When she sees me, she stops right where she is for a second or two then keeps coming my way.

"Hey, Ash, need something?"

"Brenna, hi. Thought I'd stop by, knew Bray was doing her thing today with your club. Wanted to make sure both of you are okay. Alder would have been here but they made the hike up to the cabin today. We've not heard anything as of yet. Mind if we talk for minute, or I can come back a different time."

She looks at me and nods before she steps up and plops down right next to me. I can tell she's nervous and hopefully in time she'll get over that. I reach to my side and pick up the bag Mom wanted me to give to her. When I hand it to her, she looks in and with big eyes looks up at me, a smile starting on her face.

"Are these your mom's homemade apple and blueberry pies? Oh my God, my mouth is watering already. Come on, let's talk inside so I can eat a piece of both. You want a small slice?"

That makes me laugh. Just like Brenna, even back in the day, if she liked something she'd share... but just a little bit. Hearing me laugh, she looks at me and then it hits her what she just said. She grins then jumps up and goes to the door, unlocks it with a key code, then walks in and hits an alarm panel. Once we are both in, she hits the green button and then heads right to the kitchen. She pulls out a gallon of farmer's milk and two plates. By the time we are at the table, both plates have a good slice of each pie and glasses filled with milk beside them.

I wait and she doesn't disappoint. As soon as she puts a forkful in her mouth, the moan that follows has my body reacting immediately. Yeah, Brenna is very vocal or she used to be. I look down and start to eat my pie. It's comfortable for about three minutes then I can tell she's starting to struggle with why I'm here.

"Brenna, I owe you an apology. No, listen, last night we had a mare in trouble during foaling. I called Ollie to see if Paisley could maybe come out. Not only did she come out but in a helicopter with Phantom. By the time they got there, Panther, Shadow, and Avalanche were there, as your brother called them since they were closer. Long story short, they all managed to save not only the mare but the foal too. It made me think and remember that we are not alone. Why we acted like we were I'll never know, but none of what happened was on you. I acted a fool the first time I came here when I saw you and Avalanche together. It would have served me right if you two were a couple. Though I will say, I'm beyond glad you're not together. I'm here tonight to see if we can somehow move on and try to get to know each other again. As friends. I miss you in my life, Brenna. Even before we got together as a couple, we shared a close friendship. You were my best friend. Is it possible to work to that again or did I totally fuck this up?"

My eyes never leave her face as she looks around, doing everything not to gaze into my eyes. Oh well, I tried. I stand and pick up my plate when she reaches over and puts her hand on my arm.

"Sit, Ash. I don't know what to say. I've tried to hate you for the last couple of years and, if I'm honest, I never truly did. You were also my best friend and my first everything. I'm afraid to let you back in because if we end up apart again, it will kill me. And we can't promise we won't hurt each other because we just don't know. That's where I'm at."

I sit back down and place the plate on the table. Then

I turn to face her, grabbing both of her hands in mine. I take a deep breath and then take a chance.

"Brenna, my life's been shit since we broke up. The only thing I have is the ranch and even that is a pain in my ass most days. I did build a house, one I thought you'd like. Besides that, I live, breathe, and almost die for that ranch. I've not been a saint since we broke up, I'll be honest, but I've never had another girlfriend or fiancée. Best I could call it was hookups when I needed, you know, some relief."

I can feel my face getting hot and she's looking at me, trying not to laugh at my discomfort.

"Go ahead and laugh. Not only was it far and few between, I'd drive into the city so it wasn't someone from around here. Mom has been on me to try and find a bride to help me, but there's only one woman I want as my bride. No, I won't put any pressure on you, Brenna. I'm just trying to be honest and upfront. Now, I know you've had a really long day, I'll get outta your hair. Maybe we can grab a bite to eat sometime. Your call. I'll leave the ball in your court."

Again I stand, and this time after I lean down and put a kiss on the top of her head, I walk to the door. Before my hand can reach out, she calls my name again.

"Hey, want to stick around, maybe watch a movie? I've got to take a shower. Long story, but little Teddy's dog, Tuna, isn't doing well and I went over to help just when she lost her cookies all over the house. Teddy is a wreck and Taz is pregnant. Enforcer was out so I cleaned up the mess then got the rug cleaner out and washed the great room rug 'cause it stank. Then before it got dark, went in the backyard and cleaned up. Now not sure you know, but they have three big dogs, so yeah, I filled an entire garbage bag full of crap. Teddy tried to help but, poor kid, dog poop and him don't get along. By the second time he threw up, I sent him in the house. Told him to take some warm rags and wipe Tuna down. Once I finished, Enforcer was back home, so then I stopped at the ranch here to check on Bray. She was playing board games with Squirt, Kitty, and the twins, Dottie and Dani. So, need to get the smell of dog puke and crap off of me. I have some homemade lasagna in the freezer if you want to throw it in the oven. Won't take me but a few then we can hang out and watch a movie. Even eat together. If you want?"

Looking at her face that shows her anxiety and a little excitement, I thought what the hell. This is what I want anyway. So, I nod and she smiles.

"Go take your shower, don't rush. I'll put the food on and see what else you have to go with the pasta. Mind if I get something to drink?"

"Oh my God, I'm a horrible hostess. Yeah, there's beer in the fridge and hard liquor over there in the corner on the bar cart. Help yourself. I'm going to get started."

I watch her walk down the little hallway to the door off to the left. Once she's gone, I walk to her fridge, look in the freezer, and grab the lasagna. Then I preheat the oven and walk to her bar cart. I pick up a tumbler, grab the Jack Daniels, and walk back to the kitchen. I look for some Coke which, thank God, she has, so I mix myself a Jack and Coke. Rarely do I drink, but I need just one tonight. The stress has been building and with our asshole father doing whatever he's doing, we are on pins and needles.

After I make a salad, I set the table and check the lasagna, which needs more time. I go sit on the sectional and flip the television on. Brenna has a cute place, it fits her. I must have dozed off because the next thing I know, Brenna is shaking me, telling me dinner is ready. I look around to get my bearings before I stand and walk to the table. She has everything already out so I sit down.

"You were out, I almost didn't wake you up. Then your stomach growled and that told me you need to eat. Hard day?"

I laugh for a few then dive into what's been going on since that day I first came to her. As we ate, she listened and even asked a few questions. I've never had this with anyone. Can't talk to my mom about this shit or Rowan, he's too young—well—teenager young. Then my other brothers are trying to work and have lives. It feels so good to have someone listen, but I also have to do the same so I ask her about her day.

"Well, started out really bad. Bray was doing her intake today and Shadow and Glory wouldn't let me in with her. I mean, they actually physically removed me. I was so pissed but as time went on and I sat on my ass outside the room, it dawned on me it's about Bray, not me. I should be supporting her. Well, leave it to Taz to figure out a way for me to support my sister. I spent almost three hours listening to Bray describe what the Thunder Cloud Knuckle Brotherhood did to her. Ash, if I could, I'd go up to that part of your ranch where they are and I'd kill each and every one of them. I told you what I did after, so think we are caught up. Do you want to call it a night so you can go home and get a good night's sleep, or are you up to watch a movie?"

I don't want to leave yet so I vote for a movie. We first clean up then fight over a movie. We decide on an action flick. Each of us with a drink and a bowl of popcorn Brenna made, we sit on the sectional with our feet on the ottoman. She throws me a blanket and then pulls one for herself. My eyes are so tired that I kind of lean to the arm of the sectional, putting my legs and feet on the ottoman. Brenna moves the bowl of popcorn so I can stretch out, and I do just that. Not sure but it probably takes only ten to twenty minutes before I am totally out on Brenna's sectional. Don't know what she does because I am sleeping but when I wake up a few hours later to pee, I am covered up by two blankets and my boots are off and by the door. A glass of water is on the end table.

I get up and go to the bathroom off the kitchen. When I am done, I walk to the kitchen window, move the blinds, and look out. Damn, it's dark here too. Moving away, I let the blinds go and I head back to the sectional and sit. What do I do, leave or go back to sleep? I don't want to fuck this up, but damn I'm exhausted. So, I send my mom and kid brother a text. Also send one to my foreman so he can make sure someone is up early to feed the animals. Then I take my jeans off, placing them on the chair, and remove my flannel but keep my T-shirt on. Then I fluff the pillow off to the side, lay my head on it, and by the time I pull the blankets over me, my eyes are already closing. And for once I sleep through the entire night.

FIFTEEN
'RAVEN'
BRENNA

Something is ringing but it isn't my phone. My head is stuffed up so it takes me a minute or two to wake up enough to get out of bed. By the time I make it to the hallway, the ringing stops. I walk to the main part of my cabin and the phone starts ringing again. Shit, must be Ash's. I look around and when I see his pants, I move quickly to them, reaching in the back pocket, pulling his phone out.

I look down and see Rowan's name. Oh no.

"Hello, Ash's phone."

"UM, who is this? Can you get Ash? This is his brother, I need to talk to him now."

Not sure if it was the phone or my voice but I can see Ash is waking up. I walk over and give him a hard shake. His eyes pop open and he looks up at me. I put the phone in his face.

"It's Rowan, he says he needs you."

Ash jumps up, swings his legs over the edge, and answers the phone at the same time.

"Rowan, what's up, bro?"

I can't make out what Rowan is telling him, that is until Ash puts it on speakerphone.

"Hey, Ro, slow down. Take some breaths. What the hell happened now?"

"Like I said, Ash, I got your text late last night and thought I should maybe go down to the barn to be close to the momma and baby foal. So I did, made me a bed right in the stall. The next thing I know I'm hearing horses neighing and shit. Then I smelled it. Fire. I got up and I pushed the emergency button you put in there and the alarm rang throughout the ranch. Mom was there first then some of the hands. We managed to get all of the animals out. Mom has the foal in the house with the momma in the garage for now. I'm sure the momma horse will find her way into the back porch in a bit. I called Sheriff George, he's on the way. Ash, it looks like someone set the fire. I took pictures but you might want to see it and be here for the sheriff. Who answered your phone, by the way? It was a girl. Come on, you can tell me. I won't tell a soul."

Ash laughs then gives his brother the business. He tells Rowan he's on his way. When he hangs up, he looks up at me.

"Someone tried to burn our barn down. Gotta go, sorry, Brenna."

"Hang on, Ash, don't run out all half-assed. Let me call Tink and maybe even Ollie. If you wait for a few, I could follow you home, maybe help out, if you want. If not, I can still make those calls. I can even call Panther since he's closer to your ranch." His head jerks back like I hit him. Guess it was kind of a surprise. To me too, but I didn't want him to run out all discombobulated.

"Um, sure, if you want to make those calls and feel like coming along, better move that fine ass of yours. I got to get on the road."

That's all I have to hear. I literally run back to my room, trying to dial my phone and get dressed at the same time. Panther and his crew are going to head to the Sterling ranch immediately. Ollie is loading up the helicopter with supplies, then with Phantom and Paisley, and will be flying over. Finally, Tink told me to head there, and she'll get some of the club sisters together, then they'll head that way in a bit. She's got to get someone to stay with Bray before she leaves. Once I got all the calls done, I quickly walk into my bathroom, brush my teeth, and throw my mass of hair into a low ponytail to keep it out of the way. I grab a pair of worn jeans, my cowboy boots and put a long sleeve T-shirt on then my kutte. Not sure how Ash's family will feel, but I go nowhere without my club kutte.

Rushing down the hallway, I don't see Ash at first, but then he moves and I see he's making coffees to go. Thank God, I'm useless without my coffee. I grab my laptop bag, which is full of just about everything I use when not in my office at the clubhouse.

"Ash, do you have Wi-Fi at the ranch? If not, I can

bring my mobile router/hotspot. It generally works anywhere. I'm ready if you are?"

He nods then grabs both travel mugs, walks toward me, and hands me one. Then he grabs his coat and walks out the door. I follow close and lock the door after I set the alarm. Can't be too careful nowadays. We've had so much bullshit happen at the ranch lately, we are all very careful.

I'm so much in my head, I don't realize Ash stopped until I plow into him from behind. He turns, grinning at me. I shrug my shoulders. What can I say, some things never change.

"All right, Brenna, I'm not gonna follow the speed limit. So either keep up or meet me at my ranch. For Rowan to be worried and nervous, something else is going on."

Then out of nowhere he leans down, placing a very soft closed-mouth kiss on me. Before I can react, he pulls away and touches my face.

"Thanks for coming with, means a lot."

He turns and hurries to his truck, jumps in, and takes off like a bat out of hell. I jump in my cage and follow. When we get to the gates of our ranch, there are a few Intruders on guard so they open the gate so we can leave. I feel eyes on me but don't look around because there are a few of those assholes in Tank's club I'd like to whack up against the head.

Time seems to fly by as I try to keep up with Ash, though he drives like a maniac. Knowing that Rowan called Sheriff George, I hope we don't meet him on the way because Ash would so deserve a ticket for reckless driving. And I get it, he's worried about his family and their homes, but killing himself or someone else won't help.

Just as we are coming up to the turnoff to his ranch, I see a bunch of vehicles blocking the entrance as well as sheriff cruisers and I think even Panther's huge truck off to the side. Hearing the whirring sound, I look up and see the helicopter kicking ass toward the ranch. As we slow down, I see it's the Thunder Cloud Knuckle Brotherhood blocking the way. Shit, trouble is going to start, I can feel it. Ash jumps out of his truck and just by the way he's stomping toward the crowd, he's looking to bust someone's head open, for sure.

I turn my cage off and get out of the car just as Ash gets in some old guy's face, cussing and carrying on. The old dude just smirks and it dawns on me that it's Cliff Sterling, Ash's dad. He looks ready to start a revolution with the gun swung on his back. In fact, all the men and women blocking the entrance have guns on them. Thank God I put my Springfield Armory Hellcat in the holster at my back. In my cage I have a Steyr AUG SA USA rifle stashed in the back. Tink and Glory made sure every sister has one in their personal vehicle and with all the Devil's Handmaidens vehicles too.

I'm trying to get my head in the right space, which is right behind Ash, gun already in my hand at my thigh. The mood in the air is violent as can be. Then I feel it, like the devil himself is looking my way. I shift my eyes until they meet Cliff's. His face is scrunched up, guess he's trying to look badass, though it isn't working, because his son is right in his face.

"What in the ever-lovin' fuck do you think you're doing? This is our ranch and you have no right to be on it or try to keep folks out. Now move your asses before this gets nasty."

Cliff looks around then back at Ash with an ugly look on his face.

"Whatcha got, son, two Indians, some white trash with those two, and that useless woman behind you. Oh, the helicopter but it's going to be busy with the burned down barn. Sorry to hear about that, hope you got all the animals out first. Now, once and for all, we are gonna settle this bullshit. This is my ranch, not yours, and from now on I'll give the orders not you, boy."

Before anyone can say a word, the helicopter comes swinging down and lands right in the middle of the field. As the blades start to slow down, out hops my brother Ollie, Phantom holding a huge as fuck gun, and I think her name is Spirit. She's worked with Shadow so I know she can hold her own. Especially since she's outfitted like she's going to war. The last guy to get out I don't know, but he just looks like ex-military, especially with his big gun held across his waist. Leave it to Ollie to try and calm shit down.

"Ash, we heard you had some shit go down. We came to give you a hand. Paisley is already doing assessments of your animals. Barn is gone. I put a call out to Tank. Once he gets ahold of Pussy, he can send him out to get lumber. We'll have a new barn up in no time and this one will be bigger and better. Now, what's going on here, your mom was asking for ya."

Cliff is eyeballing my brother and his team with some fear in his face. The brotherhood looks like they are ready to start a war just because they can. Sheriff George comes by, greeting just about everyone, except Cliff. That pisses the man off, but surprisingly he holds his tongue.

"Now, like I said, this is my ranch and I want all of your asses off of it. Especially soldier boy and his minions. No need for you fuckers to be here. Don't you need to be at your place to hold hands with your damaged soldiers while they pet and feed sick old dogs and such."

Before anyone can even say a word, my brother Ollie, who is forever calm, reaches out and grabs Cliff by the collar. When he winds back, I know he can't hit the asshole as that will give the bastard what he wants. So, I rush forward and before he can throw a punch, I grab on to Ollie's forearm, pulling it back.

When he's back under control, I glance at Ash's dad, who is studying me. Not sure he knows who I am, well, until he starts running his mouth.

"Oh, lookee here, it's Brenna O'Brien. Ash's first piece of ass. Didn't leave a lasting impression, obviously, since he broke it off with you at that engagement party your parents threw. Just heard through the grapevine that after the breakup you lost my grandchild. You better pray to whatever you think is sacred because if I find out you did something to lose the child, no one will be able to hold me back, I promise ya that. Now this doesn't involve you or your brother, so once again get off my property."

I hear something and when I look there's a 4x4 flying down the road. When it gets closer I see Rowan, Gertie, Ash's mom, Joshua, Ash's biracial little brother they took in to save his life, and Joe, one of their hands. When they stop, Gertie jumps out, gun in her hand, and walks right to Cliff.

"You get off my property now and take the scum of the earth with you. Cliff Sterling, I've had it with you. I'm done, if I have to sell this property, I will, but definitely not to you or any of the Thunder Cloud Knuckle Brotherhood. Do you hear me? Done, and I win this time. Remember, this is my ranch, was my mom's before me and her mom's before her. I never put your name on the deed or property so you've been squatting on my land. You've never paid rent or even asked to be on our land so, Sheriff George, I'd like to press charges. Not sure what but I'm sure you can find something that will fit this situation. Now we have a burned-down barn to deal with and have to find shelter for our animals. I don't want to see any of these people near my ranch again. This is a formal warning in front of the sheriff and his deputies."

She turns, walks back to the 4x4, and gets in. Something has me look at where Cliff and all the brotherhood are standing. When I see a gun aimed at Gertie's back, I don't think, I raise my Hellcat and fire not once but twice. I blast the hand and the gun goes flying then when the person goes to run, I graze their hip so they fall to the ground.

Sheriff George walks to me, grabs my gun, and tells me to stand down. Not sure he saw what I did, I try to explain.

"Sheriff, they had the gun aimed at Gertie's back. I couldn't let him shoot her in the back."

"Raven, it's not a he but a she."

When I look, I'm shocked to see a young woman, probably the same age as Squirt. She's holding her arm, crying softly, and not one person from that group is by her. They've turned their backs on her. Son of a bitch.

"Raven, I don't want to but have to. You're under arrest for firing your weapon."

"No, don't arrest her please, Sheriff. They made me do it and I'm so sorry. I would never have shot Mrs. Sterling. She's been nothing but good to me and my sisters. I don't want to be here anymore. They won't let me leave. Please help me. No, help us."

As Sheriff George starts to listen to the young lady, I walk over to Panther, Avalanche, George, Dallas, and Chicago. Panther looks my way and gives me a head lift. I walk over to him and he leans down, whispering quietly.

"Shadow is out there in the back forty or whatever it's called. She's trying to see if there are any more victims. I couldn't stop her and this fiasco played right into her hands. Fingers crossed she finds something and can safely bring them out. She's gonna be pissed but Jersey followed her in, he didn't want her by herself.

Yeah, my guys have kind of adopted your enforcer, Raven, what can I say. You okay?"

As we stand and talk about what's going on. I have no idea what's going to happen to me. So when Sheriff George approaches me, I take in a deep breath and wait.

"Raven, you're free to go. Though I have a favor to ask. See that girl you grazed and those three little girls with her? Those are her sisters. She's pretty tight-lipped, but she did share what that brotherhood has made her do to keep her sisters safe. Sounds like, and we have no proof, the Thunder Cloud Knuckle Brotherhood killed her parents and took over their cabin on this side of the mountain. She doesn't even know how long they've been with them. Can you and the Devil's Handmaidens take them in and help the girls start over? I know it's a lot, but I got nowhere else to send them."

Just as I go to answer we hear a commotion and, holy hell, no way. One of the brotherhood is pointing an AK-15 assault rifle at the girls. The older girl stands and puts her three little sisters behind her. I don't want to see these kids gunned down but not sure what to do. That is until I see Avalanche and Panther rounding the trucks and cars to get behind the man with the rifle. Before I can blink, Avalanche grabs for the gun while Panther puts the man in a chokehold. He squeezes his neck and the man goes down immediately.

Ash walks up to me, though his eyes never stop moving.

"If you don't want to get any more involved, Brenna,

I understand. I need to get to the barn. Thanks for everything though."

He walks away, jumps in his truck, and manages to get past the group of assholes and barrels away. I run to my cage, jump in, and before I go down the road, I stop by Sheriff George.

"How bad are her arm and hip? If not too bad, have them get in my cage and once I'm done helping Ash and his family, I'll take them back to the ranch. Unless you want to drop them off, whatever works, Sheriff."

When I pull up to the burned-out barn, I have one young girl in the front, her arm bandaged up with a towel. The younger three are in the back huddled together. What did I just get myself involved with? Better put in a call to Tink and Glory. Again.

SIXTEEN
'RAVEN'
BRENNA

This day is nothing short of a miracle. Started out crazy, escalated to loony tunes, and by the time I'm sitting my ass on a chair finally able to take a breath, I can't believe the sun is going down. A lot was done today too.

First and foremost, Sheriff George removed the Thunder Cloud Knuckle Brotherhood, who were blocking the road to the ranch, for criminal trespassing. Who knows if it will hold but it got those assholes off the property. Then after viewing the burnt barn, Ash, Rowan, and Gertie wanted to move, not sure how many, animals so they could be closer to the house. Now all their cows, no way, but some of the other animals it could be done.

When Ash said his mom had the mare who just gave birth in the garage, I had no idea he meant a pole barn where they stored their cars. Well, his mom's, Rowan's, and some of their recreational pieces too. So, after moving the cars to the actual garage and all the other stuff in there to one corner of the pole barn, bales of straw were brought in so they could first section off different areas by stacking straw bales. Then within the areas the bales were cut open to make bedding for the animals. Rowan, along with a few hands, made sure each enclosure had buckets of fresh water as well as some hay and feed for the animals.

By the time the animals were settled, which took a while, and the foal and momma horse were in the enclosed porch, everyone was standing around the burned-down building. I could see Ash was suffering, though it could have been a hell of a lot worse. But without this barn, which was pretty close to his mom's house, they either have to have all the animals farther away or try and get another barn up before winter hits.

Looking around I see Panther, Avalanche, Dallas, Jersey, and Chicago, along with my brother, Ollie, sitting around a picnic table, sheets of paper in front of them. Almost like blueprint papers. Way above my abilities, that's for sure. Tink and Shadow came and picked up the girls and took them to the ranch. Probably doing intake right now. Neighbors, neighbors, and more neighbors spent the day dropping off dishes, casseroles, and tons of vegetables. Gertie was so overwhelmed she was handing food to those who were leaving, trying to explain she didn't want it to go to waste. And she fed everyone who was there today multiple times.

Now we're in Gertie's kitchen, all sitting with either a beer, water, or iced tea in our hands. Little Joshua is so frigging cute, he's curled up in Reed's arms asleep. Rue just got here a bit ago, so the only Sterling brother missing is Alder. Still haven't heard back from him yet, though he's with some deputies and forest rangers. Sheriff George told Ash if they weren't back by tomorrow, he'd get some men together and ride up there to check on them.

I can feel my body starting to shut down. I'm exhausted and still have to drive back to the ranch. I could fall asleep on this very uncomfortable chair for all I care. Must have shut my eyes for a second or two because when Ash's voice is in my ear, I jump and knock foreheads with him before he literally lands on his ass. Everyone at first is shocked then one by one they start to snicker, chuckle, or outright laugh, including Ash.

Rubbing my head, I look around and a grin appears on my face. This is what I love, when I can put a smile on anyone's face either by joking or being a goof. Though this one, damn, Ash's head is hard as a bowling ball. When my eyes reach his, he's smiling until he looks at my forehead.

"Shit, Brenna, you're gonna have an egg up there. Mom, can you get her some ice, please? You should have remembered I have a head like a rock. Are ya gonna be okay?"

Smiling because he's so concerned, I just nod then grab the bag of ice Gertie hands off to me.

"I'll ice this for a minute or two then I got to get home. Don't want to be on the road in the middle of the night, it's way too dark on those Montana roads."

Gertie gives Ash a look with eyebrows up into her

forehead and hairline. Wonder what that's about? Then it hits me when Ash turns to me, a question in his eyes.

"Brenna, you're more than welcome to either stay with me or here with Mom and the boys. Or if you feel like driving, I'll follow ya so you can get home safely."

Gertie jumps on board, telling me it's better I stay tonight and leave after breakfast in the morning. I'm looking between the two of them, feeling like I'm getting set up. Then Reed and Rue jump in too.

"Go see Ash's new house, it's finally done. He's got like four or more bedrooms, so he's got plenty of room. With Rue, Rowan, Joshua, Mom, and me this farmstead is full. You're exhausted, Brenna, go ahead. Put a call out to one of your club sisters, tell them where you are if that makes you feel safer, though out of all the Sterling boys, you got the safe one there, for sure. Now I'm spent gonna go to bed. Night, y'all."

I watch Reed, then Rue, get up and head upstairs to the bedrooms they probably had as kids. Rowan is cleaning up the kitchen with the help of Gertie. They wouldn't let me lend a hand, something about being a guest. Whatever.

"So, what's it gonna be, Brenna? Home or my house? Not to rush ya, but I'm so fuckin' exhausted. I'll follow you if you decide to go home, no worries."

It would be selfish to go home knowing he's going to follow me, so I softly say to him, "I'll stay with you tonight, if that's okay." He literally almost jumps up and down for a second before he gets himself under control. Gertie and Rowan are giggling at him in the kitchen. I walk to first Gertie then Rowan and say my goodbyes. Before I can turn, Joshua is cruising toward me, arms up, a huge smile on his beautiful face. How could anyone want to hurt this child? I lean down and pick him up into my arms. He proceeds to place kisses all over my face, which has me smiling and laughing. Gertie comes and grabs him, pulling him into her.

"Joshua, be a good boy. Brenna is going to go to Ash's but you will see her in the morning, Son."

He makes a face then looks at Ash, sticking his tongue out.

"Uhhh, think my little brother has his first crush. You mad at me, lil' man?"

Joshua glares at him then looks to Gertie and says, "Down." She puts him on his feet and he stomps his way down the hall to the stairs. He pounds up the stairs, never looking back. I actually hear him slam his bedroom door, which shocks everyone in the kitchen.

"I'm so sorry, Brenna, he's usually such a good little guy. Maybe all the craziness of today has him off his game. I'll go up and read him a story. Then I'm going to go to bed, if it's okay with y'all. This old body needs some downtime. Goodnight, and thanks for all of your and your club's help today. It feels nice to have community around us for once. I pray Sheriff George can keep those jackasses in jail or transfer them to prison, I don't care as long as they aren't here."

When it's just Ash and me, he turns to me.

"Ready to get some sleep? That's all I'm offering

tonight, Bre, 'cause I don't have the energy for anything else. Let's go home."

"Like I said, I'll stay, Ash, to sleep. I'm not ready for anything else, don't know if I'll ever be. That night shattered my heart and not sure if it can be repaired. And I don't say that to hurt you because you're a victim too. But to drive myself to the ranch and then have you drive back is crazy. Let's get some sleep. Tomorrow is a new day, right?"

I start my cage and when Ash starts to drive down the secondary road on his property, I follow him. I forgot how big their ranch truly is and from what I've heard today, this family has been working their asses off to keep it up and running. At the same time trying to fight their father and the brotherhood he calls his friends and family. Something has to give and in my opinion there's only one option. Get rid of the Thunder Cloud Knuckle Brotherhood.

As we take the turn, my eyes almost pop out of my head. Holy cow!! Ash's house is a log cabin and it's beyond gorgeous. The logs and materials fit right into the natural scene. I'm speechless because it almost looks like the log ranch I wanted when I was a young girl. Probably still have the plans in one of my bins at my parents' house. Wait a minute, is this my house? No way.

"Ash, is this the house I showed you we were going to live in when we got married and saved some money. Is this my house?"

"Brenna, you don't listen when I talk to you. Told ya

I built a house I thought you would want and love. Did I do it?"

It's hard to breathe as my eyes shift between the log house and Ash's face. This stuff only happens in those books the young sisters read. And never would I have thought this kind of stuff would happen to me. Maybe I'm delusional from lack of sleep.

'Breanna, hey, you okay? We can change anything you don't like, promise. Let's go inside and maybe tomorrow, after we both get some sleep, you can tell me what you don't like."

He grabs my hand and walks me to the door. Or I should say doors because it's the double door entrance, which I totally love. Also has to have screen doors which helps get some fresh air into the home. Ash lets me go in first and again I can't catch my breath. It is definitely my dream home. Wood ceilings, drywall, and beams. The fireplace is stunning while, if I'm right, the floors are white oak. My God, how, when, and why? I don't even know where to start. Then I feel arms wrapping around my waist from behind. It's been so long since a man has even touched me that I feel the shivers running up and down my body.

"Please don't be mad. When I realized you were my 'one,' thought I would need everything I could get on my side to win you back. Go ahead, look around. If you want something to drink, just grab it. Not to be rude but I gotta jump in the shower. If you want to take one, let me show you the guest suite. Come on, Brenna."

Walking down a hallway, the suite is beautiful: earth

tones, a large bed, and nightstands. A reading nook and a television mounted to the wall. I follow him into a small hallway that leads to the master bathroom with a standing tub. My God, when's the last time I took a bath?

"Take your time, there's some stuff in the drawers and a brand-new robe on the back of the door. Meet ya back in the kitchen, we'll grab something to snack on."

He leans down and presses a kiss to the top of my head. Then he turns and walks out and down the hall back toward the great room. Slowly, I walk into the bathroom and shut the door. It's so gorgeous but not overdone. Walking to the tub, I start to fill it up and notice a basket with stuff in it. When I look inside, everything in there is stuff I use. How the hell did he even know?

I riffle through everything and grab a bath bomb. I open it and then toss it in the tub. Next, I take my clothes off and roll them neatly. I enter the shower area and realize this is one of those fancy ones. Takes me a while to turn it on, so I walk out, turn the water off for the tub, and then try to shower quickly before I go in the tub. Yeah, my sisters and mom always laughed at me but don't want to soak in my own yuck. A quick shower then when I go in the tub, I'll be much cleaner.

I wash and condition my hair, then run a hand towel filled with Bath and Body Works Sweet Pea body wash and clean my body. When I finish, I wrap my hair and head over to the tub, I'm exhausted. God, I'd hate to drown because I fell asleep in a tub. No not going to happen. Just for a few minutes to relax my muscles and as Taz says, take some cleansing breaths. All I can do is hope she's right about that.

Not sure how long I've been in the tub but it's phenomenal. I feel so relaxed and all the tightness is just about gone from my body. I get up—not gracefully at all—step out of the tub, and grab a huge bath towel, wrapping up in it. Once I'm just about dry, I put on the robe and remove the towel around my head. Next, I braid my hair so it's not all over. When I finally open the door and see Ash sitting in one of the chairs at the table in the corner, for some reason I let out a scream. His head jerks back then his eyes take me in. The look in them has tingles running up and down my body. He's in sleep pants and a tight T-shirt, feet bare. And those gorgeous eyes are running the length of my body before they stop on my hair in a braid.

"Um, everything okay, Ash?"

"More than okay, Brenna. You have no idea how long I've waited to have you in this house. Maybe not in this room, but hey, beggars can't be choosers, can they? Now, you want to raid the kitchen?"

He smirks at me as he stands and walks my way. When he's next to me, he grabs my hand and together we walk into his kitchen to see what we can snack on, which is cool with me because believe it or not, I'm starving. I figure we'll get something to eat then finally get some much-needed sleep.

SEVENTEEN
'TAZ'
RAQUEL/QUE

My God, I thought the intake interview with Bray was hard, son of a gun, these four girls are killing me. We should have been done hours ago but first we had to take a break for lunch. Then the littlest one needed a nap, probably because she's not been sleeping well, so we let the two older ones just hang out and watch television, while the oldest one asked to read some magazines we had lying around. Then when the little one got up, they had to have dinner.

So finally, we are all together trying to finish the intake. I think both Vixen and I have been very patient but now is the time to shit and get off the pot. I look down at the papers in front of me. The oldest is Hazel, the next is Eleanor, then Aspen, and the youngest is Everly. The four are cute as buttons, but I can see something bad definitely happened to Hazel and maybe even Eleanor. Hazel is not Squirt's age of almost twenty, she's only fifteen. My God, this poor child. Eleanor is thirteen and the two youngest are seven and five. This next section is going to be rough so I look to both Hazel and Eleanor, giving then big eyes. Hazel looks to Aspen and Everly then back to me. When she nods, I'm beyond grateful. She's a good older sister.

"Aspen, Everly, I'm going to call Squirt to come by and take you around the ranch. Does that sound good? You might even see a few animals if you're lucky."

They both look to Hazel with pleading eyes. She grins their way and nods. Both girls jump up and down, holding on to each other, smiling. Good, the first of many good things to come into their lives. I pick up my phone and hit Squirt's number.

"Yeah, Taz, need something? A run for some crazy-ass food you're craving? Let me guess, hot dog banana splits. Or Twinkies with ranch dressing. No, fried chicken and tater tots soaked in ketchup and mayonnaise. Which one is calling your name?"

I laugh because Squirt is a mini-Raven when it comes to being the club clown. Though Squirt doesn't have the same delivery and sense of humor as our sister Raven does.

"Squirt, need a favor. We are still doing the intake and I was wondering if you'd be able to take Aspen and Everly for a bit of a walk, introduce them to the ranch and maybe even some of our animals. That'll give Vixen and me a chance to get some info out of the two older girls. Can you help a sister out?"

After she tells me she'll be here within the next half hour, I thank her then hang up. I look to Vixen and nod.

After we sit around talking about jack shit, passing time until the youngest are out of hearing range for what is to come next. When Squirt shows up, I know why it took her so long. She's carrying two of the new barn kittens in the carry thing across her chest. Also, she's brought Dani and Kitty along, which is good, all three are great with kids.

"Hey, I'm Squirt, that's Dani and Kitty. Do you like kittens? If so, I brought two for you to cuddle with while we walk around. These are cat slings and we will fit them on you then can put a kitty in each. Sound good?"

I smile because Squirt has come a long way since she was found. I'm proud of her, even after her one misstep when she dragged the prospects to Texas for a book signing. What a total fuckup, but hey, we were all young at one time. The little girls are giggling and playing with the kittens as both Squirt and Kitty are putting the slings on them. Once those are in place, they each pick a kitten and we help them get the little cats settled. Both kitties fall back asleep instantly, which has the little girls laughing. Squirt gives me a nod then they all head out to go look at the horses, cows, goats, and the two alpacas we brought here from the Blue Sky Sanctuary. I'm sure they'll have tons of fun.

"Thank you for getting them out of here. I don't ever want them to know what I did to try and keep them as safe as possible. Not sure why Eleanor is still here, really don't want her to hear this either. Nothing against you, sis, but just, no, don't want you to hear."

"Hazel, do you think I don't know? I slept in the

same room with you. Was there when they would pull you out and when they would drag you back and drop you on the bed. I've seen the bruises, bites, and all the other stuff. Also didn't know how to tell you, but they were grooming me to be next. No, don't lose it, Hazel, I thought if I let them, they would lay off of you but it didn't work that way. So better if we both stay and tell our stories. Maybe the Devil's Handmaidens will have a better chance to take them down."

Watching these two very strong young women, my heart goes out to them. What the fuck is wrong with grown adults to want to hurt and abuse these poor children? My God, what's come of our world?

"Okay, let's take it slow. We'll ask some questions and if you can answer good, if not, no worries. Let's do the best we can and remember we have no judgment. Most of us come from very rough beginnings so we understand."

Hazel gets an ugly look on her face.

"Rough beginnings. What? Didn't get the horse you wanted or lost a job? I can't speak for Eleanor, but I was repeatedly gang-raped just about every night. And I let it happen because they said if I didn't, they'd go grab my younger sisters and make me watch. So how bad could your younger years have been in comparison?"

Before I can say one word, Vixen is up and—wow—to my surprise, pissed as hell.

"Hazel, we don't try to compare each other's nightmares to see whose is the worst. I get your pissed, upset, confused, and everything else you can think of.

Don't take that shit out on the people trying to help you. Now to give you some reality, I left home young, ended up in Vegas where I was taken under the wing of a pimp. Yeah, that's right, little sistah, I was a whore or prostitute, whichever word works for you. He called us escorts but not sure why. That's not the worst either. He would let his girls get pregnant then he'd steal the babies once we gave birth and would sell them on the black market. He took my twins on the same day they were born and I didn't see them again until they were brought here because that brotherhood who had you was working with the pimp who had me. They wanted my twins so they were brought to the ranch so we could protect them."

"Did you protect them?"

Vixen looks at Eleanor and smiles.

"We sure did, Eleanor, and now they live with me and my fiancé. So yeah, bad stuff happens but remember good stuff does too. Now without the attitude, Hazel, let's get started, shall we?"

I watch as Hazel drops her head for a second then lifts her eyes to Vixen then me.

"I'm sorry I acted like a bitch, this is so much, and I want to forget not keep reliving it. That's not your fault. I'm in pain too, but I'll try to be nicer though."

Knowing the grazes on her arm and hip must be burning and hurting, I get up, walk to the little kitchenette, and open one cabinet, pulling out some Tylenol. I grab two of them and bring them to Hazel with a cold bottle of water.

"Should help take some of the intensity off you, Hazel."

She nods then throws the pills in her mouth and follows it up with two huge drinks of water.

"Okay, ready as I'm ever going to get."

Then for the next two and a half hours, we drill first Hazel then Eleanor 'til they are exhausted and so are we. The stuff these kids told us makes me want to do something I've never done. Hurt someone. No not hurt, torture then kill them. There is no reason for those adults to do what they've done but then again, I don't understand any person who could abuse a child or animal.

After we are done, the four of us head to the ranch. Tink has already had two adjoining rooms made up for the girls. Each room has two beds so that should work. The little ones are almost asleep in the great room on the sectional. Must have run them out of all their energy. Hazel and Eleanor plop down and just stare at the television that two of the Intruders are watching. Some shoot 'em up movie. I'm just about to go into the kitchen to grab some snacks when I hear Eleanor start to scream. Turning, I see her pointing at one of the Intruders.

"Oh my God, you aren't trying to help us, are you, Taz? Why is he here? Please don't let him take me again. I'll do anything, just don't make me go with him."

When I look to the sectional, I see Malice and Presley sitting there. For a second, I wonder who she's talking about but Presley is Squirt's ol' man and doubt he's doubling as a human trafficker. So that leaves Malice, the one Intruder just about each and every one of my club sisters have had a run-in with. He shifts his eyes from Eleanor to me and he smirks. Asshole.

"Eleanor, which one are you talking about? The first guy is Malice, the second is Presley."

"Definitely Malice. I've seen him at the camp multiple times. He's mean and never lets up. Again, why is he here?"

I see Vixen on her phone and I reach behind me to pull my automatic out and point it at the brother. He sees it and his eyes turn mean.

"Remember when I said there is evil in the world. Well, some of that evil can play like they're good, even though they are really bad. I'm thinking that he's one of those people. Now you get up and kneel on the ground, hands on your head. Do it, Malice, don't piss me off, *brother*."

Slowly he stands then hits his knees, hands linked behind his head. Vixen comes up behind him with zip ties and uses them on his wrists. He tries to turn but can't so he shifts to make it difficult. Vixen reaches around and grabs his junk, that has him howling.

"Now listen to me, asshole, you'll do as I say or I'll rip this appendage off and shove it down your throat. Got it?"

He nods and Vixen is able to get his wrists in the zip ties. I'm shocked, never heard her so vicious or violent but good for her. Just as she's pushing back to sit, the door opens and in walks Enforcer, Yoggie, and Glory. All looking mighty serious.

"What the fuck is goin' on here? Why you got our brother zip-tied?"

Watching my man Enforcer, or Travis to me, walk to me and put his arm around me, reaching for my gun, I let out a sigh. Now he's going to take over for sure. These badass alphas can be a pain in the ass at times.

"Malice, got anything to say? You've been on our radar for a while, but I prayed you weren't a deviant and now we hear you are."

Malice looks around the room at first with that irritated look on his face, but then he drops his head. When he looks up something is tearing him up, it's all over his face.

"Fuck, was hopin' to get away without an explanation. Damn these women in the Devil's Handmaidens always fuckin' shit up. Truth is I'm working undercover for the sheriff. Yeah, that's right, and the reason I can is because my twin brother was a part of the brotherhood. I know, don't know why. It was him, my sister-in-law, and my nephew. At first, I guess he thought he could handle it. When they tried to take his wife, he fought back and eventually lost. He grabbed my nephew and fled to the sheriff for help. George is a good man and he got his deputies together and went out to that property behind the Sterling's. They found a burned-out pile of wood. And in the center was my brother's young wife burned to death. My parents have him locked down in a psychiatric ward in a hospital in Billings. They also have my nephew, who's trying to survive without his mom and, right now, also without his dad."

Malice takes a deep breath then looks around the table, stopping on Hazel or Eleanor.

"Be honest, I might have acted like a dick but I've never laid a hand on either of you. In fact, I'm the one who was sneaking food into that shit room they had the four of you in. Enforcer, Taz, and Raven, I've never put a hand on a minor... ever. That is some sick shit, but I've seen what the Thunder Cloud Knuckle Brotherhood is capable of. Me, I used scare tactics to keep the group of kids assigned to me, that I'm supposed to be using and abusing, so I can school them into keeping quiet. Yeah, I've slapped a few—just to leave some bruising—but nothing sexual at all. Sheriff George and the FBI know I'm undercover. Now that you three do, I'm sure in no time at all the entire Devil's Handmaidens and Intruder clubs will know. Can I please go talk to Tank first? I owe him that, at least, for all he's done for me. "

I'm flabbergasted so I look to Travis. He's watching his club brother. Until he's not.

"Let's go, I'll take you to Tank, Malice. And you're right, he deserves to know the truth. Then you're going to share everything you know about the brotherhood, got me? Don't make me turn you over to Shadow 'cause, motherfucker, I will without a thought."

Malice turns a bit pasty then gives Intruder a scared look. Well shit, I'd be worried too if someone was going to turn me over to our club enforcer. Travis leans down, gives me a kiss, then whispers for me to get my ass home, feet up. He lets me know Teddy and the three dogs are at Glory's house, which means Lilly must be watching all of them.

Well, this intake took a serious turn. I reach for my phone to text Tink. She definitely needs to know what Vixen and I uncovered today.

EIGHTEEN
'RAVEN'
BRENNA

Slowly I feel myself waking up but as soon as I do, confusion sets in. This is not my bed and the light shouldn't be getting in as I have darkening blinds. I pry my eyes open and the instant my eyes are focused it hits me, I'm in Ash's guest room at his beautiful log house. Stretching to get my blood flowing through my body, it hits me, I feel pretty good. Must be this frigging awesome mattress. Like sleeping in the clouds.

I swing my legs off the bed and move toward the restroom. Once I've peed, brushed my teeth, and washed my face, I head back into the bedroom only to realize I have no clothes, except my dirty ones. *Shit*, I think to myself as I walk back to the bathroom, only to notice my clothes are gone. Come on already, the morning just started.

Grabbing the tie of my robe, I tighten it, then open my door to the smell of food cooking. Damn, that smells excellent as my tummy growls in agreement. Ash cooks too, hmm, what a guy. Though I can't let my walls down because if I do and he does something like the last time, he'll gut me forever.

Walking through the hallway, I'm looking at pictures hung up along the way. Most are of his family, mother, brothers, and probably his uncles and aunts on his mom's side. Then I come to a complete stop because there are three photos bunched together. One is of our engagement party, one is of me by myself on my folks' front porch, and the last is me coming out of the clubhouse, hands full of laptop, tablet, and iPad. This last one is recent. What the hell?

Ignoring what that could mean, I hit the kitchen to see Ash working over a couple of pans on top of the stove. He has a television on softly with the news playing. I stand here for a second or two just watching him. What a mess. This could have been our lives but instead we both got hurt, not because of what we did but because his father is involved with very nasty folks.

Ash must have heard me sigh because he turns and flashes that gorgeous smile of his.

"Damn, mornin', *A stór* (uh STORE is Irish for my treasure). You have no idea how long I've dreamed and waited to see you come walking into this kitchen just like you are. Shit, sorry, Brenna, brain is still recovering. Didn't mean to say that out loud right to you. Shit, I'm a moron. How'd you sleep? Can I get ya some coffee? Breakfast will be ready shortly. Your clothes are on the dryer, if you want to get dressed first."

I can see he's uncomfortable, but in a way, so am I,

though him calling me that again has my heart doing flips. He used to call me that way back when, and every time it made me feel so special. How did I forget his nickname for me?

"Yeah, Ash, I'll take some coffee. Just point me in the direction, I can do it myself."

"Know that, Brenna, but this morning I'll take care of it for ya. Three creams no sugar, right?"

I nod then walk toward the laundry room to grab my clothes. I walk into the half bath and get dressed then walk back to the island. This is a chef's dream kitchen. The island alone is huge and I love the two colors of cabinets. The island is wood and the other ones are a very light green. *It's beyond gorgeous*, I think as I pull a stool out and sit my butt down.

"How long have you been in the house, Ash?"

"Not long, maybe three or so months. Took a while and some of the stuff was on back order. It was worth the wait though. Whatcha think, Brenna?"

"My God, Ash, it's a dream house. It's perfect. I mean, look at you and how far you've come. You built your own home and I live in one of Tink's cabins."

"Don't do that, Brenna. Those cabins are sweet and if I remember how you used to be, you have a nest egg somewhere just waiting to be used for your dream house. Am I right?"

He doesn't wait. Just puts a huge mug of coffee in front of me, then goes to the toaster, pulling out four slices of toasted bread. He butters them and puts them on the island next to two kinds of homemade jelly and jam.

"Please tell me you don't can too? Come on, you're killing me. I'm lucky that I can cook decent."

He smirks then outright laughs. *That's an awesome look on him*, I think quickly then push that thought out of my head.

"Naw, Mom does all of that. My pantry has more of her canned goods than a grocery store probably has. Though I'm grateful, especially during our Montana winters. Her canned goods back in the day saved us all. I mean, she had five boys to start with then added a sixth one. And honestly, Brenna, I've never heard her complain once. She's beyond phenomenal. That's why I want this to end. She needs to move on and have a life of her own, no matter what it turns out to be."

"I totally understand, Ash, I'm going to go to my office in the clubhouse today and do some research and catch up with Freak from the Intruders. He was put on doing the background searches for all of those taken into custody. Hopefully, he can find something or an opening we can use to get one of those bastards to talk to us."

I watch all the emotions run across his face. It takes all I have not to run to him, putting my arms around his body and holding on to him tightly while he works through all the emotions, but I have to remember what went down years ago. That crushed me. I don't think I ever recovered. I'll do my best to help Ash and his family with the Thunder Cloud Knuckle Brotherhood situation, but got to protect my heart.

When I look toward him, he's watching me intently. I give him a small smile, which he returns.

"Let's eat, Brenna, since we both have shit to do. Hope this is enough for you."

We both sit after he plated a ton of food on both plates. It wasn't until I was looking at the food I realized how truly starving I am. So without further hesitation, I pick up my fork and start to dig in. Damn, everything is so good, I just keep shoveling it in until I hear Ash snort then chuckle. Looking up, he's holding his coffee mug in one hand and his phone in the other. My God, I think he's either taking a picture, or worse, a video of me eating like a pig in a trough.

"Ash, for Christ's sake, put that damn phone down. No, better yet give it to me so I can delete whatever you have on it. What are you thinking, man?"

Instead of answering me, all he does is grin then take a huge swallow of coffee. He pushes his phone to me. When I wake it up there's no security to get into the phone, so the first thing I see is a picture of his house as a screensaver. Awe, cute. Then I start looking for what he was doing. Yeah, there it is, he took a few pictures then a video. When I go to delete everything, I sneak a peek at him and he looks anxious as hell. It dawns on me he didn't take these to show to anyone to make fun of me. He wanted pictures of me so he took them for himself. Oh shit, there goes my frigging heart again. Instead of deleting, I close down his phone, and slide it back to him, saying nothing. Then he blows me away with his sincerity.

"Thanks, Brenna, for not deleting them. It means a lot. Now eat, will ya, still have more on the stove."

Just when we start to dig back in, I hear a knock on his front door before the beeping and boots on his wooden floors. I look up to see Rowan and Joshua walking our way. The little boy is all smiles and Rowan has a smirk on his teenage face.

"Mom told us to make sure you were feeding Brenna this morning, so the two of us took a ride on the four-wheeler to check on both of you. Good morning, Brenna. I see my older brother went all out with his favorites. Guess we'll head back, come on, Joshua. I got some chores that I have to tend to."

Feeling like Ash's little brother wants to stick around, I look at Ash and do a half-assed chin lift at him then his brothers. He smiles hugely at me then looks at his two brothers.

"Hey, there's plenty, pull up a chair and I'll fix you both a plate. Joshua, you want some eggs or pancakes?"

"Both pease."

Joshua is so cute. Then it dawns on me, he's the same age or very close to what our baby would have been. That hits me right in the gut and immediately it feels like I have acid in my stomach. Shit, I've been around other younger children and it never hit me like seeing Joshua just did. I feel two hands on my shoulders and when I glance up, Ash is looking down at me, concern on his face. Then he mouths, "Are you all right?" I take a breath then nod, but he looks to Joshua then me, and back at his little brother. It's almost like I see the light bulb go on above his head. His hands squeeze my shoulders then he leans down and kisses the top of my head before walking away to fix the plates. I hear a kid's giggle and look to see Joshua staring at me.

"You kissed her hair. Why?"

I don't say a word, figuring I'll let Ash handle this one. As he makes his way to the table, he puts the plates down then scrunches down to his little brother.

"I kissed her because I like her a lot, and she was sad for a quick minute. When you care about someone, you show it with your actions. Like when you fall and Mom cleans and puts a bandage on your sore."

Ash leans and ruffles Joshua's hair before going back to the fridge and grabbing some orange juice. He pours two glasses and places them in front of the boys. Then he sits back down and resumes eating. Watching them all eat, it's like being with my family. We never wasted food growing up. We weren't poor but we sure weren't rich. Mom and Dad did their very best, but they had eight children, so the meals Mom cooked were made to stretch a long way. It hits me right then how lucky we were. No, we didn't have a new house, fancy cars, or even designer clothes. What we had no amount of money could buy. That thought brings a smile to my face as I grab my mug and slug back some coffee.

Joshua is staring at me and he is as cute as a button. His skin tone is almost like a light caramel and his hair is more curly than kinky. What grabbed my attention is his eye color. They are a weird grayish blue and look awesome with his skin tone. Damn, Gertie is going to have her hands full when that one grows up, for sure.

After we finish, Rowan and Joshua leave to take care of chores. Well, not before I get a hug, snuggle, and kiss from cutie Joshua. Rowan just smiles and says see ya later. I help Ash clean up the kitchen then get myself together, put my shoes on, and tell Ash I am going to leave. He walks me to the door then onto the porch, not saying a word. When I get close to my cage, he grabs my hand, stopping me.

"Brenna, I want you to come back. Will you? I don't care if it's for a meal or to watch a movie or play a game. It felt good to have company last night, especially since it was you."

I squeeze his hand and gently try to explain where I am at.

"Ash, not sure that's a good idea at the moment. So much is going on and, I'm sorry, don't want to hurt you but this thing between us is confusing as hell. I thought I pulled myself together after I lost our baby, but seeing Joshua it dawned on me. He's close to the age our baby would have been. That just about crippled me at your kitchen island. So let's play this by ear. Maybe I can come out if it's not just us but more of a group get-together. Would that work?"

"I'll take whatever you'll give me, *A stór*, and I'll be happy with it. There is no time clock on us, and shit, it's been years, maybe we aren't even compatible. All we can do is see, right? Now be careful and text me later. Let me know you're okay."

Then he leans down and gently kisses my nose before rubbing his nose against mine. He waits until I get in my cage, start it up, and do a three-point turn. As I am driving away, I look in my rearview mirror. Ash is standing, his hands in his pockets, watching me. That right there gives me butterflies in my stomach. Shit, I'm so screwed.

NINETEEN
'ASH'
ASHTON

Damn, am I tired, and it ain't even noon yet. This is gonna suck if we have to keep the animals sectioned off like this in Mom's pole barn. I mean, fuck, she has the mare and foal in her three-season room with an electric heater to make sure the foal is warm enough. That room will never be the same, though Rowan and Mom laid down huge, thick plastic first then some lime before putting down the straw. When I went to check on them today, Rowan was already in there mucking it out. I mean, horses piss whenever and wherever they want. That is way worse than their shit.

Now that everyone is taken care of here, got to go and make sure all the other animals are also okay. Then need to check on the herds. Fuck, not sure I'll make the day and not sure why because I slept really good last night. I mean, Brenna was in the house and safe. Only thing that would have made it better is if she had been in my bed, but can't rush this shit.

"Ash, honey, come on in and grab some lunch. Also, you got to stay hydrated, Son, you're busting your hump, sweating like a pig. Wash up and come in. We'll wait for you before we start."

I walk over to the spigot and turn it on. Then I rinse off my hands, arms, and face. Afterward I run my wet hands through my hair to try and calm it down. Looking down, I again wet my hands, shake them off, then run them down my T-shirt and jeans. I start to walk back to Mom's house, wiping my hands on my jeans once again. I grab the screen door, walk into the mudroom, first take my boots off, pushing them to the side, and then go directly to the sink. I turn the water on, wet my hands, then grab the bar of soap. After scrubbing for a couple of minutes, I rinse and grab the hand towel that hangs off the hook on the wall behind the utility sink.

Walking into the kitchen, I see Rowan, Rue, Reed, and Joshua already at the table. Shit, had no idea my brothers were here.

"Hey, y'all, what's going on?"

Reed's head snaps up and I can tell something is going on, I can feel it in my gut.

"Bro, no one has heard from Alder yet. Mom's really worried and I'm not far behind her. Sheriff is coming up with some men to go up and search the area. I'm gonna go with them."

I'm watching Rue, who's looking right at me but something is missing, and I can't figure out what it is. Reed is also watching me but not saying a word.

"Mom, can I go with Rue to look for Alder?"

Mom turns from the stove, glancing at Rowan then Rue and back to Rowan.

"Don't think so, Son. This isn't for fun, it's serious business. No, I'm not saying you won't take it like you should, just I'd rather you stick close to the ranch and me. I feel safer when you're here, Rowan, and so does Joshua."

I know Mom added that at the end to make my little brother feel better. And looking at him, it worked. Lost in my thoughts, my head jerks when I hear something hit the table. I focus and can't believe the huge pot of soup Mom just put down. Then she adds freshly made bread and finally it looks like sliced beef for roast beef sandwiches. Damn, she must have been up at the crack of dawn to do all of this.

We sit and Mom says grace before we all dig in. About halfway through, there's a knock on the door. Rowan gets up but Mom puts a hand on his shoulder, shaking her head. He lets out a huge sigh but doesn't argue with her. She goes to the pantry, opens it, and puts her hand on one of our portable gun safes. She pulls her weapon out, puts it in the back of her jeans, and walks to the door. Rue gets up and follows, hand to his holstered gun under his flannel. I look to Reed with huge eyes and he returns the look. Seems like he doesn't know what the fuck is going on either.

I hear Sheriff George's voice as he heads into the kitchen. Mom has tears on her face and Rue has his hand on her shoulders. Fuck, please don't be Alder. Then the sheriff shares the news.

"All right, boys, some hunters were out before dawn this morning. They were up by that cabin but it was the smell of burning wood that had them hightailing it to the area. When they got there, Alder and his crew were hog-tied around a dying fire. They are beat to hell but besides that seem okay. Also by the fire were the women who were held there with Bray. They are in serious shape; one is being air lifted to Bozeman from what I hear. I called Brenna's sister, Bray, to come into town, see if she can talk to them, make them more comfortable. It's gonna take a lot of therapy to help them poor women. Anyway, Alder is at the emergency room in town. Wanted to let ya know. He's gonna be sore and bruised but otherwise okay. Now, I gotta go down by where the Thunder Cloud Knuckle Brotherhood was staying and make sure no one is back there. I got Judge Jones to give me a criminal trespass citation. Also giving them a ten-day notice to vacate the premises. We are gonna follow the law but saying that, there is no way in hell—pardon me, Gertie—that I'll allow them to stay if I have to physically remove each and every one. Now gotta get going. Gertie, need a favor. Can I get a refill for my travel mug? This is turning out to be a very long day and will need my caffeine to keep myself moving and clearheaded."

"Sure, George, go get it. I'll also make up some beef sandwiches for you to take along. Go on now, get that mug."

The sheriff shakes his head then moves through the house back to his squad car, coming back in with his huge as fuck travel mug. Mom looks at it and grins, then goes and starts a fresh pot of coffee. We talk as Sheriff George waits for Mom to fill him up. When she finally hands him his travel mug, she also hands him a small cooler. He looks at her then a look of confusion appears on his face.

"George, there's ten sandwiches in there. Some waters, granola bars, and homemade cookies. No, don't say a word, you're doing this for our family, the least we can do. Right, boys?"

We all agree then strangely enough, Mom walks out Sheriff George. I look to both Rue and Reed. They shrug their shoulders, shaking their heads. By the time Mom comes back in we are all done, dishes are loaded in the dishwasher, and Rowan is finishing up the pots and pans. She looks around but seems to be avoiding our eyes. Oh shit.

"Rowan, can you take Joshua into the great room for a second? Want to have a word with Mom."

He looks at me then at Mom. He waits until she nods then he picks up Joshua and they both leave. The three of us are staring at Mom, not sure how to start this fuckin' uncomfortable conversation. Thank God she does.

"I'm not going into details. I've been down that road with Rowan. So this is all you three are gonna get. Sheriff George has been coming around lately to visit. We are not dating or how do you young folks say 'hooking up or bumping nasties.' He's a friend and I'm overdue to have a friend, a man friend, in my life. End of conversation."

Then she walks out. Rue, Reed, and I watch her 'til she disappears around the corner. My eyes meet my two brothers, but it's Rue who beats me to it.

"Bumping nasties. For fuck's sake, I'll never be able to unhear our mom saying that or the picture that popped into my head. Holy shit never even gave this any thought. But Mom's right, she deserves it and she could do a whole hell of a lot worse than Sheriff George. Don't you agree?"

As we hash it out between us, at one point Rowan comes in and sits at the table. We shut up but he smirks before he drops his bomb.

"Sheriff George is a good guy. He's been over for both lunch and dinner. He always brings Mom flowers or chocolate, and Joshua and I always get something. He listens to me when I talk, which is more than I can say for any of you. You still treat me like I'm a six-year-old not sixteen-year-old. Plus, you're always too busy for me, while he makes time to listen and give advice. So I like him and I think him and Mom are cute together. More importantly, he's good with Joshua, doesn't treat him like less. And our little brother adores our sheriff. Just thought you should know."

Before he can scramble out of here, I reach out and grab his hand. He looks to me and sits back down.

"Damn, Rowan, sorry if my head's been up my ass

and I've not been around for ya, bro. I'm always here for you, just like these guys and Alder are. Sometimes when you grow up, responsibilities hit you so hard you feel like you're drowning, but that ain't no excuse. Thanks for sharing with us. I totally appreciate all you do around here, lil' bro, for Mom, Joshua, and all of us. Never doubt that, little brother. Now do you want to take a ride with me to check on the herd in the northern pasture?"

Must be the teenager hormones 'cause I can see how excited he is, but he's trying to play it off.

"Yeah, I guess, as long as Mom is okay with Joshua staying here with her. I'll go run it by her, give me a minute or two."

I watch Rowan walk away and when I turn, Joshua is staring at me wet eyes. What the fuck?

"What's wrong, buddy?"

"I wanna go witt you and Rowan on da horsies."

Oh fuck, this kid's always paying attention. Well, I mean what can it hurt? He can ride with me and that gives Mom a break. I go and pick him up, shifting him to one hip then follow the path Rowan took. When I get to the three-season room, Mom is sitting on one of her chairs watching the momma horse and foal outside hooked up to the clothesline. Rowan is talking to her as she looks out on the ranch. Mom looks tired, damn it. Yeah, Joshua can come with us I decide.

"Rowan, dude, hang on. Joshua brought it to my attention that I didn't ask him to go ride horsies with us.

So the three of us will go check on those cows. That sound good, Mom? Gives you some time for yourself."

She nods but it's the look of gratitude in her eyes and the small smile that lights her face up. Yeah, gotta do this more often so she has some time to do what she wants. She's our mom but she's also a woman living and working on a ranch filled with men. Unfortunately, I've only been looking at her as our mom, that has to stop. We talk for a quick minute then the boys and I jump into my truck after I put Joshua's car seat in it. Then we make our way to the huge horse barn about a half mile from my home. While Rowan and I get the horses ready, Joshua has a ball with the two donkeys he and Rowan named: Batman and Robin. They were out in the small pasture off the side of the barn. Watching him laughing and running around makes me happy. To be so innocent and young. I just hope we can protect him from the hatred and despair out there for as long as possible.

When we were ready to head out, I lift up on my horse, Warrior. I get situated then look to Rowan, nodding. He lifts our little brother up into my arms and I place him right in front of me, close to the horn on my saddle. Then I take the breakaway and wrap it around his tiny waist and hook it to my belt loop. If something happens, I'll have a chance to keep him with me. If not and say Warrior goes down, the breakaway will give if Joshua falls or moves suddenly off the horse. We played around with this when he was a baby because as soon as he would see a horse, his arms were up in the air.

As we head out, my thoughts go to Brenna. I hope she's having a good day. Not sure how to play this, but I'll send her a text once we get to the pasture. Just a check-in. After that thought my attention is on both of my brothers.

TWENTY
'RAVEN'
BRENNA

Well, looks like it's another day in the life of a Devil's Handmaidens sister. Got back to my cabin, took a quick shower, then got dressed. Made a travel mug of coffee and grabbed an apple. Before I left, sent a text to my club sisters, letting them know I was heading into town and the clubhouse, as I needed to get to my office and do some work. When no one seemed interested in heading in with me, I figured either they were already there or had other shit on their agenda. So in my cage, as I'm heading into Timber-Ghost, my thoughts go to Ash. As soon as I'm wondering what he's doing and if I should text him, I push that thought out of my head. What the ever-lovin' fuck is wrong with me?

Even knowing the whole story, there is still a small part of me that's truly hurt. Either he didn't think enough of me or didn't love me with his whole heart because he walked out and never looked back. I mean never. We've seen each other from a distance since that day, I mean, we live in the same damn town. I would always walk away if we were at a town parade for like July Fourth or the Christmas bazaar. Then there was all the shit we put on at the Wooden Spirit Bar and Grill, one of our club's businesses. With that thought, think I'm going to stop at the gym before I head to the clubhouse. Need to grab some of the last two months' receipts. How did I forget to tell Ash I'm a business owner. Well, with the help of my prez, Tink. She backed me without a second thought.

When I came up with the idea of a gym, a real one, I talked it over with Tink. She loved the idea, as the building I was interested in was huge, so we could split it into one section for men to try and fit their workout requests, while the other section for women would have some machines but also Zumba, Pilates, and we start hot yoga next weekend. That Stephanie, my manager, found Luni is a miracle. Everyone was asking about it and I was feeling kind of bad not being able to provide members with something they wanted to try, but fuck, we live in Montana. From what Stephanie told me, Luni was in a bad relationship and when she left her ex-boyfriend, she came home to her parents' ranch. When she lived in Billings, she worked at a gym and taught hot yoga. She actually came in to speak to us about maybe considering it and she walked out with a job. We'll see how that goes.

Taking a sip of my coffee, I take the sharp corner slowly and when I'm back on the straight road I see something on the side of the road. Awe shit, someone hit a deer. It's dead, most of its guts are on the road. I swerve to miss a huge pile of something, not looking. When I see a place to pull over, I do. Grabbing my phone, I put a call to 911. When the emergency operator answers, I let them know a huge buck was taken down and it could be a hazard on this road since it's the only one that brings you into town. She told me she'd get some of the road and sanitation guys to go out and clean up the mess.

As soon as I turn on the street the gym is on, I know something is wrong. As I pull up, no lights are on and the front door is wide open. I pull my cage in quickly and pick up my phone. I hit number one speed dial and after just one ring, I hear Tink.

"Hey, Raven, what's up, girl?"

"Tink, we got trouble. I'm at the gym, needed to pick up some receipts for this month and last. Looks like no one is here and the front door is wide the fuck open. Anyone close to town? I'm gonna go in, would love someone on my back."

"Shit, Raven, stand down, wait until someone can cover you. Noodles, call Sheriff George, tell him we got trouble at Raven's gym. I know Peanut and Kiwi are at the Wooden Spirit, let me get ahold of them. Shadow and Panther were going to the bank today so I'll have Noodles reach out to them. Someone should be there as quickly as possible. Don't take any chances, sister."

Without another word, she hangs up and I've got dead air. I put my phone in my back pocket and grab my automatic out of my side holster. Reaching into the glove compartment, I pull out two extra clips. I look around and the street is completely dead, which again is really strange. Something is telling me to get in there so I exit my cage and carefully and quietly make my way to the door. As I move to walk in, I hear screaming and then men laughing. Oh fuck, no way, motherfuckers, not on my watch in my gym.

Turning, I hit my truck and use the key to open it. I pull out the Steyr AUG SA USA rifle after I reholster my automatic. Moving quickly, I again hit the door and now all I'm hearing is the laughter. I give my eyes a second or two to adjust, then I move in. Nothing in the main area, but the 'party' sounds seem to be the on the men's side of the gym. As I walk that way, I see in the hot yoga area something is lying in the middle of the room. A person who's not moving. Son of a bitch, I don't want the person who was screaming to suffer another second, but I got to check on this one, so I move in. When I get close, I can see it's Luni. She's beat to shit, workout pants tore off of her, and just looking at her, I can tell she was raped. I feel for a pulse so I grab the phone and text Tink to get an ambulance on route.

Turning Luni on her side in case she starts to vomit, I again make my way to the men's workout area. Looks like all the lights are on so as quiet as possible I make my way to the huge open area. What my eyes fall on has me taking in a huge breath and not letting it out. The motherfuckers in there, I swear to Christ, I'm going to kill them all.

Not sure, but I think they are all Thunder Cloud

Knuckle Brotherhood. When someone starts giving orders to the two assholes holding Stephanie down, I just about lose it. Well, until I see who it is. How is he even out, thought Sheriff George arrested them all. Guess it's time to make my entrance.

"Motherfuckers, step back right the hell now. Don't tempt me to blow your balls off. I said move, you stupid piece of shit. Bastards, do it. Everyone up against that wall. NOW!"

Hearing my voice, they all turn in my direction, immediate hatred in their eyes. I don't take my eyes off of any of them as I make my way to the wall next to the entrance, so no one can sneak up on my back. When Cliff Sterling's eyes meet mine, he smirks. *Jagoff, give me one reason to blow your goddamn head off,* I think to myself. One of the assholes starts toward me, so I let loose with a quick finger pulse. Bullets hit the rubber matting on the floor. It's the particulates of rubber hitting their bodies that has them screaming. I hope they hurt like hell. I quickly look over to Stephanie and see she's on her feet, pulling her ripped workout pants back on. Her face is swollen and starting to bruise. When she sees me looking her way, she gives me a tiny smile. I return it with one of mine.

The assholes must think I wouldn't see them advancing on me. I swing the Steyr AUG SA USA rifle to the side, grab my automatic, and aim at them.

"Keep coming, motherfuckers, and I'll start blowing brain matter all over the place. Try me. Now, like I said, everyone up against that wall. Kneel, cross your ankles, hands interlaced behind your heads. Do it."

A few of them head toward the wall when two start running at me. I don't even think about it, I aim and in a second, one is down. The other starts to slow down when Cliff tells him to advance. He's a young guy and I can see the fear in his eyes. I look at him then the ground. Thank God he got my message and immediately falls flat on the floor, hands on his head.

Seeing movement out of the corner of my eye, I see Cliff grabbing for a gun. Holy shit, he's going to kill this poor confused kid because he didn't give his life for the cause. Nope, not happening. Again, I aim and when Cliff's hand lifts, I am ready. I pull the trigger and my bullet hits its mark. His arm. Immediately he starts to swear and cuss like a trucker, while I didn't think my automatic would do so much damage even with a graze. Oh well, I don't personally give a shit how much Cliff suffers. Then I hear noise coming from the front of the gym.

Turning I see Shadow, Panther, Avalanche, and Jersey running toward this part of the gym. I look back and smirk largely at Cliff.

"See, asshole, good always prevails over evil assholes like you."

He belly laughs then glares at me.

"Bitch, you have no idea. In a million years you won't be ready for what's about to hit this hick-ass town. Startin' with my family then hitting yours. NO one will be left out; I promise you that."

Before he can say another word, Avalanche walks right up to him, pulls back, then punches Cliff right in the face. He actually lifts off his feet and falls straight back down, out like a light. Thank God, I was sick of hearing his voice.

"You okay, Raven? Fuck, we got here as fast as we could. Left the banker at his desk, took off running. Oh shit, go take care of your girl, we'll take care of these bastards."

"Shadow, need you to check on Luni. She's in that room we were going to use for hot yoga. She's been violated from what I saw, so go gentle. I'll get Stephanie and we'll meet you in that room. Panther, don't let anyone walk in that area over there. See where it's wet? Evidence, want Sheriff George to get DNA so we can bury these dicks."

I walk to Stephanie and when I'm close enough, she flings herself into my arms, violently sobbing. Trying not to fuck up evidence at first, then I realize she needs comfort more than worrying about getting shit on these assholes. We'll have more than enough. I hang on to her until she starts to slow down then stop. I lift her face and I'll never forget the look in her eyes.

"Stephanie, you won. No, don't. You did what you had to do to live and it worked. We need to get to the hot yoga room Shadow is checking on Luni. She's in bad shape. Can you make it, Stephanie?"

She nods and we slowly make our way to Shadow. When we get there, Shadow is hanging on to Luni, who seems to be disoriented. Stephanie looks at her than me.

"Why is she here, Raven? I didn't see her when I opened, and I know I locked the door and put the alarm on before I went to the back to check everything was ready for when I opened the gym. Next thing I know, someone grabbed me from behind and threw me on the ground. I couldn't fight them off, Raven, too many of them. My God, what is Benji going to think? He won't be able to handle this. He's going to ask what they did. Raven, oh my God, I can't lose him."

I pull her close, look her directly in the eye, and give it to her gently.

"Stephanie, you didn't do anything wrong. What they did is on them. Benji loves you, so don't worry about anything. If he doesn't understand, then I'm sorry to say he's not the man for the phenomenal woman you are. Right now, we need to take care of you. I got to ask and even though I saw your pants torn off, did any of them take it to the max? Did any of the Thunder Cloud Knuckle Brotherhood force themselves on you, did they rape you?"

She starts to cry before she nods. We both jump when we hear the ambulance siren. I hold on to her tightly as Peanut and Kiwi come running in, guns in front of them. Well, Peanut has her Steyr AUG SA USA rifle pointed in front of her. Kiwi has a large automatic in her hands. When they see me and take in the scene, both of them come instantly to the two women who have been violated. Peanut takes Stephanie from me, holding on to her. Kiwi is already by Luni.

When I start to move away, a hand grabs mine. Stephanie looks at me sadly.

"Thank you, Raven, I can't imagine what would have happened to Luni and me if you hadn't shown up. I'm thinking you saved our lives."

I just smile her way when I hear my name yelled out loudly. When I turn, I see Sheriff George making his way to me.

"Gonna need your statement, Raven. Now would work for me, I'll get you over to the hospital if you want or we can stay here. I put a call in to that FBI agent who's been following our progress with the brotherhood. You okay?"

"Yeah, I'm fine. Let's go to my office, if you don't mind. Not what I was expecting coming in today. Before you ask, no one knew I was making my way here before I went to the clubhouse. With everything going on, forgot to get receipts for this place. If I don't get them to Taz regularly, she loses her mind. And it's worse now that she's pregnant. OCD all the way."

We walk into my office and before I even make my way to the desk, Sheriff George grabs me, pulling me back out.

"Don't touch anything, Raven."

"Why? What's up?"

'Shit, woman. All of you Devil's Handmaidens are like my family, don't really want to talk about this, but here goes. Look in real quick."

I do and at first don't see anything, then notice the top of my desk looks wet. Well, there's puddles of a cloudy liquid on my desk and something is running down my chair. When I turn my eyes to the sheriff, he looks down. What the hell? Then it hits me why Sheriff George is embarrassed and doesn't want to talk about it. Someone ejaculated all over my office furniture.

"That is seriously gross. Good thing the dumbasses left their DNA. Makes it easy for you because it's there for the taking. Guess they aren't as smart as they all think they are. Definitely not the smartest ones, that's for sure"

Sheriff George watches me for a second then looks around before he pulls me in, giving me one of his awesome hugs. Then he leans down and whispers only for me to hear.

"Definitely a badass."

With that I let out a loud laugh, which has people walking by turning their heads to look in my office like I'm nuts. Maybe I am, but I totally needed that laugh. That is until in the next minute when all we hear are assault rifles and screams coming from the front of the building. Sheriff George looks at me and I nod, walking to the large locked safe against the wall behind the door. Using my fingerprint, I open it and pull out two assault rifles and two body armor vests, handing both to him. As a team we put the vests on first, then move out quickly to try and save as many people as we can. That's my prayer because my chosen family is out there and the thought of any one of them getting injured, or worse, is something I can't even let into my head.

TWENTY-ONE
'SHERIFF GEORGE'
GIORGIO DE LUCA

Son of a bitch, let my guard down for five minutes and all hell breaks loose. I'm so fucking sick of these racist bastards. I know these thoughts go against the badge I wear each and every day, but this has to end. And soon, before my little town becomes a war zone and ends up on the national nightly news for all the crazy motherfuckers in our country to see.

Carefully, Raven and I make our way down the hallway to the sounds of screaming, laughter, and gunfire. Since we have no idea what we're gonna walk into, I make sure to be first out. Before we blindly walk in, I turn to Raven.

"Give me a minute to get a handle on what's going on, Raven. No, don't argue, I'm the sheriff of this town and believe it or not, I know what I'm doing, child. Just gonna take a peek then we can decide what's the best way to approach this. Might want to put a call out for help, 'cause we have no idea how many injured or dead."

That last word has Raven close her eyes and shiver. Fuck, didn't think on that one. As I move out it hits me, Raven has a third of her club sisters out there and more are on the way. I've got three of my deputies out there and as far as we knew, before we went to the office, two injured women. I move silently toward the end of the hallway. Once there I take a deep breath and slowly lean forward to see what the hell is going on. What I see has my mind go blank for five seconds. Then I quickly turn around and move toward Raven. This is worse than I even thought it would be. She's waiting for me impatiently.

"Raven, you got a back door?"

"Running away, Sheriff?"

I shake my head, closing my eyes for a split second for patience.

"No, what I'm thinking is one of us goes out the back, gets into my vehicle, which thanks to Tank is bulletproof. Then we make a grand entrance. That should give the other one enough time to take a few of those Thunder Cloud Knuckle Brotherhood down. They've got everyone in your main room. Now, don't run out there, but what I saw was Stephanie, Kiwi, and Peanut have been stripped down to their underwear. Shadow looks to be unconscious, covered in blood, half unclothed. Panther, Avalanche, and Jersey are also beat to shit but awake and warily watching the brotherhood. Tink is who they are working on right now. No, don't,

Raven, let me finish. The assholes have her kutte and T-shirt off, but she has her jeans and boots on and a bra. She's up against I guess one of their, don't know what to call it, so I say like you do, prospect. They are fighting. And from what I saw Tink is winning, kicking his skinny ass."

At that moment we hear a gunshot then nothing else.

TWENTY-TWO
'RAVEN'
BRENNA

FUCK!!! I look to Sheriff George then my head drops. When I look up, I've pulled my big girl panties on.

"Which do you want me to do, crash the front or take out as many of those assholes as I can? I'll do whatever you want, but we have to move. Oh, I put a call out to Tank, he's engaging all of the Intruders, but it's going to take time we don't have. Also left a text for Ash but didn't get an answer, as of yet."

We take a minute or so to go over our plan. Then as I figured would be the case, so I was as safe as he could keep me, Sheriff George hands me his key fob and I backtrack past my office to the back door. First, I disengage the alarm for the door then slowly open it, checking to make sure no one is in wait. When I see it's clear, I run around the building, my intention is to go straight to the squad vehicle. I come to a complete stop when I see Luni talking to a bunch of the Thunder Cloud Knuckle Brotherhood. She's got a weird smile on her face as one by one the men give her a very intense open-mouth kissed. Motherfucker, that bitch is one of them. Probably a brood mare and, obviously, a whore to top it off. Can't let this get to me. I've got a job to do and Sheriff George is depending on me to get it done.

So when I look around, I'm thrilled the patrol vehicle is directly to my left. Keeping an eye on the bunch of assholes, I quietly move to the driver's side. Knowing once I hit the fob it will alert the crowd, I try the key first. The door opens and I instantly push the button to start the vehicle so no alarm goes off. When the engine engages, I slam the door as every head in front of the gym turns. By this time, I'm backing up and angling the wheels toward the biggest window. Taking a deep breath, hoping this works, I shift the vehicle into drive, hit the gas, and pray Sheriff George's plan works.

As I approach the building, the group of assholes including Luni separate, screaming and swearing at me. Luni looks shocked like a kid caught with her hand in the cookie jar. Watching my gym, I try to stay relaxed, and at the last minute I push on the gas pedal harder. First, I hear the crush against the brick under the window. Then the glass doesn't look like it will break until it first shatters and holds together until the weight of the SUV forces it to break and fall open. I don't slow down one bit, so when everyone starts to turn, I aim toward the largest group of Thunder Cloud Knuckle Brotherhood. Not sure who or how many are hit. I finally shift my foot to the brake, just as I see one of the brotherhood aiming an assault rifle at me. When the bullets hit the window, I naturally lean to the right but like Sheriff George said, the window holds up. By the time I've come to a stop, everyone is running around. I see Tink's hands swollen and her face a bloody mess, trying to drag Shadow out of the way. It takes everything in me not to jump out and grab Tink to push her into the back seat. She's our prez so her safety is our mission, especially since Rebel, whose job is specially to keep our prez safe, isn't here. I'm like Rebel's backup, Tink's bodyguard if that's what it's called, we just know it as keeping her safe.

Next, I see Sheriff George and two of his three deputies herding the injured brotherhood members over to the corner. Looking like it's under control, I'm thinking maybe I should get out to help when I see the sheriff look at me shaking his head. I roll the window down and hear my name being screamed.

"Brenna, get your fine ass over here now or else I'm gonna have to do something you'll regret. Bitch, I said now."

Knowing it is Cliff, Ash's father, yelling I slide down in the seat. My eyes start to shift when I see he's coming up on Tink, who's still trying to help a now conscious Shadow to her feet. I blow the horn to get everyone's attention. I look to our sheriff then at Tink. He sees what I do and screams for Cliff to drop the gun and get down on his knees. At the same time Ash's father moves quicker than I thought he'd be able to and grabs Shadow from behind. Usually, our prez could take that motherfucker down, no problem, but she's tired and beat to shit. When I look to Shadow, I see her staring at me. When I give her big eyes, she winks at me. Son of a bitch, thought I was the club clown. Then Cliff looks my way.

"Last chance, Brenna. I'll blow this bitch's head off, then next up will be the club freak of your girly band of do-gooders. Need you to get out of the vehicle slowly, else those other two of your 'sisters' over there will be next. Now last time…GET THE FUCK OUT OF THE CAR NOW, YOU CUNT."

My eyes take everything in and I know, no matter what, I'll never be able to live with myself if anything happens to my sisters or the police. This situation seems to have escalated since Ash came clean and told me the whole situation. Cliff has always scared me but looking at him right at this moment, he looks totally insane. He puts an arm around Shadow's neck and starts to tighten it. I can see her struggling and that right there tells me what I have to do.

Slowly, I take the seat belt off, letting it retract. Then I open the door and hear Sheriff George tell me, "No, Raven, stay put." When Cliff sees the door open, he loosens his hold on Shadow. Her ice-blue eyes search me out and she barely shakes her head. She doesn't want me to get out, but I won't let that jagoff murder her in front of me. With all eyes on Cliff, the men from the brotherhood start to get behind him, all armed again. Sheriff George and his deputies have about half of them in the corner either cuffed or zip-tied.

Getting out of the patrol car, the one thought that

comes to mind is I'm sorry I was such a little kid when Ash tried to explain everything to me. If this goes south, I might never get the opportunity or chance to see if Ash and I could rekindle our relationship from back in the day. I know we each have feelings for each other.

"That's right, Brenna, get your ass over here. No, wait, open that vest and let me see you are unarmed, then get over here."

As I open the bullet-proof vest and then turn around before I start to walk toward Ash's dad, I see the second before they both move at the exact same time. Shadow elbows Cliff right in the gut while somehow Tink manages to drop to her knees and reach over to grab Cliff's junk. From the shocked yell of pain, I'm thinking she succeeded. Then all hell breaks loose as the brotherhood starts aiming at people at random, pulling the triggers. I watch one of the deputies go down, not sure if he is killed. Next one of the men turns to where Sheriff George is and lets loose, killing all the brotherhood in the corner. One puts a gun to Shadow's head.

"Tell your fuckin' president to let him go now, or else she'll be wearing your brains all over her."

Shadow knows she's fucked so she looks down and gives Tink a nod. Our prez slowly releases Cliff's shit and gets to her feet. Before anyone can do anything, Cliff grabs the hand of the guy with the gun aimed at Shadow. He aims it directly at Tink and fires, just as Shadow flings her arm in the air, knocking the gun up. Shock appears on both Shadow and Tink's face as blood starts to appear on Tink's T-shirt. Motherfucker, I'm not sure if it's a graze or a gut shot. Either way, this is not good at all. I move quickly and get right next to Cliff.

"I'm here, let's go now. In a minute or two the place is going to be crawling with county cops, the Intruders, and the rest of my club. And I'm sure my brother, Ollie, and his folks are on their way. Not to mention the FBI and CIA. Best to call it a draw and move out."

Not expecting it when Cliff backhands me so hard, I literally fall right on my ass. I feel the wet instantly and figure he either broke my nose or put enough pressure to do some damage. I wipe my face with my forearm and look down. Yeah, it's broken with that amount of blood.

"You will learn now you are nothing. I don't want to hear your voice, just do what you're told. If you don't, you'll get more of that. My son should have reeled you in back in the day. Too fuckin' big for your breeches, whore. Now let's get in that vehicle so we can get the hell outta here. Men, pull back. We'll meet at the rendezvous. If you want one of the whores grab her now or move your asses. Obviously, between this whore and the sheriff they made a few calls, so time to get our asses outta here right now."

As I go to move, Cliff grabs my arm, pulling me way too close to him. Then he leans down and tells me to kick Tink in the stomach. When I refuse, he leans around and aims the gun at Shadow, who has her hands on her best friend's wound, trying to stop the bleeding. Seeing where I'm at, I look at Tink, who returns the look. She pushes Shadow's hands away and she waits. I mouth,

"I'm sorry" then pull back and kick her. She moans as Shadow first growls then screams. Cliff laughs then drags me by the arm to the very back of the sheriff's SUV. He throws me in and not sure where he got them from, but he zip-ties me. Before he shuts the overhead door, I see Tink writhing in pain. I'll never forgive myself for what I just did, even though it probably saved both my prez's and enforcer's lives. Not paying attention, I don't see Cliff's hand coming toward my face with his gun still in it. When he hits my temple, I'm out immediately.

TWENTY-THREE
'ASH'
ASHTON

Damn, forgot how much fun it was to just hang out with my younger brothers. Can't pick which is cuter or funnier. Joshua is such a smart little kid and obviously idolizes Rowan. And I can tell Rowan loves our little brother. They are in tune with each other, which is weird since one is a toddler and the other a teenager. I guess stranger things have occurred in life relationships.

After we checked on the cows, we just horsed around while checking the fences. I marked where we had either some loose barbwire or posts going down. That will need to be fixed quickly, so I'll get back and let one of the hands know and they can put it on their list of shit to do. A list that is never-ending.

I haven't checked my phone in some time so while the boys are off and the horses are drinking water, I pull my phone out and see I have messages. When I open that app, I see the first one is from Brenna. I click on it to read it and, fuck, I can't believe my eyes. How the fuck does this keep happening? That son of bitchin' group of demented assholes.

"Boys, mount up, we got trouble."

I watch Rowan pick up little Joshua and fling him on my saddle then run to his horse, jumping on. We ride like the devil is on our asses. I don't want to return Brenna's call until I'm able to be in my truck on my way. Even riding like crazy, it takes some time to make it back to the barn. Three hands are there and must realize something is up because as soon as I pull the reins in to stop, one is at my side while the other grabs Joshua. Rowan is right on my ass.

Jumping down, I reach for my phone and push Brenna's number. I hear 'her' pick up and before she can say a word, I start babbling.

"Brenna, my God, are you okay? *A stór*, I'm on my way. Is your club and sisters there for backup?"

"Well, well, well, if it isn't my dumbass son. Bet your surprised as fuck to hear me on your whore's phone. Well, better listen closely, son, or else you might never see her again. Well, alive and in one piece. Should have kept your mouth shut but, no, not you. Have to be righteous at all times. All my sons are stand-up good men, which pisses the hell out of me. In this life, gotta be hard if you want to get anywhere. Now, this is what's gonna happen, Ashton. I have Brenna and she's already in bad shape. She's kinda sleepin', yeah, that's what I'll go with. I need the following for me to even consider releasing this troublemaking bitch. First, I need cash. Second, I need your mother to sign over that section of land to me. Third, I need that little colored boy brought back to me. Fourth, I need Bray back. And finally, fifth, when you drop off the brat and Bray, include your mother in the mix. If all of my demands are met then I'll think about returning your *A stór*."

"If you lay one finger on Brenna, I swear to Christ, Dad, I'll not only put you in your grave but before that I'll turn Brenna's sister Shadow on you."

"I'd like to see you try since she's either cryin' over her president, who's gettin' cold or being rushed to the hospital. Actually, a bunch of those Devil's Handmaidens women are gonna need some fixin' up. Sayin' that, *son*, I wouldn't dare put my hands on your bitch but can't say my brothers won't have some sadistic interest. You saw Bray, so you know they aren't the gentlest men out there. Treat women worse than dogs. I wouldn't take too long to get my demands in order. I'll be in touch. Don't worry, Ashton, Sheriff George knows what's goin' on, he had a front seat view."

Before I can say a word, he disconnects.

"MOTHERFUCKER."

Both Rowan and Joshua rush over to me, hugging on me. I feel it but push it back. Now is not the time to lose my shit. Gotta think and get ahold of all my brothers. Feeling two more arms coming around my back, I can smell her lily of the valley perfume. That does it and I feel the wet in my eyes hittin' my cheeks. I push them away and take a minute to feel the love from my family. Then I turn to Mom.

"Something went down in town. Brenna, Avalanche,

and one of Sheriff George's deputies texted me but I didn't see them 'cause I never checked the phone. The Thunder Cloud Knuckle Brotherhood somehow got their hands on Brenna and the ol' man reached out giving me his demands. No, Mom, not gonna tell ya what he wants 'cause he ain't gonna get it. I need you guys to grab some shit, I'm going into town and all of you are coming with. No arguments. I'll talk to the ranch hands, try to explain what's going on. Make sure they're safe."

Mom is watching me closely, her hand holding on to mine. I squeeze it as I tell my younger brothers to pack some shit together. They run off with only Rowan understanding shit is about to hit the fan.

"Ash, honey, tell me now what your father's demands are and what does he have to hold over your head?"

I don't want her to know but I'm not skilled for this kind of shit. I'm a fucking rancher and right now I have people's lives in my hands, not to mention if I do the wrong thing, I could lose Brenna before I ever get her back. It feels like I'm gonna stroke out so I do what I always do, trust my ma.

"He has Brenna. No, please don't, Mom, I'm hanging on by a thread. If I do the five things he wants, he'll consider letting her go. But I know by the tone of his voice and just him being an asshole that he's gonna kill her."

"What does he want?"

"You know, the usual, cash, the land he's been doing

only God knows what on, Bray back, Joshua, and well... you."

She doesn't even blink from what I can see, she's holding her breath. Her head drops for a second or two then she lifts it up and when her eyes meet mine, the flames shooting out of her beautiful eyes shock the shit out of me. This woman is beyond strong. She's got the backbone and determination to face anything thrown in her way. Especially the asshole who's abused her and made life harder than it ever should have been.

"Well, like you said, he isn't getting what he wants. I want you to reach out to those nice men, Panther and Avalanche. Didn't they say if you need anything, call them. I'd also call Tank and Momma Diane. It won't hurt. I'll put a call in to Brenna's parents. Oh, call her brother, Ollie, he's got that sanctuary filled with ex-military. I'm sure he's gonna be involved in getting his sister back. I'll go get some things together and check on the boys. Ash, Son, look at me. We will get through this and you will get your chance with Brenna. Don't give up. Not on us, your family, Brenna, your future, and all the people and friends who are there to have your back. Now make your calls."

Mom turns and heads back to the house. The weight of the world is on my shoulders at the moment and I don't know the half of what went down. I grab my phone, plop my ass on a bale of hay, and search for the phone numbers. When Avalanche's pops up, I hit it and wait.

"Yeah, what's up, Ash? We got World War Three happening, is it important, brother?"

"My dad called. He's got Brenna and is going to kill her if I don't honor his five demands."

"FUCK! Okay, get your ass into town. I'll let Sheriff George know you're coming in. Ash, make sure to grab your mom and brothers 'cause I don't trust these motherfuckers as far as I can throw them. We got some dead here and quite a few injured. Brenna's president, Tink, was shot, she's on the way to the hospital. Gotta go, just get here."

Holy shit, I think to myself as I run—yeah, literally run—to my truck. The drive home was done in half the time. I run into my home and go directly to my bedroom. I pull a travel bag out and throw some clothes into it, go into the bathroom, and grab the essentials. Running back into my bedroom, I go into the closet and open the gun safe. I pull out five handguns, two hunting rifles, and one assault rifle. First, I throw my travel bag in the truck. Then I load up the firepower. Finally, I grab the last couple of items before I set my alarm and head back to Mom's.

When I get there, I rush out of the truck, taking the handguns with me. Mom is opening the door when I tell her I need a minute. The boys are in the great room so I go and sit with them, asking Mom to also take a seat.

"We got a family problem. Our father is starting some shit in town and people have been hurt. No, Rowan, not going into the details. Now, not sure if Mom said but we are heading into town ourselves. Going to the Sheriff's. Now listen closely. Mom, I know you have a gun but want you to carry this one. It's a Glock and I've brought extra clips for you. Keep them in your pocket or somewhere where you can get to them quick and easy. Rowan, I'm trusting you. I've seen you hunt and you've never fucked around with the weapons. This one is for you, again, here are extra clips."

Little Joshua is cuddled up next to Rowan half asleep, thank God. Don't want him to remember any of this bullshit. Together we load the truck. Everyone gets in and I start to head down our driveway to get into town. On the way I talk to a couple of hands and tell them to do their usual, but if they want to leave or if they're in any type of danger, get the hell outta there.

Not wanting to drive like a maniac, I make it into town under my normal time by five minutes, so yeah, my foot was hittin' the pedal hard. We leave everything in the truck except our guns and Joshua's stuffed baby dinosaur. My head never stops moving as I walk behind Mom with Rowan holding Joshua, walks in front of her. Once we enter the station, the receptionist sees us and waves us to the locked door. I hear the lock open and we all go in and sit down. She tells me the sheriff will be with me shortly. Mom is sitting with the boys while I stand and start pacing. It doesn't take long before Sheriff George is making his way to where we are. He comes directly to me, hand out.

"Son, we'll get her back, that's my promise. It's my fault, should have made her stay in the office and lock the door, but she wouldn't have listened with her sisters out there facing danger. I don't have a lot of time, so come on back, all of you."

We follow him to a conference room and every one of us sits while he closes the door. When he pulls a chair out and sits down, I can see the worry and exhaustion coming off of him. Fuck, that's not a good sign. Shit.

"I'm gonna share what I know, leaving nothing out. Rowan, this is a lot so if you want to step out, no judgment, son. I'm just glad little Joshua is asleep on that couch over there. He's been through so much already. Now, seems like we had a mole or whatever you want to call it at Raven's gym. The new girl, Luni, was a plant by the Thunder Cloud Knuckle Brotherhood. She even let them beat the hell out of her and Stephanie so it looked legit. She was the one who let them in and when Raven stopped in to pick up the receipts, all hell broke loose. Your father was there too, Ash. Sorry, Gertie, you know I thought he was an asshole, now I know he's not only an asshole but a coward too. I have a deputy being airlifted, who's only been on the job six months. A good kid. About I don't know, ten or twelve of the brotherhood were gunned down by their own brothers. Kiwi and Peanut are pretty bad off, got their asses beat to shit but don't think there was enough time for those bastards to violate them. Zoey was down when I got there, they used her as a punching bag. I'm guessin' when she went down, they chose Tink to take her place, thinking because she's so small that their boys would be able to take her. From what I'm hearing, she knocked out two of the brotherhood and was on the third one when all the shit hit the fan. Your dad, Cliff, grabbed Zoey, trying to get Raven to get out of my vehicle. When he put a gun to my daughter's head, she had no choice but to get out. Raven was willing to sacrifice herself to your father but it wasn't enough. He was gearin' up to hurt Tink and Zoey when they fought back. They almost had control of the situation when he aimed his gun and shot Tink. Thank God Zoey was able to jerk his arm at the last minute so his shot was off, but still she was rushed to the hospital. Haven't heard anything yet. I'm on my way there when we're done."

I look at the sheriff, confused.

"Sheriff, who's Zoey?"

Both Mom and he answer at the same time.

"His daughter, Shadow."

"My daughter, Shadow."

Well, guess my little brother is right, something is going on between Mom and Sheriff George. I'm glad, she deserves a life, after all, she raised all of us on her own. Though I push that thought to the back of my mind, too much going on right now.

"Might want to head to the hospital too, Ash, that's where everyone is meeting up. Raven's parents and siblings, and Ollie is bringing everyone from the sanctuary, you know they are all ex-military. Panther called the rest of his people. Tank and his club are on the way in. I put a shout-out to the FBI, who is surprisingly putting a call out to the CIA. Everyone wants a piece of the Thunder Cloud Knuckle Brotherhood. That's all I got. Want to follow me? I gotta get going."

I look to Mom, who is watching the sheriff. For the first time I see the unguarded look in her eyes and, yeah, it's a good thing. When he looks her way, he winks quickly, not realizing I saw that too.

"Mom, you want to go to the hospital or do you and the boys want to stay here?"

"We'll go with. Probably safer with everyone who's gonna be there. I can also be there for Brenna's folks. I'm sure Paddy and Bronagh are besides themselves. It's partially my fault. Sorry, boys, should have put a bullet in your father's head ten or so years ago. Now let's go, time's a wastin'. Rowan, please get your little brother. Ash, you guys go on out, I need a word with the sheriff."

Not wanting to waste any time but knowing Mom wouldn't ask if it wasn't important, we all leave and head back out to my truck. It's not even five minutes later, when Mom comes out quickly and gets in the truck. Sheriff George hits his lights and sirens then comes flying by us from the back of the building. I throw it into gear and hit the gas. Fuck, probably the only time in my life I can drive like a maniac and blow through stoplights and signs. All it does is piss me off and has me worrying about Brenna. Hang on, promise we'll find you. Just hang on.

TWENTY-FOUR
'RAVEN'
BRENNA

Something is wrong. I'm not at home or at the clubhouse, that much my mind can figure out. I'm freezing and not sure why. My head is pounding and my body is aching. I don't move because as I'm trying to process everything: it hits me what happened and who took me. My head hurts because that asshole Cliff hit me up against the temple with a gun in his hand. I can tell I'm in my bra and panties, on a floor That's why I'm cold.

When something crawls across my leg, it takes everything in me not to try to jump up and scream. I try to hear Shadow's voice when she trained all of us, back in the early days, on how to survive torture. I thought she was a total nutcase, but now all I can do is cross my fingers and hope her training will get me through whatever I'm about to face.

My hair is covering my face so I slit my eyes to try and see where I'm at. It's dark, though there are windows because some light is coming through. I'm not alone because I can hear others breathing, moaning, and crying. Not sure if they are part of the problem or in the same situation as me so I don't let anyone know I'm awake, even though my body is hurting like hell. Shit, guess I should have taken my brother Ollie up on his 'soldier training.' He said every one of his people was trained to be able to stay still without moving for hours, if not days, while living on barely no food and minimal water.

God, just the thought of water has my mouth feeling even drier. Though the thought of food makes my stomach turn, so I probably have a concussion. Hearing crunching outside, I don't brace but I'm on guard. I hear keys and then the door opens and I hear people walking in. Something lands pretty close to me and it moans. Again, I don't respond.

"Bitch is still out. What the fuck, Cliff, how hard did you hit her?"

"Didn't think it was hard, but who the fuck cares? Her being out makes it easier for us. Now what are we gonna do about Luni there? Bitch didn't follow her orders. Can't let that pass. We need to talk about this but until we figure it out, leave her with these other bitches. We got shit to do."

Great, now I have to deal with a traitor too. I can't let my guard down around her, no matter what. She took a beating and let them violate her, well, made it look like they did, so she's not right in the head. I'm surprised because Stephanie and I both liked and took her at face value. We believed her. The door slams shut and the fear that was permeating the room settles down. Fuck, these women have been here a while. From what I'm feeling, they are going to need the help of the Devil's Handmaidens if we get out of this.

Thinking about my club, my mind instantly goes to Tink. I hope and pray she's going to be okay. Never in a million years did I think that Ash's dad was that far gone. To shoot a woman who he watched grow up. Well, shouldn't be too surprised, look who he's hanging around with. I'm sure he's done his own personal torture on some of the victims the brotherhood has had over the years. He was ready to kill little Joshua, and from what Ash said, it was Cliff who beat Patsy Woods to an inch of her life, while her father and brothers watched.

Another thought comes to mind. My own parents are probably losing their minds. First Bray and now me. I don't want them to worry or suffer, but it's out of my hands. With them on my mind, I drift and before I know it, I'm out again.

* * *

Not sure how long I was unconscious again but this time when I start to come to, I'm not on the ground but something is under me, maybe a sleeping bag. And there's a blanket or something over me. I can hear whispers but can't make a word out. My ears seem to be ringing so that doesn't help. Someone is brushing the hair off my face. They have really rough hands but I know they are trying to either be nice or see if I'm awake.

"We know you're awake, Brenna. Your breathing changed when you started to come to. No, don't try to ignore us, just know we know. We moved you out of the doorway, put you in the far corner on one of the sleeping bags. You felt like ice so we threw a blanket on you. Sorry to say, none of that shit is very clean but it's all we have. I know you won't believe me but I'm sorry. I could tell you a ton of different lies, but it doesn't matter. I've been here for years and have had three children. Lost one, but the other two are alive and well. The reason for that is I do what the men tell me to do without question. It's how I've lived all these years. Many women and children have come and gone. And by gone, I mean they were killed. After I had my kids, didn't want to orphan them, so when the opportunity came and some of us were offered the ability to spend more time with our babies if we cooperated with them, I jumped at the chance. So instead of seeing my babies once or twice a day, they were able to live in a rundown cabin with me and a couple of the other women who agreed to the terms. So you can judge me, but now, because of what I did, they might kill my children."

Listening to Luni try to explain herself, honestly, even though I have a soft heart, I don't care. At this moment, not only everyone in this piece of shit 'cabin' is at risk of being murdered but so are all the children. These assholes aren't going to want to take the time to bring everyone along. I take in a deep breath and just when I get ready to lash out at Luni, I hear another voice.

"Luni can be a bitch but she's not lying. Or not this time at least. We all have to do what we have to do to survive in this disgusting pit of hell. So we can either all fight against each other or we can band together and try to figure out how the hell to get out of here. I, for one, want to get out, find my kids, and hightail it away from the brotherhood. I'll be glad if I don't see any of them again, ever."

One after another the women start whispering their names, how long they've been held against their will, and the story how each and every one of them have come to be prisoners of the Thunder Cloud Knuckle Brotherhood. I can't believe the length of time some of them have been held captive. I open my eyes and see women in all shapes and sizes sitting in a semi-circle around me. I can't make out their faces too well, though I can see they are two or maybe three deep. Trying to look around this cabin or building, looks to be on the larger size so that's why they can cram so many into it.

I see a hand coming toward me and on instinct I go to cover my face. Someone pats my shoulder gently while the hand by my head opens and I see a piece of hard candy. I look up the arm to the woman offering it to me.

"We don't have any water, but this will keep your mouth wet and the sugar will help with your blood sugar levels. Your eyes are glassy and your lips are dry. Promise it's just candy, nothing else. Here, look."

She takes the piece of candy out of the wrapper and puts it in her own mouth. She pushes it around a time or two then takes it out and offers it to me. At any other time, I'd never take it after it was in someone else's mouth, but fuck, this isn't a normal time. I slowly and tentatively reach for it. When I put it in my mouth all I taste is butterscotch, which is my favorite. All at once my childhood flashes before my eyes. All the times Mom would buy these for me. The goofy shit my siblings and I did. The way our parents, even though strict, were also so loving. As memory after memory runs through my mind's eye, I don't even realize that tears are running down my face. Not until a sob comes out of my mouth.

"That's it, let it out. Once it's out then let the anger take over. Brenna, right? I'm Olive, and trust me, we've all been where you are right now. Fear, tears, anger, and rage. As long as you don't get to despair then surrender, because then they win. Okay, let's back off, give Brenna some time. Let's hope tonight isn't a party night so we can get some sleep. Otherwise, it's going to be a long night of pain."

They all mumble something but I don't care. I close my eyes and cuddle myself into a ball. This is not how my life was supposed to go, for Christ's sake. All that we as a club have done over the years, isn't it enough? Why do we all have to experience such devastating events? Life can suck big time, for sure.

I hear someone crawling toward me, but I still stay in

a ball, head tucked down. I don't want to make friends or be open to anyone here because I don't know who to trust. A body gets close and I can feel someone breathing at the back of me. Again, not sure what's going on, but if I have to, I'll do what Shadow told us to do. Escape your body and what's happening to save your mind. At the time I thought she was talking bullshit but if I make it out of here, she'll be the first one I give a huge hug to. Then someone whispers in my ear so softly I barely hear the words.

"Brenna, it's me, Olive. Give me your hand. No, don't argue, please. You don't have to trust me but even though you don't know me, I want to get out of here as much as you do. You're Bray's sister, aren't you? No, don't say it. I was with her when that forest guy came in and saved her. And damn was I glad. They almost broke her so it was good he took her out of there. Though the rest of us suffered for days after because we didn't fight them off and keep her with us. It was worth it, swear to Christ. So here, take this, put it under your head or keep it in your hand. Worst case, put it in your bra. Not your panties because if tonight's a party night, those won't stay on very long. They don't care if the bra stays on but the panties always go."

I reach behind me and feel her place something in my hand. It's kind of long and when I run my finger over it, I can feel a sharp edge.

"It's a small pocketknife. Saw it out on the table one day and stole it. Not the first one I took so you take that one. I have two more on me. Just in case you get the opportunity to use it, don't hesitate. I've already sworn to myself that if it gets too bad here, I'm going to kill my kids then myself. No, don't, I have four little girls. What do you think will come of them in this environment? Hell, thank God they are little because these men are truly evil. The things I've seen them do; I'll have nightmares for the rest of my life if I ever get out of here."

"Olive, if we get out, I have somewhere you and your girls can go. We'll help you, I promise. And if I don't get out but you do, still go to my club sisters, they will honor my promise."

"Bray was so proud of you. She talked about you and the Devil's Handmaidens Motorcycle Club all the time. Told me she wanted to try and join but she was weak, surely not as strong as her baby sister. And after what we've gone through, she didn't think she'd be able to handle what you all do, ya know, saving victims. Thanks though for that. Means the world that even though you don't know me, you care enough to offer. I'm going to ask you, if I don't make it but my girls do, that you take them and help them. Promise, Brenna."

"I do, Olive. I promise."

She stays close and the last thing I remember is her turning over, her back to mine. Then I fade into the blackness again.

TWENTY-FIVE
'RAVEN'
BRENNA

Cold water hits me in the face, forcing me to wake up. Shivers run up and down my body as I try to focus. There are lights on now and I can hear the women crying as they huddle all around where I'm at. The sleeping bag and blanket are soaked so I throw the blanket off and struggle to sit up. Once there, I move off the sleeping bag, pulling my legs up to my chest, the little knife in my hand before I slip it in my thick socks.

"Oh look, the little princess is up. Someone grab her arm, drag her ass out of the corner. Now, motherfuckers."

Before I can do anything, someone reaches for my arm. As they go to drag me out, I feel one of the women grab on to my other arm as another woman grabs on to my leg. Fuck, they're going to tear me apart.

"Bitches, if you know what's good for you, let the whore go. She wouldn't worry about you, so don't give her a second thought."

I knew before they slowly let me go that they would. I get it, when you've been beaten and abused for so long, you have hardly any fight in you anymore. As I'm being pulled out, I look and see Olive watching me, tears in her eyes. She mouths, "Be strong," to me. I try to smile but I just can't. God, I'm not going to survive this.

Once outside there are torches all around the campsite. A huge fire is going far to the left and the number of men standing, sitting, and walking around is staggering. How have they been able to hide out with no one noticing? And why didn't they bounce on my radar? I've been doing searches for anything out of the ordinary. With all this going through my mind, I'm not paying attention. Well, until my arm is dropped on the ground. They might have pulled it out of the socket. Next, both legs are being pulled apart. That's it, I start to fight because, shit, I'm backup as muscle for our club. I'm not a withering flower but a badass motherfucker. One foot hits someone in the balls and he goes down. My other foot slams into someone's face. By the time the second one hits the ground, I'm rolling onto my knees then am on my feet. The dirt is hard on my socked feet, but fuck it, what do I have to lose? I go to move my arm and, luckily, it's not as bad as I thought. Quickly I look around and see the crowd coming toward me. I shift so my back is toward the row of trees and brace myself. There is no way I'm going to be able to fight my way out of here but before they rape or kill me, I'll do some damage, promise that.

They are playing with me because instead of rushing

me only two or three come at me at a time. This goes on for a bit but between the beatdown from Cliff, my possible concussion, and the hits I'm taking now, my strength starts to wane. When I miss the next man up, I don't see that two have snuck up behind me and are standing by the trees, waiting. Knowing my battle is up, I wait 'til the next guy comes at me. I grab him by the neck and not sure why, but I snap it and drop him. That has them coming at me all at once. I get a few hits and kicks in before I'm on the ground again, getting my ass kicked literally.

"Enough. I said enough, motherfuckers. I don't want her dead. Not yet."

Barely recognizing the voice, Cliff continues.

"Now, like I said before, you can play but no sex. I mean it, assholes. She's gotta be in one piece or my son will not go along with the plan. Saying that, you can touch, slap, punch, or kick, just don't kill her. Or go grab another woman and have your way with them. I don't give a shit if you kill them. We can always find and get more of the expendable women we have here. When you're done with her, bring her to my cabin. If I'm asleep, throw her in the corner, I'll have a pad there for her. Make sure you cover her up, don't want her to die from hyperthermia during the night. Now, have some fun but don't go overboard. Brenna, enjoy your evening, bitch."

I hear him walk away as many hands are on my body. Shadow's words echo through my brain. *If it's too much, sister, just close your eyes, take deep breaths, and let your brain fly. Find your safe place and go there. No one can hurt you there.* So as I feel my pants and underwear being ripped from my body, I do exactly that. I close my eyes and go to my safe place. I don't feel a thing.

Not sure how long I've been in my head but when someone cracks me in the face, it startles me. Not wanting to open my eyes, I keep them scrunched close. Until another crack lands, this one harder. I open my eyes to see Cliff bending over me.

"Brenna, get up. If you need to piss, let's go now. And I'm gonna give you some wet ones, need ya to clean yourself up. Don't want all that filth in my cabin. They dumped you outside of it and your moaning woke me up. Be thankful 'cause there are wolves, bears, and other animals out here. Damn, woman, you stink. Let's go."

Again, this asshole drags me to the outer perimeter of the campsite.

"I don't care what you have to do crawl, walk, or just piss here. I'll be right back."

Knowing I don't have a lot of time, I do crawl into the brush and without underwear, get up to my knees, squat, and pee. Once I'm done, without toilet paper, I just drip then crawl back to where I was. Cliff is waiting, a smirk on his face and a package of wet ones in his hands.

"Not so high and mighty, are you? Didn't think you would be. Wait, it will only get worse, I can promise you that. Now, wash that shit off of you and get your ass into my cabin. I'm tired, want to catch some shut-eye."

He tosses the package at me. It hits me in the shoulder and lands on the ground. I grab it and peel it open, taking a few of the sheets out. Slowly I start to wipe my body, knowing I'm wiping off a lot of semen and probably spit and shit, but I keep my mind as blank as I can. From what I can tell I wasn't raped or sodomized, so that's something, I guess. Glad I was out of it because what I don't know won't come back to haunt me. Knowing he's watching me; I try not to let it bother me. I don't hunch over or hide anything. I pile the dirty wipes off to the side and continue to clean up. When I'm done, I pick up everything and look to Cliff. He throws me a plastic bag so I put everything in it.

"Stay here."

I watch him walk over to a huge dumpster that he flings the bag into. Then he walks back to me, giving me a hand up. I almost fall flat on my face but he grabs ahold of me, giving me time to find my feet. He walks me to his cabin, shuts the door, and points to a far corner. I make my way there and when I turn, something hits me in the face. I grab for it and feel it's a soft T-shirt. I don't look at him but put it over my head slowly. When it's in place, I look at where I guess I'm sleeping. Shocked to see what looks like a thick, kind of clean, sleeping bag and a newer thick plush blanket. Next to the blanket are wool socks so I carefully sit down, remove my filthy ones, and pull the socks on, realizing I no longer have the knife from Olive. I can feel Cliff's eyes on me but I look over the sleeping bag making sure there are no critters. Then I lie down, back to Cliff, and pull the blanket over me.

Lying here, I don't move and barely breathe. I listen and can tell when he's fallen asleep. Then and only then do I allow myself to let the tears fall out of my eyes. I do it quietly and without my body moving. I don't want to give this asshole the satisfaction that what happened tonight put a crack in my armor. By tomorrow I'll have it patched up so I can face another day. I think about Ash and wonder what he's doing. How did this ever get so far? My God, how do people turn into monsters? This man sleeping, lying a few feet from me, was going to be my father-in-law, instead, years later, he's my captor. Never in a million years would I've thought I'd be here.

Pulling my hair up and using some of my hair to tie it into a messy bun on top of my head, I put my hands under my head. My hair feels sticky but I try not to think about that, nothing I can do about it right now. Feeling my head pounding, not sure from what, only God knows. I could use another butterscotch but that isn't going to happen in here. I try to imagine one of our club's potlucks we have at the clubhouse when we invite the townsfolk to join us. I can visualize all the tables of food and drink. Digging deep in my memory, I bring up the taste and textures of my favorite dishes. I can almost smell and taste them. I throw in a huge glass of ice water with lemon, and those are my last thoughts before I fall into a fitful sleep. One that keeps me under throughout the night.

TWENTY-SIX
'SHERIFF GEORGE'
GIORGIO DE LUCA

Son of a bitch. This has turned into a circus. There are so many goddamn people here wanting to help, we had to take over the cafeteria. So now I wait for Tank, Momma Diane, and the Intruders to take seats along with the O'Brien clan, including Ollie and his folks from the Blue Sky Sanctuary. Ash, Gertie, Rowan, Joshua, and Rue are sitting with the O'Briens. Makes sense.

Along the other side is the Devil's Handmaidens, including Zoey still covered in Tink's blood. Panther, Avalanche, Jersey, Dallas, Chicago, and George are sitting with the women. Actually, Panther has Zoey in his arms. Need to check on her before this starts. My remaining deputies are around me. Some of the townsfolks also showed up, wanting to throw their hands in to help. FBI and CIA are on their way. Yeah, a clusterfuck. Before I start, I do what I need to do. I walk over to my daughter, who happens to be the enforcer for the Devil's Handmaidens.

"Zoey. Honey, how are you holding up?"

She looks at me with the same ice-blue eyes I see every time I look in a mirror. Though hers are truly icy at the moment.

"Hey, Dad, I guess okay. Hanging in. Have you heard anything about Raven yet?"

"I'll fill in everyone in a few minutes. Any news on Tink?"

Zoey's eyes look down at the blood still on her hands. Well, what the fuck? Why didn't they let her wash up?

"You want a minute to wash up? I'm sure the hospital can give you some scrubs."

Her head jerks up just as Panther shakes his head at me. Oh fuck. I wait for it.

"Absolutely not. This is Goldilocks's blood, Dad, not washing it off. What the fuck, why would you ask me that? For Christ's sake, can we get on with this? I've got to get back up there, be there for her."

Panther pulls her close and I see her deflate.

"Zoey, Noodles is up there. We'll be back there as soon as we can. The surgeon said she's going to be in there for a couple of hours. Try and relax, no, don't get all pissed off, Nizhoni, I've got you. Lean on me. You are not alone."

"Zoey, I'll try to make this quick, just wanted to check on you."

I stand to leave but she grabs my hand. I look down and see she's looking up at me. Damn it, I reach down and give her a hug. The room instantly goes eerily quiet.

What the fuck, a father can't hug his daughter? Jesus Christ, small-town shit, I guess.

Making my way back to the front, I turn to my deputies first then to the room. Clearing my throat, I jump right in.

"Folks, we have a sensitive situation. As everyone in this room knows, we've had this situation for the last couple of years with the Thunder Cloud Knuckle Brotherhood. We've found out Cliff Sterling is part of that group. No, don't look at Gertie and her boys, that has nothing to do with them. So, this is what we have so far. A woman who has ties to the brotherhood worked her way into the Devil's Handmaidens gym employment. It was a plant. This morning, on her way to work, Raven decided to stop by to pick up the receipts for Taz to process. Upon entering, she had up front eyes on what had happened or what she thought had gone down. Both of her employees were beaten and violated. The brotherhood was in the process of torturing Stephanie, the manager. Raven sent out emergency texts then went in, trying to assist. Long story short, it turned into a massacre. We have some down on our side, a deputy had to be airlifted out. Tink is, at this moment, in surgery upstairs. Tank, Momma Diane, we appreciate both of you stepping away to be here. She's in our prayers."

Everyone looks at Tink's parents to see Momma Diane trying not to cry, while Tank looks like he's ready to explode. I move on.

"Ash got a call from his father with demands. Not going into those because they won't be happening."

"Why not, Sheriff, maybe if we give him what he wants, he'll let Raven go?"

"What he wants, Stan, are other people in our community. Would you like me to give Cliff your wife or daughters? Didn't think so."

The post office employee puts his head down as his wife shoves her shoulder into his. *That's gonna be a fight on the way home, for sure,* I think to myself.

"Between all the resources we have in this room, we need to come up with a plan and quick. From what I've been told Raven and Freak have been working nonstop to try and find where the brotherhood's main lair is. It's not where Alder found Bray. It's got to be pretty close though because with Cliff's involvement it's most definitely on the Sterling's land. We have maps of the Sterling ranch. Ash, Rue, and, Gertie, can you come up here, please?"

I watch the three of them make their way to the front. I spread the blueprints and maps my deputies found.

"Now looking at this, where would you think they would be hiding out? Think about it, boys, you've done the fencing and managed the herds for years. Ash, you were out today with the boys checking on the cows in the northern pasture. Did you see anything out of the ordinary? Have any of the hands talked about weird stuff happening?"

I wait for a bit to give them time to think. Looking

around, everyone is on the edge of their seats. Rowan raises his hand from where he's sitting.

"Yeah, Rowan, got something, son?"

"Sheriff, don't know if it means anything but maybe two weeks ago when I was on the four-wheeler, I saw some tire tracks going toward what we all call Sterling Mountain. Ash can show you where it's at, but the ground had a lot of tracks. At the time I didn't pay much attention 'cause I looked around, didn't see anything. It just popped back in my head when you were asking Mom and my brothers where they might hide out. Dad used to take me up there when I was a little kid, before he left. He said it was his favorite place on the ranch."

"Thanks, Rowan. Ash, Rue, where is that on this map?"

As they both show me where it's at, I glance at Gertie, who's watching Rowan holding Joshua's hand. I know she's worried about her boys, but they take after her and not her asshole husband. Ash points to the map and I look back down. Damn, that's on the exact opposite side of their ranch. The spot where they've been squatting is close to the main house and Ash's home. Sterling Mountain is almost by the Yellowstone River. Now I can see why no one has seen the comings and goings of this branch of the brotherhood. Too far off the beaten path.

"Are there any buildings out there that you know of?"

Ash looks to Rue, who shrugs his shoulders. Then

Ash looks to his younger brother. Rowan, still standing, nods.

"Tell us, Rowan, what do you know."

"Ash, haven't been up there in ages but I did sneak that way a few years ago. Didn't go all the way but from where I was, thought there were some cabins and a few lean-to type buildings. Also, off to one side I saw the makings of some kind of road. I ran when I heard a loud machine struggling my way. I never told you or Mom because thought you'd be mad at me for going that far."

He puts his head down. Shit, the kid is feeling bad. Can't have that when it's him giving us all the information.

"Rowan, son, don't feel bad. You are actually helping us a lot. Now sit down for a bit, might need to ask you some more questions in a while. Now, Tank, can Freak figure out a way to get eyes on that area? Don't tell me but if a satellite is up there, can that be used as eyes in the sky, or however they say it?"

Before I finish, Freak has two laptops open and is pounding away on a tablet. Tank looks to his brother then at me.

"Sheriff, he'll do his best."

I nod at Tank, knowing his mind is not here. And he's still recovering from his heart attack. Hearing someone walk in, I see Reed making his way to his little brothers. Tank and Momma Diane look at him and he shakes his head. No news yet. Glancing at the Devil's Handmaidens, it dawns on me Squirt, or as I know her, Hannah, isn't here. She's probably with Noodles.

Hannah is Tank and Momma Diane's other child. Well, actually, she's their granddaughter but that's another story.

"All right, we need to find a way to get up there without drawing attention. Now who lives on the other side of the mountain? Are there hunting or hiking trails up to the mountain? Most of our mountains have them, especially when by rivers or lakes. Sherman, aren't you on the other side of Gertie's property? Or is it Phil? Come on, let's put our heads together, we need a way in. Once we are in, with the size of our group, we should be able to stabilize the area and the brotherhood quickly. We've got to be careful because they have innocents up there besides Raven."

"Sheriff, when you have a plan in place, if it's okay, I'd like to send some of my people ahead so they can get situated. The ones going will be my sharpshooters. It can give us an advantage and also some cover if things start to go south."

"Yeah, Ollie, that's a great idea. We'll take all the help we can get. Now for a distraction, it won't be out of place if a few large farm machines are moving along. There's always a farmer or two on the road. It can be used as cover, if any of the farmers in the room are willing to let us use your machinery?"

I hear a bunch of yeses and yeahs. Then a few speak up.

"Not only can you use my tractor and baler, but I'll personally run one of them myself. Brenna used to babysit my kids, back in the day. She doesn't deserve this, none of those folks do. Let's put these fuckers, sorry, 'cuse my language, down."

More and more farmers are offering up their equipment. Ollie comes up front with his dad, Paddy O'Brien, and all his other sons Orin, Oliver, Bennett, and Brooks. Tank, Intruder, and Yoggie make their way to the front, as I watch Momma Diane make her way over to Bronagh, Onyx, and Bray. I'm shocked to see her here but it's her sister too. On that thought, something comes to mind.

"Bray, honey, are you up for some quick questions? Nothing except location and stuff."

She looks at her mom, sister, and Momma Diane. Onyx takes her hand and Bray's eyes come to me and she nods.

"Before Alder found you, were you in the same place? Wait, didn't you say that you were moved around?"

"Yeah, Sheriff, all the women were moved, not sure how often or where we were taken. When they moved us, we were blindfolded and drugged. So, by the time we came to, we had been put in a new place. Well, a new building or cabin. Only time we were allowed outside was our three to four bathroom breaks and if they wanted to have one of their parties."

Hearing that, every man in the room just about comes out of their skin. I hear Ollie and his brothers growl. Mr. O'Brien's eyes never leave Bray. She never puts her head down but doesn't look around either. I'm not gonna ask the question 'cause I have a pretty good idea what the parties were.

"Did anything stand out to you on the bathroom breaks? Landscape or flowers, hills or highways? Anything at all?"

She takes a minute or two to think then she lifts her head.

"There was one place we went to a few times, and I could have sworn I heard a waterfall. When I asked, got myself a beatdown so I never asked again. But yeah, I think it was close to water."

I smile at her just as her mom stands, makes her way to her daughter, grabbing and pulling her close. Turning, I glance at the men around the table with me.

"Okay, go to the Sterling Mountain and look for water or waterfalls. That's where we start. Ollie, how long will your people need to get situated? Farmers, figure out amongst yourselves who wants to volunteer with their machinery. Devil's Handmaidens, we're gonna need your help with the victims up there since that's what you all do. Whatever that means, get ready, please."

I take a breath just as a bottle of water is pushed in front of me. I turn to see my deputy-in-training, Yoggie, handing it to me. I thank him, open it, and drink half of it down. The pressure is overwhelming 'cause if I fuck up, lives could be taken. Brenna could be killed. I can't have that on my conscience.

As we plan, I realize we still haven't heard anything on Tink. I take a second and say a silent prayer.

TWENTY-SEVEN
'ELLINGTON' "L"
NOODLES

I'm fuckin' going crazy. What the hell is taking so goddamn long? And why hasn't anyone come out to give us an update? If they don't soon, I'm gonna go back there 'cause not knowing is slowly killing me.

"Noodles, she's going to be okay. Maggie is tiny and mighty, remember?"

I turn my head to look at Hannah, who's sitting next to me, holding on to my hand for dear life. Shit, she's got to be goin' out of her mind too. I mean, even though it's confusing Maggie is Hannah's biological mother. Her parents, Tank and Momma Diane, decided to raise Hannah as their daughter, making her Maggie's sister. Maggie is also Tink, the president of the Devil's Handmaidens, which is the club Hannah is prospecting for. So, she's surrounded by all that is Maggie/Tink.

"How ya holding up, Squirt?"

She gives me her glare for a second before I see the

fear in her eyes. I pull her into my side, giving her a squeeze.

"Noodles, she is going to be okay, right? I mean, she's the glue that holds all of us together. If something happens to her, everyone and everything will fall apart."

I got nothin' so I just hold her close. We sit together for I don't know how long, until I see Cynthia and her two kids rushing into the surgical waiting area, arms filled with bags and boxes, which I assume contain food.

"My God, I just found out, Noodles. How's she doing? Hi, Hannah. We brought some food and coffee since food at hospitals usually sucks. Where is everyone else?"

"Downstairs with the sheriff. I'm sure they will be coming up shortly. Thanks for coming and bringing all of that food. I wouldn't mind a cup of coffee."

Cynthia immediately puts stuff down on the small table. Then puts the three boxes of coffee down and pulls one of the paper bags toward her, emptying it out with sugar packets and creamer cups along with stirrers. She knows I take it black so she grabs a cup, fills it, and puts the cardboard holder around it and a lid on. She passes it to me as her daughter is setting out the food. She puts out donuts, granola bars, bags of apples and oranges, along with a huge bunch of bananas. I see her son coming back, his arms filled with pizzas. Yeah, Maggie's reach is far. She gave Cynthia a chance and this woman appreciates it very much, every single day.

Cynthia hands Hannah a cup of coffee already fixed

with her extra, extra cream. Hannah softly thanks her, which has Cynthia reaching down, grabbing the coffee, and placing it on the table. Then she pulls Hannah up and hugs her close. As soon as she does that, the young woman loses it. Oh fuck. Both kids come up next to their mom, placing their hands on Hannah's waist. No one says a word until Hannah gets herself under control.

"Honey, we are here for you, no matter what you need. Now sit down. What do you want to eat? No, you need to eat, got to stay strong so when Tink needs you you'll be there. Tell the kids what you want. I'm going to run back out to the car and get the other boxes of coffee. I'll drop them downstairs. Noodles, where are they all at?"

I tell her the conference room and watch her walk away. The kids are now on either side of Hannah, so I stand and start pacing yet again. I glance at the clock, and shit, she's been in there for four plus hours. The television shows if the patient is still in surgery and Maggie's name shows she's in a surgical suite. What the hell are they doing?

I run my hands through my hair, just as out of the corner of my eye I see someone walking our way. I turn and see it's Shadow. She's by herself, no wait, there are more behind her. I see Maggie's mom. And Gertie Sterling, along with her youngest, Joshua, in her arms with his stuffed dragon. As they make their way to the waiting room, some of Maggie's club sisters are also walking this way.

Shockingly, Shadow walks right into me, arms around my waist. I grab her, holding on to her tightly. This is new but I know how she feels, so we hang on to each other.

"Any news yet, Noodles?"

"Not a single fuckin' word. I'm ready to pull my hair out."

I see Maggie's mom move back out the door, heading toward the nurses' station. She is talking and waving her arms. Hannah gets up and quickly makes her way to Momma Diane. The nurses are trying to calm her down, but I think Momma Diane is at her wits' end. I head over to them and when I get there, I pull Maggie's mom into my arms. As soon as her head hits my chest, like Hannah, she loses it. I can't say shit, my throat's closed up, but I let her have her moment. Before I realize it, all the Devil's Handmaidens sisters who are up here on this floor are surrounding us, hands on Momma Diane. It takes her some time but she lifts her head, looks around, and face-plants back into my chest. We're standing like this when Tank, Panther, and Avalanche show up. Instantly, Tank starts to lose it, thinking the unthinkable.

"Holy shit, what happened? Diane, my God, did we …"

"Jay Rivers, stop. Don't even think it, let alone say it out loud. No, we've gotten no news. I just had a moment. It's over now, let's all go sit down."

At that moment Cynthia comes back up, more bags in her arms. How much stuff did this woman bring? When Momma Diane sees all the stuff, she grabs

Cynthia, giving her a kiss on her cheek. The two women put their heads together and whisper back and forth. Hannah comes back and grabs my hand. Panther and Avalanche, along with Shadow, pull chairs around so we are all sitting together. Everyone else either grabs a chair or sits on the floor. Once the waiting room is filled, they start sitting or standing outside in the hall.

A nurse makes her way down and I think she is gonna tell us we all can't be here. However, she walks to the far end of the room, fucks with the wall, and to my amazement starts to push the wall into itself, opening it up to another room with chairs and even a few recliners. She turns, looks around the room, and shocks the shit outta all of us.

"Went to school with Maggie. Her Devil's Handmaidens have helped this hospital out many times. Not to mention all the money they've donated without taking any credit. Please make yourselves comfortable. If you need anything, just come get me or ask for Mona."

She walks up to Momma Diane, giving her a hug, telling her she'll try to see if she can get an update. Tank is now sitting with his wife, well, until Enforcer starts shifting shit around while some of the Intruder prospects push two of the recliners into the room. Enforcer tells both Tank and Momma Diane to sit down. At first Tank starts to fight it but when his wife puts her hand on his arm, he shuts up, sits down, and reclines the chair back, putting his legs up. The room quiets down and again we wait for news.

About twenty minutes later, Mona comes back in,

asking Momma Diane if she can speak freely. She gives her a nod of her head. The nurse continues.

"From what I can see and have been told, everything is going well. They are still finishing up on Maggie, but nothing out of the ordinary. The doctor's will be out when they finish to talk to all of you. That's the best I could do. Wish it was more."

As Maggie's parents thank Mona, I lean back, head against the wall. Fuck, I can't even think what I'll do if something happens to Maggie. My God, she's become my life. Then that ex-SEAL in me wants to be a part of what's goin' on downstairs. I want five minutes with Cliff Sterling to pull his arms and legs off and fuckin' break his neck. This is all on him, for fuck's sake, he shot my Sweet Pea.

Panther leans in, hands on my knees. Avalanche is next to me and he puts his hand on my shoulder. Very quietly they start to chat and Shadow puts her hands on Panther's. I close my eyes and listen to the rhythm. Not thinking anything could, it relaxes me so I can take a deep breath. Not sure how long they do it but when I open my eyes, directly in front of me is Panther. His green eyes are blazing.

"My friend, she will be okay. You have to believe it, manifest it, so it will be."

I nod as they all lean back, letting me go. As strange as it is, once they let go, I feel alone and lonely again. I look over to Shadow to see her watching me. She gives me a small smile that doesn't reach her eyes, but I appreciate her trying.

Time goes by and everyone just settles in. Hannah leaning against me falls into a fitful sleep. Not sure where Presley is, but I'm guessing he's downstairs. I saw Enforcer take off, telling Tank he'd be in touch. Surprisingly, Panther and Avalanche stick around. Probably for Shadow.

I just start to doze, head back against the wall, when I hear a voice say, 'Maggie Rivers's family.' Instantly I'm wide awake and on my feet. As I go to make my way to the three doctors standing in the doorway, Tank is trying to put the recliner down and having a problem. I stop and walk over to give him a hand. When the doctor repeats Maggie's name, I lose it.

"Motherfucker, just give us a minute, will ya? We've been here for over five hours and not one goddamn update, so you can now wait on us."

I never lose it, so everyone is shocked. Well, except Tank, who has a shit-eating grin on his face. Great. When I get his recliner down and he's up on his feet, he puts his huge paw on my shoulder, giving it a squeeze. Momma Diane gets between us, grabbing each of our hands. When Tank walks by Shadow, he grabs her hand as I grab Hannah's. Everyone else in the room follows behind, as those out in the hallway move closer to the doctors.

"This is all Maggie Rivers's family?"

Momma Diane looks around then her eyes meet the doctors.

"Not all, but yeah, we are her family."

"Do I have permission to share PHI with this crowd?"

Tank growls as his wife gives permission.

"All right, Maggie was shot in her left side. It nicked her spleen and bounced off her ribs, breaking three. We tried to save her spleen but with the damage and loss of blood, we had to perform a splenectomy. We also had to perform a partial nephrectomy. Sorry, we had to remove part of her left kidney because of damage. The blood loss was significant and we had to do blood transfusions during surgery."

No one says a word, so I dive right in.

"Doc, is she gonna be okay? What does all of that mean? Can you break it down into normal laymen's language, please?"

"Sure, we removed her spleen and a small part of the bottom of her kidney. She's going to be transferred to ICU and will stay there for a couple of days, as long as she doesn't get a fever or have an infection start. Then she'll be transferred to a regular room. We will have her up soon to walk to make sure no fluids or blood clots develop. She should recover just fine and be able to live a normal life."

I let out the breath I've been holding in. *Thank God*, I think just as one of the other doctors step up.

"Now in regard to Maggie's medical history of trying to get pregnant with the different options including the pills and insemination and now the shots she's been on for IVF, we'll have to put a halt on that for the time being. We want her fully healed before any transfer of eggs can happen. This surgery will have no effect on her ability to get pregnant or carry full term. She just needs to heal. I was called in because during the surgery Dr. Fhatijic saw a slight twist in one of her fallopian tubes. I went in and untwisted it with no problems. Once she's healed you can resume your pregnancy plans."

She steps back and the next doctor steps up front.

"I'm the nephrologist and just want to reassure you that Maggie can have a normal full life with one and three-quarters kidneys. She will need to see me so I can make sure all is working fine, but I see no problems. I'll be checking in all night long to make sure the other kidney is working one-hundred-percent. The kidney we did surgery on will take a while to heal and get back to normal. Nothing to be too worried about. We will make sure the nurses give you all of our contact information and if you need any or all of us, just reach out, please. And on a personal note, Maggie and her club not only saved my wife from a psychopath but because of them we met, got married, and now have twins. So, I'll do my very best because I owe her everything good in my life."

Listening to the doctor, it starts to hit me how very special Maggie truly is. Her dream to find her daughter turned into a mission to save victims of human trafficking and domestic abuse. I doubt Maggie or her club sisters realize how much they have touched the people who have been saved, survivors, and their families.

As the doctors ask if anyone has any questions, they

wait, then turn and go back into the unit. I feel someone grab my arm so I turn to see Tank looking at me.

"Y'all are trying for kids? What? Something wrong with your swimmers, SEAL?"

Leave it to Tank to bring a laugh out of me. Gotta love him.

TWENTY-EIGHT
'OLLIE'

My head is pounding as we wait for everyone to get to the rendezvous site. We went back and forth for hours and decided we shouldn't approach at night, no matter how much my dad, brothers, and I fought to just go. It's not just Brenna up there and with Sheriff George, and now the FBI on board, I'm surprised they are even allowing us to be involved. Though if they said no, I'd go rogue without a fuckin' doubt.

The final plan is a multiple layer of attacks. From farmers on tractors, to folks on horseback, and so many people in different groups, it's crazy. And to top it off, I'm gonna have snipers to cover everyone's ass. If only I could get a message to Brenna so she'd be prepared, but that ain't gonna happen. Some of the women like our mom, Ash's mom, my love Paisley, and a few of the townsfolk and farm women are staying in town at the hospital so they can be on hand if this takes a major shit.

Tink will eventually be okay from what I've been

told, though she lost her spleen and part of her kidney. Shadow and Tank are out for blood, so Cliff better hope someone else finds his sorry ass. His boys also want to end him, especially Ash. He's going crazy not knowing what's happening to my sister. I've got a different outlook on him now that I know what went down before. His father is one sorry son of a bitch, for sure. I brought Ash and his brothers with us because my men and women are the best to handle them.

For now, at this crazy hour in the morning, we are waiting for dawn and some morning light before we make the final journey.

"Ollie, got a minute?"

I turn to see Ash, Reed, and Rue all standing looking at me. Alder is in town, well actually in the hospital, not in any shape to be here, though he wanted to be. Oh shit, here it comes, been waiting on them to ask.

"Sure, guys, but before you ask, I can't guarantee Cliff will be yours. No, listen, this operation isn't just mine. Believe me I get it, for fuck's sake, she's my sister. We just got my other sister back from the Thunder Cloud Knuckle Brotherhood. From the little I've heard, they fucked her up royally, might never be the same. I want that jagoff too, but the mission—and this is hard to even say—isn't just about Brenna. We don't know how many innocents are up there and we have to do our best to make sure they all come out alive. Now did you want to talk about something else?"

They all look at each other, then at me, shaking their

heads. Ash remains but his brothers go back to the area they've been at since we got here.

"Ollie, I know this is hard on you, but try to understand how we feel. It's our dad doing all this shit and has been for years. I just found out and don't tell anyone about this, ma will kill me. That motherfucker raped her for years. She was afraid to say anything as he'd sneak into the house after everyone bedded down for the night. No, not talkin' when we were kids, I'm talking recently. Rowan wasn't even a teenager yet. So yeah, I want to put my hands around his neck and watch his eyes dim then go out. But I understand where you're coming from, so I'll follow your lead. Can you tell me what we're waiting on? Because God only knows what they are doing to her. My mind is goin' all over, Ollie, and bottom line, it's my fault because he's my father."

"No, you're wrong, Ash, it's all on him, not you or your brothers or mother. He's a grown man who's made decisions in his life, letting money turn him into a monster. He wanted to try and take the easy way out. Well, life doesn't work that way. To get whatever you want it takes hard work, time, and patience. You know that, not gonna preach to you. We should be good to go within the next hour or so. I gotta check a few things but when we go, your family will go with me and my team. Our objective is to hit the main area, which I'm hoping that's where they are holding Brenna. Brother, I get it because I can't shut my brain off at all either. We'll get her out and help her deal with whatever was done to her. She's an O'Brien and one of the strongest women I know. Have some faith."

He nods then walks back to his brothers, while I turn and grab my cell phone. I hit dial and wait for a response.

"Spirit."

"Yeah, just want to confirm you understand your orders. When we advance, I want the five of you to take anyone out who isn't with us and has a weapon on their body or are using an innocent to protect themselves. If by chance your location is breached, relocate and get back in the firefight. Understood?"

"Yes, sir. We have your back."

"Thanks, I'm out."

I walk around, checking in with everyone here, until we hear a vehicle making its way up the slick road. I turn to see a huge-ass pickup truck shifting off the road to the grassy area. Being it's dark out, I can't make out who's in there until Panther, Avalanche, George, and Shadow jump out. They walk right to me. Panther starts immediately.

"Ollie, I left Dallas, Jersey, and Chicago back at the hospital for security. They are armed to the fullest. Tank is on his way but left some of his brothers there. With him are some of the Devil's Handmaidens, though not a lot. The majority are on guard duty on Tink's floor in the ICU, while the others from the gym are being treated themselves."

"Understood, didn't expect to see any of you, especially you, Shadow."

She looks at me and I swear those icy-blue eyes are the coldest I've ever seen them.

"Just so we're clear, Ollie, that motherfucker Cliff is mine. Nope, don't want your lip. He shot Goldilocks and for that he's going to get my own personal type of hell, up close and very personal. That's the only reason I'm here. I don't care what you or his sons say, he's going to end up in my wet room, might as well accept it. Now, when do we go?"

Again, I'm explaining the plan until I hear even more vehicles, thank Christ not bikes, coming our way. This is such a shitshow, won't be surprised if half of our folks get shot. When a mission is this big and you have defiant, stubborn, rebellious people thinking with their emotions and not their heads, shit is bound to happen.

Once Tank and all the other people hunt me down, once again, I go over the plan. I can only pray this is it, no more helpers are on their way. There is no way we'll be able to sneak up on this group with all these civilians. Yeah, Panther and his group are ex-military but everyone else is just common folks with huge hearts.

Sheriff George makes his way to me, a bottle of water in his hands. You can see the pressure on his shoulders, but I give him kudos, he seems to have most of this under control. The wildcard is the bikers, especially Tank and Shadow. Just gonna have to take it one minute at a time.

"How ya holdin' up, Ollie? I see your dad and brothers are here to back your play. That's good, they're all excellent men and will follow your lead. Not gonna ask you to go over that fuckin' plan again 'cause I'm about to shoot the next person who asks me to. Now we wait, that's all we can do. Our farmers should just about be on the move, probably in the next thirty or forty minutes, as that's what a regular farmer would do. Thanks again for having two of your people on each tractor to protect our townsfolk. They mean well, but they sure as hell ain't soldiers. All right, let me check on everyone. I'll be back before we start on our way. Again, thanks, Ollie, for everything you're doing, my man."

"Sheriff, she's my sister. I'd run through a burning building or jump outta a plane without a parachute to a certain death, so really there's nothing I wouldn't do to protect anyone who is part of my family."

The sheriff gives me a chin lift then starts to walk away. Hope someone has eyes on him when we proceed, since it's clear he and Gertie have something goin' on. I'm sure Cliff, if given the opportunity, will try to take our sheriff out. On that thought, I look around until I see Phantom, who has eyes on me. I give him a come-here motion and within seconds he's standing right in front of me.

"Need a favor, brother. When we advance, I want you close to the sheriff. I'm thinkin' Cliff would like nothing better than to take him out since he's got to know that Sheriff George and Gertie are getting close and starting something. I don't know what that is 'cause not my business, but Cliff is a psychopath so let's just prepare for the worst. Don't want the Sterling boys to lose their momma, and can't believe this is coming outta my mouth, but don't want Shadow to lose her father either. Phantom, we need to end this shit or we're gonna lose our town and more. These assholes need to go down today. Might not get rid of all of the entire brotherhood, but we'll end the jagoffs in our town and hopefully this part of our state."

"You got it, Ollie. I'll bring Mutt with me so we have the sheriff covered from all angles. I'll call Hellcat, tell her to get to the hospital and keep eyes on both Gertie and Bronagh, just to be safe. We got guards on Tink, as does Tank, but don't think anyone thought to keep eyes on the mothers."

"Good thinking, Phantom. Glad one of us is on our game. Goddamn, brother, I'm fuckin' exhausted. This is worse than some of our missions back in the day."

"Ollie, my man, this one is beating your ass 'cause it's your kid sister. Take a breath and remember your entire team from Blue Sky Sanctuary has your back. Just don't push us away, each and every one of us is trained for situations just like this. Let me make this call then I'll be Sheriff George's shadow. Mutt will have eyes on the both of us from a distance, just in case I'm taken out. No, Ollie, we don't know what these motherfuckers are capable of. First priority is getting your sister back and rescuing all the innocents, after that all bets are off. If each and every one of the Thunder Cloud Knuckle Brotherhood is taken out, I'm good with that, as I'm sure you would be too. Might want to put the word out to all of us that all shots should be kill ones, Ollie."

I look at Phantom, realizing this brother who I served

with for years has not only had my back as I've had his, but the whole idea of why I wanted the sanctuary is standing in front of me. A year or so ago, Phantom could barely put a couple of sentences together, let alone be in such a large group of people without going off the deep end. At least I did something right.

"Don't go there, Ollie. You got this, so get your shit together and call in the troops. Today we take back our little town of Timber-Ghost from these degenerates. Let me get these couple of things done, then I'll be at the sheriff's side, even if he blows a gasket. Ya know, Sheriff George has a pretty nasty temper when you get under his skin."

I laugh 'cause if anyone would know that it's Phantom. He makes a habit of getting under our good sheriff's skin. I nod and he walks away, his phone already up to his ear. Good call to keep eyes on Alder and our moms. That's why the only way to get shit done is when you have a team or group of folks who can cover each other's backsides.

Hearing someone walking my way, I see my brothers, Dad, and Tank. With Tank is Enforcer, Yoggie, Malice, and Half-Pint. I know eyes have been on Malice for a while, so surprised Tank brought him along. I eye Tank and he looks healthy and strong. I brace when I see the look on their faces.

"Just got a text from one of the farmers. They made it up about a third of the mountain on the other side when they hit a roadblock. Literally. Those motherfuckers are blocking the road and threatened to not only kill him but after, they'd go to his farm and rape and gut his women. Now, Ollie, he has his wife, six daughters, and two sons. Otis told them he was contracted by the forest rangers to clear the sides of the road. He told them he'd call the cops if they didn't move. Guess right now Otis said they told him to wait while they check his story."

I grab my phone and pull up Freak's number.

"Freak, get in the system, somehow, and either block a call or take it and confirm that Otis is working with the rangers to clear brush along the roadside. Yeah, they are probably trying to get ahold of someone, only problem is no one is there at this godforsaken hour. Let me know if you can bypass them."

"It's time, tell everyone to be ready. I'll be directing different groups to each area at the top of the mountain. Each group will have ex-military or a few of Tank or Tink's people. Tell the farmers and ranchers they need to follow orders to the T. I don't want to lose any of our people because they went off the tracks. Check your watches, we march out in ten minutes."

They all nod or give chin lifts before turning and walking away. I take a quick minute and reach out to Paisley. Never know what could happen, want to hear her voice.

"Hey, Ollie, how's it going?"

"Pixie, just wanted to hear your voice. We go in less than ten. Remember what I told you in case this goes south. You'll need to batten down the hatches. I love you, Paisley. You saved my life, now I'm trying to pass it forward."

"Don't do this, Ollie. I know you love me just like I love you. This is just another one of your Navy SEAL missions, you got this. I mean, look at the people taking your back. Get this done and bring your badass back home to me, end of story. Be careful and know you have a Pixie on your shoulder watching over you. I love you."

I don't want to hang up 'cause her voice calms me, but the time has come. Once again, I let her know what she means to me then we hang up. When I look up, all the groups are sectioned off and even though Sheriff George's face is red, Phantom is right next to him.

I give a nod then look up and silently say a quiet prayer that, when this is done, everyone I just made eye contact with and those I didn't are standing on their own two feet, ready to get back to their lives. I start pointing and each group moves on my command. My mind goes back to training and how they pounded in our heads that quitting isn't an option. And 'the only easy day was yesterday.' Then without thought, I take a deep breath and very loudly say "HOOYAH!" which my family from the Blue Sky Sanctuary replies back with their own version. It's time to shit and get. Then I hear Phantom and his words bring a grin to my face.

"Never give up!"

TWENTY-NINE
'RAVEN'
BRENNA

I scream when someone kicks me in the back. I flip over immediately and see it isn't Cliff but some other asshole.

"Get your ass up, this ain't no spa, sleepin' beauty. Dress and go help the women with breakfast. NOW!"

Slowly I try to get up, as my body has gotten really tight overnight from all of the physical abuse from yesterday. The kick in my back isn't going to help but I refuse to let this dickwad know that. When I'm on my feet it hits me; I'm in Cliff's T-shirt and no undies. Have no idea where my clothes are, though they are probably gone when I remember them being ripped from my body. Not wanting to remember last night and knowing I'm not going to ask for any assistance from this one, I head for the door. He grabs my arm and points to the small table in the far corner. Piled on one of the chairs are clothes, including socks and gym shoes. No wait, they look to be Chucks. I'm not going to be fussy since I love me some Chucks.

I walk over and grab the clothes. When I go to take the T-shirt off, the asshole leans against the other chair and stares.

"Do you mind?"

"Nope, not at all, go ahead, get dressed. Want to see what I'm gonna be sticking my dick in later on. Quit wasting time and do as I say or I'll dress you myself."

Not wanting his hands on me, I give him my back, pull on the undies first, then the jeans up. I thank God they have some stretch. Then I put the tank top over my head and manipulate it on with Cliff's T-shirt still covering me. Once the tank is in place, I take the T-shirt off and fold it, putting it on the table then grab the long-sleeve flannel, pulling it on. Next, I sit and pull off Cliff's wool socks and pull on the socks and Chucks, then stand and look at the asshole.

"Now you can come and thank me for those clothes."

"Like hell I will."

"Then, bitch, take them off and walk around camp naked. See how that works for ya."

Shit, what do I do? How the hell did Bray get through this for how long she was trapped with this group of sick as fuck degenerates? I picture Ash's face and know he would lose his mind if I was walking around naked because I think that would give these men the wrong idea. And I'm pretty sure if one of them grabbed me and started to rape me, no one would come to my aid. Swallowing my pride, I tentatively walk toward the big ape.

"How do I show my appreciation? What do you have in mind?"

As soon as I say it, I want to take it back. If this man thinks I'm performing any type of sexual act, he's nuts. I'll fight 'til someone kills me. He's watching me with the dirtiest smirk on his face as his eyes take me in. Then he gives me the come-here motion with his hand. I walk closer and when I'm within reach, he grabs me by the upper arms and pulls me right up to him. It takes everything in me not to fight or try to pull away. When his mouth hits mine, I can't hold it in any longer. I open my mouth, which I'm sure he thinks is an invitation, but instead I bite his bottom lip so hard I taste blood. When he pulls back, he rips his lip and I can feel skin in my mouth. I turn and spit it on the ground just as the door opens and Cliff walks in.

He looks at me then at the big ape. His eyes take in the situation and before I can blink, he whips an automatic out and shoots the asshole between the eyes. I scream and jump back, but not before brain matter hits me clear in the chest. Son of a bitch.

"What did he do to you, Brenna?"

"Um, nothing really. He tried to kiss me but I bit him. Think he was trying to intimidate me; see how far he could push me."

I feel my body starting to tremble and I refuse to look at the body off to the side of me. Cliff walks to the door and screams. When two women and three of the Thunder Cloud Knuckle Brotherhood hurry into the tiny cabin, everyone comes to a complete stop when they see the body on the floor missing part of the back of his head. They look at me and see the front of my shirts though no one says a word. Cliff does though.

"Clean this shit up. Take him to the empty grave in the woods, throw him in, and burn his body. Do it now. I'm gonna take her over to the mess tent. Want this done before I come back. Better not find anything or you'll be next."

He reaches over, grabbing my arm, and pulling me to the door. Once outside, I take a few deep breaths and try to keep up with him. Looking ahead, I see a tent with a ton of people standing around. I jump when Cliff yells.

"Donna, get me another shirt for this bitch. This one has brain matter on it."

A woman probably a little older than me turns and looks my way first, then Cliff's before she nods and walks away. He lets my arm go and pushes me at a picnic table.

"Sit the fuck down, don't say a single word. I'll be back. Don't get any funny ideas, Brenna, about running because if you try, you'll end up like that jagoff who's burning in the woods. Hear me?"

I look up at him and nod but say nothing. He turns and walks away and I fold my hands on the picnic table. My mind is trying not to flip out. With all that is going on, I look around and it looks like they are getting ready to break camp. Shit, if they take me from here, I'm never going to get back home to my club, family, and Ash. Last night, before I fell asleep, after thinking over it; I've been such a twit. It wasn't his fault what happened all those years ago and I can be a mean-ass grudge holder. Ash was trying to honor his mom and me at the same time. I don't know what Cliff held over their heads, but shit, it had to be something huge.

A tray hits the table shocking me. I almost pee myself. Yeah, got to take care of that soon before my bladder explodes. Not wanting to piss Cliff off though, I need to go to the bathroom.

"Um, Mr. Sterling, I need to go to the bathroom, if that's okay."

His head shoots up at the sound of my voice and he looks confused for a split second. My words must have penetrated his brain because again he yells for Donna, who is making her way back with some clothes in her hands.

"Donna, take her to the outhouse. Brenna, change your clothes. Give those bloody brainy ones to Donna, she'll get rid of them. You have five minutes then I'll come lookin'. You need to eat, we got lots and drink too today, don't need you passing the fuck out again."

Donna pulls my hair though not hard, almost like it's for show. I get up and follow her to a small building way back by the woods. She turns to see if anyone is around then she pushes the clothes into my arms. Her eyes never leave my face.

"Do what ya gotta fast. Change out of those tops, put these on. Be careful, there's a cell in the pocket of the top shirt. Make a call to whomever you need to, then shut the phone off and throw it in the toilet. Wrap it in the toilet paper. You better not say a word to Cliff or I'll deny it while I'm ripping your throat out. Tell them Delta said better get moving, they are breaking this camp today. Now go, he's not lying, he'll come looking for you. And that won't be good for you, take my word on that."

With my mouth wide open I rush into the outhouse, close the wooden door though no lock, and push my jeans down. Holy shit, does it hurt when I finally pee. As I'm taking care of business, I'm pulling the two shirts off and replacing them with the clean ones after I pull the phone out of the pocket. My mind is racing, not sure who to call, then like a light bulb I know who to call so I dial the number.

"Yeah."

Just to hear his voice I almost start bawling but have no time.

"Ollie, it's Brenna. No time, first Delta said to tell whoever to move your asses they are breaking camp this morning. We're on the mountain off of the Sterling ranch. There's a lot of them, probably close to fifty if not seventy-five. Innocents, at least fifteen or twenty. Not sure where they are keeping all the children though. That's how they control and manage the women, by threatening their children. I got to go, Ollie. Tell Ash, the family, my club sisters I'm fine. Fuck, how's Tink?"

"Brenna, she's gonna have a rough road but she'll make it. We're on our way, little sister, just hang on."

I don't say goodbye because don't want that to be the last thing I say to my older brother.

"I love you, Ollie. See you soon."

I don't wait for a reply, just turn the phone off, wrap it in the toilet paper, and fling it into the mess of shit and piss. I finish up and get dressed. I roll the shirts up and open the door to see Donna looking toward the camp. My eyes go in that direction and what the fuck, is that farm machinery coming up to the camp? Shit.

"Let's go, girly, shit's about to go south real fucking fast. If this turns into a gunfight try and find me. If not, see that trail behind that huge tent to the left? Run down, it'll take you to Cliff's western pasture. Just be careful, lots of roots and shit along the way."

Again, no words, I just nod. She starts walking toward the picnic table, turns, and grabs the shirts out of my hands. Cliff is stuffing his mouth with food off of his plate. I sit back down and look what's on mine. Some eggs, bacon, fruit, and toast. In a cup is some black coffee. I'll take it all, need to keep my strength up. I start to shove the food in my mouth because I'm starving and I think Delta is right. Today this ground will be covered in blood. I pray it's not mine or any of these innocent, abused women because they've been through enough. I hear a whistle, look up, and see Mr. Johansen pointing my way, waving his arms above his head.

"Brenna O'Brien, that you? Child, for fuck's sake, whatcha doin' way up this way?"

I look to Cliff to see he's glaring at me. Then he turns his head to look at Mr. Johansen. My eyes look down to see he's reaching for his gun. Oh hell no, not on my watch. Everything happens in slow motion. I fake cough and stand up like I'm trying to get something out of my throat. Just as Cliff pulls his gun out and starts to aim it at Mr. Johansen, I scream for the old guy to take cover as I jump over the table, grab Cliff's gun hand, and tackle him to the ground. We are both fighting for our lives as I hear more and more machinery moving in. Just when I think I have the gun in my control, Cliff uses his boot and kicks up, knocking me off of him, giving him the advantage. I continue to roll away from him, then jump to my feet just as he gets to his gun and aims directly at me. I stop because there's not a damn thing I can do, he's too far away to fight and I have no weapon. My hands go to my sides. I lift my head and give him the most badass stink eye I can. Not going to beg a total jagoff for my life when I know this man has no heart.

I feel something whiz past the side of my head and with huge eyes watch something hit Cliff center mass. His eyes show shock for a split second before he starts to fall backward. I'll never forget the look that comes into his eyes when he glares my way. Pure unadulterated evil. Then he pulls the trigger as he's falling backward. The next thing I know is, for some reason I'm also tumbling backward, and it takes me a second or two to realize he did it. Before he died that son of a bitch shot me. That's the last thought I have before I hit the dirt.

THIRTY
'ASH'
ASHTON

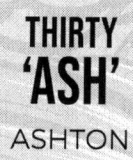

Making our way up a mountain while trying to be quiet and stealthy is an oxymoron. My God, there are so many people involved and going up from so many different directions. Not sure how Ollie is keeping track of everything but apparently, thank God, he is. From what I heard from someone, Freak was able to manage the check-in from one of the brotherhood so the farmers were allowed to continue on their way up the mountain to clear brush off the path for safety and fire prevention. Not sure who came up with that idea, but it's a damn good one.

Just as we hit a steep spot, I see Ollie reach for his pocket. He lifts a hand then answers his phone. From where I am, a few people back, I can hear someone screaming but can't make out a single word. Before any one of my brothers or I can ask Ollie what's up, he hits the button to disconnect, shoves the phone in his pocket, and starts to run up the overgrown path. Something's wrong. I've got a really bad feeling in my gut so I follow him, running to try to keep up with him. I know my brothers are also following because I can hear them.

It's like a domino effect because now you have in our group alone fifteen grown men running up the side of a mountain. When I look to my left, I see a bunch of Ollie's folks also sprinting toward the top. Motherfucker, what did my father do this time? Why can't he just die already? As soon as that thought goes through my mind, I push it out. No, I don't want to be like him at all. Even though he's a heartless prick, I don't wish him dead, too easy of an out for him. Prison for the rest of his life, totally yes. With my mind spinning out of control, I trip over a huge tree root and almost face-plant, except Rue grabs my arm, holding me up.

Just when I don't think I can keep running, Ollie comes to a sudden stop. Once again, he grabs his phone and listens for a second, then turns and when I see his eyes, I know it's Brenna. Fuck. Before I can even ask Ollie what's going on, I feel someone run past me with a couple of men behind the first person. When I realize who it is, I take off like a bat outta hell. Shadow is sprinting in front of Panther and Avalanche, with two other men from their ranch pursuing her. I need to put in more time at the gym or something. Thought I was in pretty good shape.

Suddenly, I see Shadow dive and slide to a complete stop. She looks behind her, throwing her arm up. Immediately, Panther and Avalanche stop dead right where they are. Unfortunately for them, I can't stop so I head-plant right into Avalanche's back. All I hear is a soft oomph. Damn, he's like a brick building, that's gonna leave a bruise. He turns, looks down at me, then pulls me in front of him like I'm a doll or something.

"What's going on, dude? Everyone is running and sprinting, has there been news?"

"Don't know, my job was to stick to her like glue. Shadow makes that difficult but we do our best. I don't ask questions."

I nod then turn to look at Panther, who has eyes on his woman. Her head is going from the left to the right then up and repeat. Something catches her eye because she slowly walks deeper into the woods. I can hear her sniffing and taking in deep breaths. When she turns to Panther and points, I don't know how, but one minute he was right there, the next he's gone. Then I see him deep into the woods and he's looking down at something. He kneels down and reaches for something then gets back on his feet and makes his way back to our group.

"Your instincts were right and fast. I was just picking up the scent and you already had it. About twelve feet into that wooded area is a hole about seven or eight feet deep. There are remains of a body that was burned. No, Ash, it's not a female but a male. Happened recently, within the last hour or two, still steaming. When I did a quick search with my eyes, there are a few mounds out there, so I'm guessing this is one of their burial spots."

"The smell hit me in my throat, Panther. I know the

scent of death, that's why I stopped and had you look since you're the best tracker."

I hear Avalanche clear his throat but doesn't say a word. Shadow smirks his way.

"Why are we running around on this mountain?"

Shadow looks my way with those icy-blue eyes of hers.

"Ollie got a call, the farmers made it through and one of them, a Johansen, saw Brenna. Then his phone went dead. We are almost there, so no more questions, my sister is in danger up there."

Shadow sets the pace as she continues toward the top. Looking to my left, I see Ollie and his brothers have caught up with us, so as a group we ascend through the overgrown brush. I don't know why but I start to pray that Brenna is okay, my father hasn't lost more of his mind, and no one else is injured. Yeah, asking a lot, but Mom always says squeaky wheel gets the oil, though not sure that applies to praying but I'm beyond desperate.

I can see the top from where we are. It's really steep now so we are back to walking. I think I can hear the farm machinery but it could be wind or an airplane, I don't know. Shadow throws her arm up and we stop. She motions for Ollie and he hurries to her side. They go back and forth, him shaking his head until she gets in his face. Ollie's brothers, Orin, Oliver, Bennett, and Brooks rush to stand at his side. Shadow is not letting up but before anyone can say a word, we hear it loud and clear. Gunshots. Then it's like every farm machine up there is being pushed to the limit. Everyone starts to run the plan out the fuckin' window.

When I finally reach the top, it's utter chaos. Obviously, Ollie's snipers have been busy because three-quarters of the Thunder Cloud Knuckle Brotherhood who were there are dead on the ground, either with shots center mass or a bullet between the eyes. The ones still breathing are being corralled between the farmers and their implements. Off to the far side are bunches of women, all ages, looking really rough and spooked. I see Wildcat, Rebel, Glory, and Peanut rush over to them. Some of the Intruders head over to the brotherhood being held in place by the farmers. They'll take care of them.

My eyes are skimming the area looking for Brenna or even my dad. When I see something on the ground about ten feet from a bunch of picnic tables, I squint to try and see what it is. That's when Shadow yells and takes off screaming as she's running. Then I hear Ollie's roar of utter pain, right before he calls out Brenna's name. All of the O'Brien men race after Shadow. Pushing my way through Panther and his men, I hurry to where they are at. Shadow is on the ground with Reed while Ollie is on the phone. As I get closer my heart stops dead in my chest. Lying on the ground is Brenna, perfectly still, pale as a ghost. Her own hands are holding her chest and I can see blood flowing over her fingers. Reed is pulling the backpack off his shoulders. How the fuck didn't I see him carrying it? Then I hear Ollie shouting into the phone.

"Tank, I don't give a flyin' fuck, get that goddamn helicopter up here now. Yeah, it's Brenna and she's got a gunshot wound to the chest. Lost a ton of blood, Reed is checking her out now. I'll have Rue start a smoke fire so they can find us. Hurry, Tank."

I kneel next to Reed to watch him move Brenna's hands to get a look at her wound. He presses on both sides of the hole in her chest then looks to Shadow, who immediately presses her own hands onto Brenna's chest. Reed grabs the backpack and starts throwing shit on the ground. Hearing someone behind me, I turn to see Yoggie rushing to Shadow's side. He grabs what I think is an IV and wipes down Brenna's arm with an alcohol pad before he puts a thick band around her upper arm. As he's doing that, Reed is checking her eyes and listening to her chest.

"Son of a bitch, sounds like her right lung collapsed. She's having difficulty breathing. Someone straighten her head and let's pull her body so she's lying flat. I want you to put this under her head. Best I can do right now, don't have any oxygen. Yoggie, what you got?"

Reed and Yoggie go back and forth while the ex-military person completes the IV. I feel the intensity before I even look her way. The fear and struggle on Shadow's face has me reaching over and putting my hands on hers pressing down. I don't know why I do it, she doesn't need my help but something on her face made me do it. Yoggie looks down, pushes both of our hands aside, leans in, and puts his head down on

Brenna's chest. He's there for a second or two then pushes her to her side.

"Reed, think she's experiencing a form of atelectasis. Probably has some blood or mucus behind the collapsed lung, but she's really struggling to breathe. She has to be on her side or else she'll drown in her own fluids. Where the fuck is that copter, for Christ's sake? Shadow, grab some of those gauze pads and put pressure on that wound, best you can. Reed, I've got saline running into her, got any pain meds?"

Reed pulls out a zippered pouch, opens it, and there are those medical bottles that doctors stick a needle in and draw out so much for a shot. Then I hear it off in the distance. I turn and see the smoke coming through the trees slightly.

"The helicopter is coming. Reed, how are we gonna get her there? Can she be moved?"

Reed looks my way for a second then concentrates on what he's doing. Yoggie is the one who answers.

"We'll use a blanket to put her in, then we'll carry her to the pickup site."

Shadow again has her hands on Brenna's chest. Yoggie is monitoring her breathing and checking her air passage, while Reed injects whatever he concocted into the IV. As soon as he's done, I see Avalanche holding up a blanket, not sure where he got it. He puts it on the ground where Reed was, and very carefully, we move Brenna onto it. Between Reed and Yoggie, they tell each of us where to hold the blanket. Shadow is placed in the middle on one side and I'm in the middle on the other side. Yoggie is at her head, Ollie at her feet. Panther and Avalanche are on opposite sides. Malice and Half-Pint finish up the sides. On Yoggie's word, we slowly lift her and start off carefully toward the sound of the helicopter. Avalanche and Panther are chanting while Yoggie softly counts off our steps.

In no time at all we are in a field loading Brenna onto the helicopter. There is a pilot and one guy manning a huge gun. *Where the fuck did Tank get this from*? I think to myself. Then the pilot looks out at us.

"We got to get moving. Most I can fit in here is maybe two maybe three, if one is small."

I so want to go with, but fuck, Ollie is her brother and Shadow is her chosen family, not to mention Yoggie and Reed have medical backgrounds. Without a thought Shadow jumps into the helicopter and goes right to Brenna and presses onto her chest again. Reed looks at me then pushes me toward the helicopter. Yoggie jumps in and reaches out, offering me his hand. I grab it and step into the beast of a copter. Shadow points across from her so I sit there. She grabs my hands and presses them down on Brenna's chest. Yoggie is checking her stats and the pilot tells us to hang on. Then he lifts off, and fuck, I pray to God he can fly this all the way to the hospital because the way he's flying right now is scaring the ever-lovin' shit out of me.

THIRTY-ONE
'SHERIFF GEORGE'
GIORGIO DE LUCA

My SUV could probably drive this route, even if I fell asleep behind the wheel. Goddamn, just thinking about getting some shut-eye has my body shiver. The last three weeks have been a nightmare, for sure. When we finally got to the Thunder Cloud Knuckle Brotherhood second camp, shit had already gone down. From what I've pieced together, Cliff and the brotherhood had some kinda plan but it didn't play out the way they thought it would. Not sure if Raven altered the course or if that asshole Johansen flipped it. I do know the farmers making their way up there probably saved Raven's life. When Cliff saw Johansen and the rest of the farmers, he knew his gig was done, and I'm thinking his thoughts were to take out as many innocents as he could. He didn't realize Raven would give her life so an innocent wouldn't die. She fought tooth and nail with Cliff, altering his opportunity to shoot Johansen. Then when the old prick had the upper hand, he pointed the gun directly at Raven and from what I've been told she didn't beg him, just stood there, head held high. Then Ollie's sharpshooter, Spirit, took Cliff out. Unfortunately, he committed one final atrocity. He shot Raven.

So, I'm on my way to Gertie's. I need to see her and feel something good. All the filth is getting to me. My God, what these animals have done to women and children, I don't think the devastated looks in the eyes of the victims will ever leave my mind. All I can do is pray the Devil's Handmaidens club will be able to take the victims and help them to become survivors. And the club is struggling with their president Tink out of commission for an unknown amount of time. It was touch and go for her. From what Reed told Gertie and me, she's lucky to be alive.

Driving up to the gate, I see the guards standing there. Yeah, Tank has taken protecting the Sterlings to the next level. He called in a favor from his friend, Nova, who then reached out to a friend of his who owns a security company. They are the ones at the gate and along the driveway. Since they know me, I'm not stopped but in the beginning they did check my credentials until Nova himself told them to knock it the fuck off, as they knew I was the sheriff of Timber-Ghost.

When I approach the house, I see Rowan and Joshua running around chasing each other. It's good to see them having fun with all of this shit going on. They can just be kids, finally. Even with their age difference, Rowan at sixteen and Joshua almost three, they are so cute together. Thank God Gertie raised her boys to judge people on who they are, not what they look like. I pull the truck next to Gertie's pickup. Before I can shut my vehicle off, Rowan has Joshua up in his arms while the little bugger pounds on my window with a huge grin on his face. Rowan has a smirk on his.

Waving at them to back off, I open the door and step out. Joshua has his arms out toward me so I grab him and land a kiss on his plump little cheek. He's still at the age that's acceptable.

"Unc Geo."

Yeah, Gertie has the little guy calling me uncle or as he says unc.

"What's up, Joshua? Having fun with your big brother? Don't let him cheat 'cause Rowan does whenever he can."

I watch the smirk turn into a pout. These two I've spent quite a bit of time with. Rowan even gave me the go-ahead when he caught Gertie and I kissing one night before I left. I believe his words were something to the effect of 'it's about damn time' to which Gertie told him he owed the jar. She don't give a rat's ass if they swear just not around her, one of her few rules.

I follow Rowan into the house where Gertie is setting the table. It's smells like heaven and my stomach growls loudly. Joshua laughs like a hyena.

"Hi, Lawman, sit down, lunch is ready. Whatcha want to drink?"

Before I sit, I put Joshua in his chair then grab Gertie and plant one on her to the moan of Rowan and the giggles of Joshua. We're both smiling when I pull away and go grab a seat. Gonna enjoy this hour 'cause after this, I've got to go to Ash's and that definitely won't be anything even remotely enjoyable. I've been dreading it the last three days since I got the call. I look up when Gertie grabs my plate and walks back to the stove. When I watch her pile food on my plate, I can't wait to dig in. She places a plate full of pork chops covered in bacon and tomatoes, fried okra, and Gertie's mozzarella and parmesan buttermilk quick bread. When she looks at me, she smiles.

"I got huckleberry pie with some homemade ice cream for dessert. Again, what do you want to drink?"

I ask for some milk and as I'm about to dig in, Joshua grabs my arm and shakes his head.

"Good boy, Joshua, our lawman has to learn our ways. Rowan, your turn to say grace."

I watch the three of them cross themselves and Rowan says a prayer about gratitude for the food we are about to eat. Then he adds prayers for all of those injured and recovering. They cross again themselves and start to dig in.

"Damn, I mean, darn, woman, this is fantastic. You spoil me, Gertie."

"It makes me happy, so just shut it and eat. That means you too, boys."

We eat as we also joke and the feelings inside keep growing and growing. Each of Gertie's boys is a good man. The older ones have found their calling in their professions. I know Alder is feeling some pain with what's going on with him and Bray, but only time will tell what's gonna happen. That girl has been to hell and back. After dinner and a huge hulking piece of huckleberry pie, with Gertie's homemade vanilla ice cream, I say my goodbyes to the boys just as they start to watch the movie *Up*. Rowan's a good kid to watch that movie yet again with Joshua. Gertie walks me to my truck.

"You think you'll make it back tonight, Lawman?"

"I'm gonna try but can't guarantee, Gertie. We still have a bunch of the Thunder Cloud Knuckle Brotherhood that got away. I can't let my guard down or rest until we catch them because they have it out for Tink, Ash, you, and the rest of your boys. I can't let anything happen to you because if it does, part of my heart will die. Now give me a kiss so I can get this shit done. Been putting it off too long. Yeah, don't say it, Gertie, we'll do our best for them."

She lifts up on her toes and presses her soft lips to mine. Now that Sterling is dead, she seems more comfortable in her own body. I know some but not all of what that bastard did to her. From what I do know, I wish he was alive so I could torture and kill him again and again. Need to take some lessons from Zoey because I know she can take an asshole right to the edge then she brings them back over and over until they are screaming and begging for her to end them. When Gertie pulls back, I caress her face and put a kiss on her forehead. Then I get in my vehicle and head to the next stop.

Arriving and parking in front of the homestead, I shut the SUV down and just sit there. It's a beautiful day in Montana. Clear blue sky with the sun shining. I would be able to enjoy this beautiful view if not for my next job duty. Taking a deep breath, I exit my vehicle and walk up the stairs. The home is gorgeous and not very old either. I hesitate before I knock twice on the door and wait. When no one comes to the door, I knock again. This time I hear movement behind the door. The door opens and Ash is standing there looking like he's ready to hit the floor. He's beyond exhausted and spent. Son of a bitch, I told this kid to call if it got too much, but no, better to take it on all on his own and kill himself. I push him outta the way as I'm already on my phone.

"Panther, hey. I need you to send Avalanche and one of your other guys to Ash's. Yeah, he's about to break. No haven't said a word yet, he can barely open the front door. Yeah, I'll be here whenever they can get here. Thanks."

Ash is glaring at me but I don't care. My next call is Ollie.

"Ollie, hi. Yeah, it's time. Get your parents, sisters, and brothers here as soon as you can. I don't know how bad it is, but from Ash's face it's not good."

When I hang up this time, I raise my eyebrows and he finally moves aside, letting me in. What I see has me stop dead in my tracks. His house is wrecked. There looks to be dirty plates, cups, and silverware on the end table, while I see a few beer cans lying on their sides in front of the sectional. With the open floor concept, I can see the kitchen is beyond trashed. Pots, pans, and cookie trays all over the stove and counter. The sink is full of plates and the lights on the dishwasher indicate the cycle is done. The floor has crumbs and who knows what else all over it. I turn to see Ash slumped over in one of those oversized chairs he has in the alcove of the great room. I walk over, sitting in the one across from him.

"Son, why didn't you call for some help? You know everyone would drop everything without a thought."

"I can't. You don't understand, George."

"Then make me, Ash. Are you trying to kill yourself because if you do, then what? You got a plan in place so when we put you to ground everyone can figure out what you want done?"

"No, you smart-ass, I don't have any plans in place. I'm lucky to grab a shower or use the toilet. My ranch is going to hell and I barely know my name. So what do you suggest I do?"

"I've already started it, all I ask, Ash, is don't fight it. This is gonna probably be the hardest thing you'll ever do. I believe in you 'cause I know you got this, son. You have to trust me."

Just as he finishes, a knock at the door has us both turn that way.

"Sit, Ash, before you fall on your ass. I'll get it."

Walking to the door, when I open it it's not only Avalanche and one of their crew but Avalanche, Panther, George, Jersey, Dallas, and Chicago along with two other men I don't know. When Panther's eyes meet mine, he smiles.

"Hey, Sheriff, thought you could use more than four

hands. Tell us what to do and we'll do it. Come on, men, let's check on Ash first."

Just as they move farther into the house, I hear car doors slamming. I turn back to the door to see Bronagh, Paddy, Ollie, Paisley, Orin and his husband Stefan, Oliver, Bennett and Betty, followed by Brooks. I'm sure his wife Gabbie is at the high school where she's the principal. Hangin' in the back is Onyx. I didn't expect to see Bray as the therapist from the Blue Sky Sanctuary has her over there to keep an eye on her. From what I hear she's doing a little better. I hear something like a squeak and when I look, I see Onyx is carrying a pet carrier. Oh shit.

Ash is off his feet moving quickly toward Onyx, who's placed the carrier down and is waiting on Ash.

"Is that the 'one'? Are you sure, Onyx?"

"Once again, even though this is number eight hundred twenty-three that you've asked me, this is the 'one.' Now, let's get this done."

They are walking my way, which has me tapping Ash on the shoulder.

"Which way?"

"Oh shit, come on, I'll show you."

The entire group of O'Briens follow behind Ash. I bring up the rear. Another reason to keep it clear. This is gonna go one of two ways and neither is inviting.

Ash walks down the hallway then turns down a half hallway to a closed door.

"Who's going in first? I mean, well fuck, y'all know what I mean."

To his credit, Paddy with his wife, Bronagh, step forward, each grabbing a hand.

"The three of us are going in first. What's the saying, yeah that's right, bite the bullet."

Paddy flings the door open to a state-of-the-art gym. There is every machine you could think of and those you have no idea what they are for. The woman on the machine doesn't turn or even act like she was listening, which I knew she was. This woman never misses a thing. When I see the O'Briens rushing to her, I noticed the belt that has her attached to the back of the chair of the machine.

"Awe, my baby. Brenna, sweetie, what do you need?"

"For all of you people to leave. Just get the hell out now, please."

No one says a word until Ollie and Onyx step up and crowd her on the machine. Onyx crouches down and gets right in her face.

"Enough, Brenna. I don't want to but I will if you don't stop this bullshit. When Ollie was ready to end his life, I was able to get his head out of his own ass and now look at him. There is nothing that is so bad that you disrespect yourself and those who love you. Sister of my soul, look at me. I mean it, damn it, LOOK AT ME."

I watch as Brenna struggles to not look at her sister until Onyx grabs her chin and moves her head first left then right.

"You see all of these people, Brenna, they are here because they care and want to help you any way they can. No, zip it. I get feeling down or upset, even depressed, but to blow off people who love you and want to help take care of you. Look at that man right there. He's slowly dying and you aren't helping. Either shit or get off the pot. Because if you push everyone away then when you finally decide you want, no need, someone we might all be gone and you will be all alone."

It takes a minute before her eyes shift and she takes in who is in the room. I see her eyes getting wet then they start to fall down her cheeks. For some, more tears, for others, less. When her eyes finally stop on Ash, her face turns white, eyes get big, and the sob comes out first before she breaks. Before anyone but Onyx can move, Ash is pushing everyone out of the way and when he gets to her, Brenna's sister gently puts her into Ash's arms.

"I don't want you to feel trapped, Ash. There are no promises I'll ever walk again. I'm paralyzed from the waist down. Why would you want to be stuck to someone like me? My God, Ash, you're gorgeous, smart, and a cowboy to top it off. You can do so much better; I know it and so do you. Don't let guilt ruin your life. Just let me go."

We all watch as Ash continues to hold on to her tightly, not saying a word for a bit, but when he does the room goes quiet.

"Brenna, not sure how many times I have to say the same thing. I'll take you anyway I can. You know what *A stór* means. You're my treasure. Don't go predicting the future. No one said you'll never walk again. Especially right now after they repaired your spine and are having you take it easy. You've already been on your feet and have taken tiny steps, so don't go trying to fake everyone out."

I hear all the intakes of breath. No one even knew she was able to stand with support. I'm glad Ash said it out loud because he told me last week how thrilled he was when she tried with both the physical therapist and him at her side. Prognosis from what I hear is guarded but good. The fear of what happened to her has cross-circuited her thinking.

"Ash, damn it, why did you say that? Now if I don't walk, it's another letdown or failure. I'm not sure how many more I can handle. I didn't keep Tink safe, nor did I save those people in my gym. How many were killed? Cliff shot one of his own, right in front of me. Blew his brains all over me and never blinked an eye. Yeah, he was getting frisky but still. Murder and death surround me."

Hearing laughter, everyone turns to see my daughter Zoey, or as they all know her by her club name Shadow, laughing and holding her sides. She starts to make her way to her club sister, still chuckling before she reaches down and gives her a hug. Everyone is shocked but kinda getting used to the enforcer actually having a heart. Then she grabs Raven's cheeks, bringing them nose to nose.

"I know you think you're funny but seriously, sister? You're our technology officer so how does mayhem and death follow you? Yeah, you've had a few things happen recently but it wasn't your doing, it was Sterling's and the brotherhood's. Now you can sit around and have your pity party, or you can be the Devil's Handmaiden who Tink and I knew you would be. Suck it up, friend, 'cause we have a ton of work that needs to be done. Not to mention the human trafficking circuits that are out there we need to dissolve and innocents to rescue. As far as being paralyzed, Raven, we all are in one way or another. Some physically, some mentally, and some both. Don't let it beat you down. Now everyone is gonna go outside while you and my dad talk. It's overdue and you will feel better once it's over. Then we can all visit and shoot the shit. That's an order not from me but from your prez, who couldn't be here. She does send her love and she said to expect a call from her in a day or two."

I watch as Shadow, along with Panther and Avalanche, start shooing everyone out. When it's just Ash, Raven, and me, I slowly start to walk over to her but she raises her hand.

"Sheriff, I believe I owe you an apology. Haven't been feeling myself lately. Can you meet me in the great room, please? I don't want to have this conversation here. Ash, will you give me a hand?"

Watching the two of them together, in my heart I know it's gonna be okay. Maybe not today or tomorrow, but Raven is young and a fighter. She's got this, especially with Ash at her side.

THIRTY-TWO
'RAVEN'
BRENNA

The intervention worked. It's been a couple of weeks and things are slowly looking up. Probably because I'm also talking with Ollie's therapist from the sanctuary. I knew it was something that needed to be done but being an O'Brien, I'm just as stubborn as the rest of my family is. Though when Onyx got in my face, giving me the business, knew I had to remove my head from my own ass because I didn't want her to do it. I'd never hear the end of it. It helped she brought me over the cutest little kitten ever. From the information she had and what I looked up he's a Ragdoll. I named him Vinnie. Besides Ash he's my new best friend.

That day I was shot scared the bejesus out of me. No, not so much the bullet hitting me center mass, but the crazy demented look in Cliff Sterling's eyes when he pulled the trigger. He knew his life was over and instead of accepting it and giving his family some peace, he intentionally tried to kill his son's girlfriend. I guess that's me. Ash hasn't left my side, well, until I had Avalanche, Noodles, Panther, and Enforcer force him to leave and manage the ranch. He was letting everything go so he could be here for me. I so appreciate it but not necessary. Life goes on, though sometimes you wonder why. Taz, Vixen, Glory, and Freak brought all my stuff from my office in the clubhouse to Ash's house and between them they used one of the spare bedrooms and set me up a temporary office. Freak made sure it was secure and Glory went and got a digital door lock. George and Avalanche put in a finger and eye scanner after they bumped up the security all around Ash's house. I was now tied into the Intruders security system, which Ash, Shadow, and a few others didn't understand. Even Avalanche didn't understand why it didn't just tie into all the other security systems I manage. Took a while, but I explained to them all it was tied into the Devil's Handmaidens main circuit, but for added protection Tank wanted me to feel doubly protected. Got to love the big teddy bear that he is.

So my day starts off with Ash waking me with kisses that lead to him doing range of motion with my legs while Vinnie's fluffy tail tickles my face. Then Ash helps me get up and put my back brace on before my physical and occupational therapists arrive. After a usually brutal session, they leave after helping me to clean up, then I eat breakfast with Ash or Gertie, depending on what's going on around the ranch. A few times even his brothers were around. Well, Reed, Alder, or Rowan with Joshua. Rue was back on the rodeo circuit so we don't get to see too much of him. I've been working more since we have a couple of leads on some huge human trafficking circuits within our normal range. Also, some of our other chapters have been reaching out for some research help. I know what they are all doing and I appreciate it, making sure I feel needed within my club and just the whole Devil's Handmaidens MC organization in general. And with every club duty I handle Vinnie is either at my side, on my desk or keyboard, or over my shoulder.

The one thing that is bothering me is Ash hasn't even tried to take our relationship to the next level. I mean, yeah, we've gotten pretty hot and heavy with kissing and some feeling up leading to a few orgasms that were oh so good. Just the other day while we were lounging on the couch after he gave me a shoulder massage that had gotten me all hot and bothered. Well, good news is I'm not paralyzed. Thank the Lord for that miracle. I have feeling, especially were it matters…in my girly parts. I've been relearning to walk and don't have all of my balance or strength so am limited to small walks throughout the day with a walker. Pretty sexy and I'm not sure if that's why he won't bump nasties with me. Damn, why did that pop in my head? For shit's sake. I'm an adult not a high school cheerleader. That brings a grin to my face. I've been doing that more often too. Grinning and laughing. I'm always grinning when Ash helps me over the edge with his fingers and or mouth. I've even used my hands on him but nothing more.

The best thing that's happened in the last two days

was Noodles surprised me when he walked in with Tink at his side, Shadow on her other side. Seeing her up and about broke me. I instantly started sobbing like a crazy woman. I was taking a break on the sectional and they brought her to me and then Noodles told us he was gonna go find Ash. Shadow sat in the huge chair as Tink held me as I cried, then I held her as she cried. She explained everything that happened to her and what she'd been through. My God, she's one strong woman because, shit, not sure I'd have made it through all of that. Funny she said the same thing to me. The entire time Shadow sat there watching over both of us like she was our shadow. That thought makes me laugh outright.

We both talked about what might have gone wrong with Cliff Sterling for him to act the way he did. It was now out in the open that Sheriff George and Gertie were an item. Along with that came the horror story of what Gertie had been through. Cliff was still abusing her whenever he could, holding their boys over her head. I've never wished anyone dead but I'm glad he is, just saying.

Hearing a knock on the door, the day nurse looks at me then goes to answer it. I hear my mom's voice so I adjust on the sectional, slowly shifting my legs off so I can just sit. Mom and Dad come into the great room with a huge bouquet of wildflowers and looks to be a container or two of some of Mom's baked goods. Yum, I could always use some brownie and cookie inspiration, though I'm curious what has my parents here to begin with.

"Hey, beautiful daughter of ours. How are you feeling? Brought some of yours and Ash's favorite treats, thought you both could use some of my homemade goodies. How's your therapy going?"

I know my mom and right now she's babbling. Jesus, what's going on and what has her so frigging nervous? Wonder if one of my siblings is up to no good yet again. Just as I go to ask her, Gertie and Sheriff George come in the front door.

"Oh sorry, Bronagh, didn't mean to intrude. George and I were going to see if Brenna and Vinnie were up to a drive in the country. You know, fresh air and sunshine."

They all laugh but my gut is telling me something is up with the lot of them. I'm just not in the know at the moment. When there's another knock on the front door, I just about lose it. So much for a relaxing afternoon. I gently stand and reach for the walker that I've graduated to. At least it allows me to somewhat walk on my own, though I can't go far or for a long period of time, as long as I'm not dizzy when I stand. As the therapists say, "Give it time," so I'm trying.

Everyone is standing around the kitchen island watching me as I shuffle my way to the door. When I look through the glass, my head jerks back. I open the door to one of Sheriff George's deputies; Yoggie, who I know. Yeah, the same Yoggie who's our VP Glory's ol' man. He grins my way as I hear a throat clear behind me, then Sheriff George tells me he has a few more questions. I motion Yoggie in and am about to close the door when Rowan comes jogging to the house.

"Brenna, do you have a minute? I need some help, if you don't mind. Oh, sorry, you got people here. I'll find someone else to help me."

Looking at this as a sign to get the hell out of this nuthouse, I tell him I'll be out in a few minutes. Turning, I see everyone is talking and laughing so I whistle to get their attention. When I have it, I tell them I have to help Rowan and I'll be back. Some of them have a shit-eating grin on their face, though I don't know why. Before turning to use my walker, I tell Onyx to watch Vinnie, I make my way out the door to the front porch. I don't see Rowan anywhere but I'm out here so figured should keep looking.

As much as I hate using the ramp, that's where I head. Taking my time, just as I hit the bottom Rowan comes around the back in one of the golf carts. Since my accident there are two new ones everyone uses to get me around the ranch. As much as I appreciate it, they make me feel like a cripple. That's another incentive to get my ass moving.

"Come on, Brenna, let me help you in. Take your time, once you're in I'll put the walker in the back. This shouldn't take but a second or two. I'll explain on the way."

He helps me in while explaining he's trying to surprise Gertie, his mom, I'm paying attention to getting my body in the cart. Once in, he grabs the seat belt that I hate, but Ash won that argument. Rowan clips me in then closes the walker and puts it in the back. I watch him walk in front of the cart, thinking he's such a good kid.

He turns it on and starts to make a turn to the back of the house. I hang on but take in the view, which is breathtaking. I'm so lost in the panoramic vista, I'm kind of shocked when Rowan stops. When I lift my eyes to the side, I'm shocked to see all of my club sisters sitting around a firepit or at the patio sitting on our new furniture there. My mom and dad along with Gertie and Sheriff George are also standing around. Not only is Yoggie there but Noodles, Panther, and Avalanche, along with George, Dallas, Jersey, and Chicago. Finally, off to the far end I see my siblings and some of Ollie's folks. The one my eyes catch on is Spirit. She gives me her impression of a smile, which is her lips barely tipping up. Though to see her there tells me something important is going on because she doesn't come out to stuff that often. She's kind of the definition of a loner.

Then I see it. Past the patio and back deck is an additional gazebo that Ash had added with his brothers when I finally was released from the hospital. He said it was for me to be able to enjoy the outdoors without the bugs and shit like that eating me alive. When it was completed, he showed me the gazebo and all the fancy stuff in it, including a ceiling fan to circulate the air through the screened-in windows. Though as I'm looking at it right now, it's covered with wildflowers all over. In containers all around on the ground and on top of that there are fairy lights hanging inside. What the heck is going on?

When I see Ash, my heart stops. My cowboy is in new Levi's, his boots are shined, and he's got on one of his good fancy cowboy shirts. The Stetson on his head looks new. In other words, he looks extremely hawt. And that smirk has me tingling all over. His one arm is behind his back as he walks toward me. He hands me a huge bouquet of wildflowers then he unclips the seat belt, bends down, and lifts me up and out of the golf cart. He carries me to the gazebo were Rowan opens the door. Once in, it's just us, and inside is even prettier. The table is fancy with a tablecloth and some glasses with a bottle of champagne in a bucket of ice. The entire place is lit by candles. Some real and some I'm guessing battery type.

My head jerks up to look at his handsome face but his expression is serious. He places me on the love seat covered in pillows. He lifts my legs up, placing them on a pile of pillows. Then he grabs the flowers, putting them on a side table. He sits on the edge of the love seat, grabbing my arms.

"*A stór,* life has given us a lot of bumps in our road. This last one almost killed you and that would have been the end of me. I know a lot of what happened wasn't either of our faults and we lost something more precious than words can express. Our little baby. Before I go any further, wanted you to know with the help of our family and friends, we've built a memorial for our baby by the little meadow you love that's filled with wildflowers. I'll take you there and show you when you're up to it."

I feel the tears and don't try to stop them. I'm watching Ash and he seems so unusually nervous. He clears his throat and wipes his hand across his face. Then he shifts and kneels beside the love seat. Something jumps in my chest and I feel my heart starting to beat quickly. My eyes get big as he reaches into his front pocket and pulls something out. He grabs my hands again, kissing them.

"Brenna, I waited way too long to tell you the truth, and I'm so thankful you've forgiven me. I've never stopped loving you, as you can see from the house I built just for you. Everything I've done the last couple of years has been for you. I would be honored if you would become my wife and mother of our children. This ring is the one from before but I've added to it. Back then I didn't have a lot of money so the ring I gave you was the best I could do. This one incorporates our past, our present, and hopefully our future. Brenna O'Brien, will you marry me?"

I'm shocked and speechless. I've dreamt about this since he left me at our engagement party, even though I was so pissed at him and so very hurt, more like devastated. He's the one who owns my heart, always has. He is getting pale waiting and I'm struggling to find the words.

"Brenna, it's a simple question. Yes or no? You're killing me here. Come on, put me out of my misery."

I lean forward and whisper my answer in his ear. He

grabs my arms and smashes his lips on mine. When I give him a slight opening of my lips, he plunges in, taking the kiss to another level. When we separate to grab some air, he looks toward the door and lets out a loud, "Yo." Then he yells, "She said yes!"

All I hear are screams of joy and lots of "Awesome" and "Oh yeah."

When he's done, he pulls me back to him and kisses the hell out of me.

THIRTY-THREE
'RAVEN'
BRENNA

I can't believe it's been almost two months since Ash asked me to marry him. Of course, I said yes. Why wouldn't I? Though I told him we should just elope and go to Las Vegas. Both of our moms' mouths dropped open and by the looks on their faces, I couldn't go through with that idea. Now I wish I would have.

My God, it's turning into a frigging circus. Finally, I had to put my foot down—no, I stomped my foot down—in my parents' house with both my mom and Ash's mom there, as well as my two sisters and some of my club sisters, and Momma Diane.

"Just a friendly reminder, Mom, and, Mom, this is Ash's and my wedding and this time it's going to be what we want, got it? I love you both with all of my heart, but no, we are not doing homemade soaps—sorry, Gertie—or little bottles of Jack Daniels, Mom, that Dad suggested. I've been trying to decide what to do and have come up with a couple of ideas I'll share with everyone in a bit. First, I want to go over where we are going to get married. No, zip it, both of you, and I mean that with the utmost respect. Ash and I talked and we'd like to have the wedding in the meadow on your property, Gertie. You know, my favorite spot. That way everyone we love is there, including the little one we lost. Please don't cry because I'll start and won't be able to stop."

"Next, the reception. I'm sorry, Mom, I can't have it in your and Dad's pole barn. Too many bad memories. We could have at the Sterling ranch but again we talked, and I want to have it at Tink's ranch. The Devil's Handmaidens club and sisters are a very huge part of my life. I know what you're going to say, nothing at my parents' house. Well, maybe the bridal shower if you want, Mom. The rehearsal dinner will be at the Wooden Spirit Bar and Grill. If you both want to meet me there next week, we can go over the menu with the cook. Okay, fire away?"

Mom looks at both Bray and Onyx before she asks quietly and hesitantly.

"Brenna, have you decided on the wedding party or are you not having one? Also is your dad going to walk you down the aisle?"

I get it now, Mom thinks I'm pushing them out. Silly me, sometimes I forget how she gets insecure.

"Yeah, Mom, we have our wedding party kind of picked out. It's so hard because we want everyone who means something to us to be involved, but if we do that most of our guests will be part of the wedding party.

Once Ash and I finalize everyone, you and Gertie will be the first to know, okay? Oh, of course, Dad is walking me down the aisle. Who else would I have do it?"

She just smiles and shakes her head. Now I look over to the women I've come to know and love. Tink, Shadow, Glory, Taz, Vixen, Wildcat, Rebel, Peanut, Heartbreaker, Kiwi, Duchess, and the kids: Dani, Dottie, Kitty, Squirt and our newest prospect, Addie. Not sure she'll work out, she's one of our survivors who has no one and didn't want to leave the ranch or the club sisters. For the entire club to be here is just short of a miracle. We have our part-timers working our businesses, which doesn't happen very often. There's always at least one sister helping at each business.

"I need your help with a bunch of things I want to do at the wedding. First, it has to be outside so we have to have a contingency plan in case the weather doesn't comply. Also being outside, I was thinking maybe something to cover just the area where we are and also where everyone will sit. You know, to keep the sun from beating down on us. Third, and most important, I want to get married either in the spring or fall. To me those are the best times in Timber-Ghost. Maybe we can all get together and try and figure out what will work."

I see Heartbreaker fall forward like someone pushed her. Looking behind her I see Wildcat with a shit-eating grin. Okay, what's this about? Then Heartbreaker explains it to everyone.

"Um, Raven, in my prior life before I screwed up with the drugs and shit, I was sort of a party planner. So, if you need any help, I'd be honored to assist if you want me to. If not, no hard feelings."

She steps back kind of embarrassed, which shows she still is feeling out of sorts from her falling back into her drug habit during all of Tink's shit. It's time to let it go.

"Well, hot damn, Heartbreaker, that's a serious 'hell yeah' from me. I'm thinking I can use all the help I can get. With you, both moms, and my sisters, maybe this shindig will turn out halfway decent if I'm lucky."

Taz pushes her way through and hands me a book filled with all kinds of stuff. When I open it, I'm shocked to see some of the same things I've already picked as my favorites. With stunned eyes, I look at her and she grins.

"How did you know, Taz? These are the ones I've bent the pages down in the bridal magazines."

"Yeah, I know, because I asked Ash to take pictures of all of those and send them to me. Once I had them, we all worked on it and managed to get it together. Raven, it's a starting spot, lots of decisions. Oh, we did include both Onyx and Bray in the putting of it together as they seem to know some of what you like. It was a joint effort, sister, by your sisters."

I feel them but try to hold them back, until I see my mom hugging both Onyx and Bray before she grabs Gertie and they stand together, tears running down their faces. Been a long time coming. Then I hear that voice.

"Oh, come on already, shit, thought this was going to be a fun time filled with laughs not a sappy bunch of women crying, for fuck's sake."

When Momma Diane, Gertie, and my mom glare at Shadow, she drops her head.

"Um, sorry, moms, didn't mean to use that kind of language in front of all of you. Just that this ain't fun and I got shit, I mean stuff, to do. Are we done?"

I shake my head at her but walk her way. Her eyes start to get bigger the closer I get to her. Then I lay it on her.

"Shadow, I have a huge favor to ask of you. Now listen to the whole question before you go off. Okay, I want everyone involved but for you, not sure you'll want to because if you do then there is one item you can't argue about. That item is that the day of the wedding I'll need you to wear a formal dress."

I hear everyone gasp as the room moves farther away from our enforcer. I'm pulling her leg, but I owe her for all the bullshit she's put me through. I watch her face and can see the wheels turning. She wants to be a part of it but doesn't want to wear a dress. So, I push it a bit farther.

"You do have a choice of colors though, Shadow. The main colors are teal, pink, purple, or green for spring; or orange, yellow, gray, or brown for fall. Which one do you think you'd like?"

I can feel it coming but try to keep a straight face. Well, until she literally turns around to see everyone is waiting for her answer. Thought she would have blown by now but she shocks the shit out of me. So much I actually snort after her answer.

"Well, Raven, I'm guessin' probably the yellow or

orange. They'd be the best with my dark hair, don't you think?"

My mouth is hanging open and that's when she raises her hand and gives me the bird. Everyone starts laughing and chuckling while I realize she turned the table on me. How did she know?

"Girl, you don't have a poker face. And if you did want me to wear a dress those wouldn't be your fuckin' colors, that's for goddamn sure. I think you're losing your ability to be funny. I wonder if falling back in love with your cowboy and getting it reg—umps…

I literally walk-run to her to cover her big-ass mouth. Mom and Gertie are both busting a gut while Momma Diane is watching them with a huge grin on her face. Looking around, I see everyone is enjoying the Shadow/Raven show. That is until I see Onyx and Bray watching us both with tears in their eyes. I let my club sister go and walk over to my given sisters. I reach and pull them close, hanging on tightly. I whisper so only they can hear me, "I love you both so very much." They in turn tell me the same.

After much discussion and deliberation, everyone starts to leave to go about their afternoon business. I see Tink sitting at the end of the table so I make my way to her. I need to thank her for the spread she had waiting when everyone arrived. She looks up at me, smiling.

"I'm so very happy for you, Raven. If anyone deserves a happily ever after, it's you. The ranch is yours to do with what you want. Just let me know and we will get it done. How are you doing otherwise?"

We sit and catch up for at least an hour or longer. She seems to be doing okay, getting most of her strength back, though at times she still seems to struggle a bit. Ash's asshole father put her through so much. I hope he's rotting in hell.

"Tink, not sure I ever told you, but one, I'm so sorry for what Cliff did, and two, thank you for all everyone in the club did for both Ash and me. It means the world and I'll owe you until the day I no longer breathe."

She grabs my hands before she replies.

"Raven, that is what we do for each other. Good and bad times when we are healthy or sick. Our club is almost like a marriage in a way. We always have each other's backs and never let a sister down. You've been there for me so many times, I can't count anymore. And thanks for getting back to work sooner than I thought you would. These trafficking circuits are getting out of hand, even though we took down a large majority of the Thunder Cloud Knuckle Brotherhood. Especially from Timber-Ghost, thank God. From what you've researched there are still some around this area, though in a much smaller population. Now I need to get back to the main house before Noodles sends out a search party. He's beyond a mother hen, though don't tell him I said that."

"She don't have to, Sweet Pea, I heard it with my own ears."

We both turn around, shocked to see Noodles and Ash standing in the doorway, both grinning. Damn, did we both get super lucky.

After Tink and Noodles leave, Ash takes the seat next to me.

"How'd it go? I was waiting in case you needed backup, but just like I thought, you got through it. Who was a bigger pain in the ass, your mom or mine?"

As we talk about what's coming our way, it hits me at that moment, our lives are ever evolving. I had no idea when Ash walked out of our engagement party, thinking that was it for us, then jump forward a few years that we'd be back together planning our wedding yet again. Though this time there's nothing or no one to come between us. Then after that day we will have the rest of our lives to, well yeah, just live our lives. Something I can't wait to start.

THIRTY-FOUR
'ASH'
ASHTON

Brenna was probably right; we should have eloped. I mean really, do we need all of this bullshit just to become man and wife? Months and months with both of our mothers and all of our family and friends. This is going to be the event of the year for Timber-Ghost, that's for sure. I've had my ranch hands working for the last week to get the field ready. Between the arch and what did Mom call it—yeah, a pergola—but with a cloth top on it. I'm glad we're building that because when I bring Brenna out here there's somewhere to get out of the Montana weather. As we get closer, my nerves are starting to come to the surface. Not like I'm thinking of backing out, just that all the questions start running through your head.

Looking at Brenna's favorite place, it looks awesome. Still raw because it's a wildflower field but now it's more manicured. There are stepping stones to walk into the field so guests can make it to their seats. The arch is going to be wrapped in flowers and fairy lights. Yeah, little did I know before I went to Brenna's that day, I would not only know the words fairy lights but also what they are.

My phone vibrates and when I see it's the application I've been waiting for, I look around, find Fred, one of the ranch managers, and scream, pointing to the phone. He raises his hand and motions for me to go. Turning my horse, Warrior, around I push him toward the main barn and give him his head. We are so in tune with each other, I don't even give it any mind and let my thoughts get the best of me. That day of *'love to death do you part'* is right around the corner. The thought of finally getting my dream come true by marrying Brenna and then having a kick-ass party should be one for the books.

After cooling Warrior down, then grooming him, and checking to make sure he has plenty of water and hay, I head toward my house so I can clean up a bit. Knowing Brenna is working hard with her physical therapist today, I quietly walk in the back door as the house is extremely silent. In the mudroom, I strip down to my boxer briefs and start washing the crud off of me. Once I'm able to walk through the house, I head to the master bathroom and jump right into the walk-in shower. I wash my hair then my body as quickly as I can. Once done, I dry off, brush my teeth, and run a comb through my hair.

Heading into the walk-in closet, I grab clean briefs, jeans, and a Sterling Ranch T-shirt. These were Brenna's idea and it's a great one. Every employee and family member now wears them, which has gotten our name out there faster than any kind of advertising. Especially after what went down with the old man. Every one of my brothers and Mom had one on and when the television people came to the ranch, so did the hands. Brenna explained that it looks more professional, especially when the ranch hit the television.

After I'm dressed, I move toward the in-house gym and see that it's not only Brenna but Tink and Shadow also. All three women are working out together. I'm glad because it seems like Brenna does much better with her club sisters around. I knock on the door before entering and I have six eyes on me instantly. Brenna's face breaks into a smile while Shadow smirks and Tink waves.

"Brenna, gotta run, finally got the response on the application. Going into town, be back probably around dinnertime. You gonna be okay?"

"Yeah, Ash, I'll be fine. Go. If you need anything, let me know."

"Should be fine, had Taz look at the proposal and she tweaked it a little, so it's ready to go. Love you, *A stór*, don't overdo it. You have a very important date in two days."

I lean down and give her a hot and heavy closed-mouth kiss. I hear Shadow making sounds like she is puking while Tink just giggles. Brenna's eyes are sparkling when I lift up. I wink then head out to my truck. The drive doesn't take too long, but it gives me time to think. I'm applying for a pretty big loan so I can purchase acreage from my mom. She wanted to just gift it to me, but want to do this the right way. I have some huge plans for Brenna's and my section. New ways of farming that in time will help grow the family farm. I know Reed, Rue, and Alder also are getting loans to purchase smaller lots of land, but the main purpose of us doing this is to make sure our mom is taken care of after all the years she did everything she could to raise us boys.

Now that she and Sheriff George are getting real serious, she wants some time for herself, which is understandable. Mom and the sheriff understand both Rowan and Joshua will be at the house for a while. Mom has always wanted to remodel and make the farmhouse more her style, and with the money we are able to give her, it will allow her the opportunity to do just that.

Two days and finally Brenna will be my wife. My responsibility was to figure out a honeymoon. I struggled for a while, not sure where I think she'd want to go. Spoke to both Paddy and Bronagh, along with Brenna's siblings. They each told me somewhere they've heard her say she wanted to visit at some point. Bray though convinced me on where to go. So, the plan is to fly out to Alaska and stay in a stunning cabin in Denali Park for a week. Then we fly to Canada to take a railroad trip through Vancouver, Jasper, Lake Louise, Banff, and Toronto. It's a thirteen-day trip but I'd planned for a month away. Since I can remember, we never went anywhere but local and Brenna's the same. We did get passports, just in case, when we started all the planning. That was Shadow's suggestion, which worked out well.

I have all the travel packages, tours, tickets, and transfers already. I've looked at it and am so friggin' excited. While we're gone, Alder is going to be in charge at the ranch. He's taken a leave of absence from the park rangers. Discovering the women, then the beating, has him in need of some serious time off. He's going to stay at our house in the guest suite.

Parking the truck, I walk up to the bank and open the door, stopping when I see who's there. It's not a bad thing as it's my brothers. We all hug in a manly way and then at the same time ask what the others are doing here. When we realize why we've been summoned everyone relaxes. Doris asks if she can go through this all just once and we agree.

After we are all situated in a conference room, each holding either water or coffee, Doris opens up the folders in front of her and then lifts her head looking at each of us. I can tell she's a bit nervous, though not sure why. We all make a living with what we all do and have excellent credit or the best it can be.

"All right, this is what I have. No need for a bank loan for any of you. No, wait, let me finish, boys. An anonymous person has opened up an account for the Sterling family to be used for whatever is needed. Now between the four of you, let me see, Ashton, Reed, Alder, and Rue, the total amount that all of you were looking for was two point five million dollars, using the ranch as collateral. As we all know it's worth way more, but Gertie isn't asking the going rate. This account that has been opened has five million dollars in it. No, don't ask me who funded it. One of the stipulations is that you don't know who it is. So, I suggest since there's five million, we'll transfer whatever you want to a separate account in your mother's name, and then she can do with it whatever she wants. Though the word on the street is she's getting ready to remodel the farmhouse. Good for her. Now any questions? Though remember, I'm not allowed to answer most of your questions, I'm sure."

We look at each other and then shake our heads. Doris shakes each of our hands then walks out, closing the door. Again, we look at each other, this time our faces in shock. Reed being the oldest is first to let loose.

"What the hell just happened? Thought I was approved for a loan but instead we're told that now we are millionaires. Someone please explain to me who, how, and why?"

Rue and Alder just look down, confusion on their faces. I don't know what to say, though I have a few ideas who started this and funded the account. Not many around here have that kind of money sitting around. After a long discussion, we realize we might as well go along with this so everyone can get moving on their lives and dreams.

I look around and call Doris back in and we transfer two point five million to an account that will be Mom's once she comes in. All of us are also on the account. Then we decide to put five hundred thousand in two accounts for both Rowan and Joshua. They are called custodial accounts. We are in charge of it until they reach a certain age. Doris then opens an account for each of us with two hundred and fifty thousand dollars in each one. The last five hundred thousand goes into a business account for the farm so we can maybe do a few improvements we've spoken about for years.

Once we've handled everything, we decide to hit the Wooden Spirit Bar and Grill to grab a beer together and try and figure out who did this for us. Even after two beers each, we only have general ideas on who and why. Before we separate, we make our way to the Devil's Handmaidens clubhouse. When we walk in, the women in the general area, I guess you'd call it that, turn and look at us. The tough-looking badass one comes toward us.

"Hey, Sterling men, can we help you? Is Raven okay, Ash? Need something?"

I can't remember her club name, so I'm honest.

"Sorry, can't remember your name."

"They call me Wildcat. Now what's got ya here in our clubhouse, is there a problem or did ya get lost?"

I hear some of the women chuckle at her questions.

"Is Taz in today? We've got a few questions for her."

"Yeah, Squirt, go grab Taz from her office, will ya? Can we offer you men a drink? We got water, pop, coffee, beer, and if you need something stronger, we have that too."

We all ask for a water since we have to drive to our homes after this. I hear boots on the floor, turn, and see Taz and Squirt coming down the long hallway off the left side. The rainbow-haired sister walks, no kind of waddles, her way to us. She is really pregnant and is, what do they say, glowing. My mind instantly goes to what Brenna will look like pregnant and that brings a goofy smile to my face.

"Ash, that look right there is the look of a man in love, wondering what his woman will look like pregnant like me."

My eyes almost pop out of my head. How the hell did she know what I was thinking?

"It's written all over your face. Anyway, Squirt said you had some questions. Let's go into the back conference room, see if I can help you."

We walk through the big main room, past a closed door, and then move down the hallway to another one, turn right and hit the, I guess, conference room. It's a good size so we all take a seat around a table. Taz shuts the door and sits down. No one says a word for a bit then Reed leads off.

"Taz, we were just at the bank and though we all applied for loans we were told we don't need them as someone gifted our family some money. Well, it's not some, but more like five million dollars. Now we talked about it and there aren't many folks around here we know who have that kind of money. One of them is Tink. We all know when her grandma passed, she inherited a shit ton of money. We want to know if it's Tink."

She glances between all of us then grabs her phone, tapping like a speed demon. Then she looks back up at us, even before someone replies.

"Something men don't usually learn well is this

saying about *don't look a gift horse in the mouth*. I'm thinking this applies in this situation. If that's all you need, unfortunately, this baby is pushing into my bladder yet again and I need to get to the ladies' room before I pee myself. Don't laugh, Alder, it happens a lot. Reed, explain to your brothers why this is a problem for pregnant women. Remember this when one day you have a woman who is expecting. Treat her like the queen she is. Ash, can't wait, less then forty-eight hours. I hear everything is looking phenomenal. If you need anything, let Enforcer or me know. And again, thanks for asking Teddy to be a part of the ceremony. He's beyond excited. Well, both of the kids are beyond thrilled. Olivia is biting at the bit to dress up and have her hair done. She went with us to get a mani/pedi, and damn, I think Glory and Yoggie are going to have a huge diva on their hands. Teddy keeps saying them walking down the aisle for your and Raven's wedding is a practice run for their own. Anyway, thank you for including him."

"Taz, Brenna wouldn't have it any other way. Teddy means a lot to her, as all of you do."

We say our goodbyes and head back outside. We all look at each other and shrug our shoulders. I need to have a conversation with Tink, so I tell all my brothers that's where I'm heading and if they want to come, follow me to her ranch. Thirty-eight minutes later we are slowly making our way up the driveway after being checked out by the guards at the gate. I park off to the side and wait for everyone to gather together. When I knock on the door, it takes a few minutes until Noodles opens the door. When he sees all of us, he immediately breaks out laughing like a hyena.

"I told Sweet Pea y'all are way too smart not to figure it out. Come on in, guys, I'll grab her, give me a minute. She's a bit sore from working out with Raven and Shadow."

As we take seats in the great room, I look around as I didn't realize how truly awesome the ranch home was. It's huge though it still makes you feel like you're home. Hearing someone coming down the stairs, I see Noodles and Tink. Her hair is still wet but she looks good, which I thank God for every day. Our father almost killed her for no other reason except he was an asshole. Before any of us can say a word, Tink jumps right in.

"I didn't do this for any of you. I did it for your mother and younger brothers. All these years your mom has worked off of credit at all the stores in town. She would square up after you either sold some of the young heifers, harvested the hay, or from the money you received from the dairy aspect of the ranch. Gertie has never complained or even asked for a handout, even if we all would have given it to her. That Montana woman pride. So after what happened and I finally started to feel like myself, I spoke to my parents and Noodles. Guys, I'm going to be honest. My grammy was one smart cookie. The money she left me, I'll never spend it all in my lifetime. That's why the ranch is at the level it is and we do what we do. Not for money but to pass it forward. Now the money is for each and every one of you to have a fresh start without the stain of Cliff

Sterling hanging over each of you. Why take out a loan and be immediately in debt? Please accept this as a gift, I don't know, for saving those women up there. Who knows what would have happened if you hadn't. Or, Ash, for never giving up on Raven. Alder, for finding Bray or, Reed, for what you do at the hospital. Rue, for being one crazy motherfucker getting on the back of those bulls and giving everyone the excitement of eight seconds. I want to do this so just let me. Ask Noodles, you won't win so don't even try, especially you, Ash. Don't you have better things to worry about?"

After a good thirty minutes, we all come to the agreement, that yeah, we'll accept the money, but each of us will be paying back some of it to wherever Tink wants us to. Her thoughts were to start a fund for survivors of domestic violence or human trafficking. We all agree and take a few minutes to sit around and visit.

On the way home, I have no idea how I'm going to explain this day to Brenna, but knowing her she'll take it with a grain of salt. She knows her prez's generosity better than any of us. Tink is right, I've got better things to do.

THIRTY-FIVE
'RAVEN'
BRENNA

The day is finally here and I feel calm as can be. I thought I'd be a nervous wreck but I feel at peace. Yeah, I'm worried everything won't go as planned but that has to be every bride's worry.

Thank God Onyx recommended we have the bachelor and bachelorette parties the week before. My God, what a party. First, I ended up at Tink's ranch where the club sisters, my mom and sisters, Gertie, my mom's sister, Cynthia, and a few of our long-time employees were all there. We spent hours just having fun. Food was awesome, it was catered from the bar and grill. The booze ran freely and no one was feeling any pain. Then when I started opening the gifts, it hit me why there were no young kids around. I mean, some of the gifts I have no idea what you do with them. The younger sisters were able to explain them to me in front of my mom and Ash's, which had me red as a tomato while the two of them laughed hysterically. I stayed at the ranch as, I guess, Ash was more than a little drunk, and he stayed at Panther's ranch where his bachelor party was held. The next day when we both made it home, all we did was lie around and rehydrate.

As I sit and have my hair and makeup done with my sisters and club sisters, everything seems to be going as planned. Olivia has a notebook, writing stuff down for—as she told me—her upcoming wedding. She is adorable and I think she and Teddy are beyond cute.

Mom walks up to me and sits next to me, grabbing my hands. I see both Onyx and Bray come over, along with Gertie. Mom looks at me with tears in her eyes.

"We know you might have covered this already, but we thought if not we could help out. Now I have your something new, so your father and I went into Bozeman for this. I know what your dress looks like and hopefully this will go with it. We are so happy for you, Brenna, as Ash is a good man. Dad and I wish you nothing but the best of everything."

She hands me a blue bag that has Onyx sighing. I open it after almost swallowing my tongue when I saw the name on the box. Inside is a gorgeous necklace. It is a beautiful flower made of all kinds of gems. I think the center is a solitaire diamond and around it for petals are soft colors. Then there are, I'm thinking, emeralds for leaves. It is surrounded by braided metal to hold it all together. It's beyond stunning. I put it down and grab Mom, hugging on her tightly.

Gertie is up next. She has a smaller box in her hands.

"These were my mother's. One of the few items I was

able to hide so they didn't disappear. They can be your something old."

I flip open the wooden jewelry box to see beautiful diamond earrings. The top has a diamond stud that has a hanging teardrop off of it. They are breathtaking. I thank Gertie. Then my sisters make their way to me. Onyx has a bag and Bray has a smaller one. Surprisingly, Bray is the one who explains.

"Brenna, we are responsible for something borrowed and something blue. So, this is from the both of us. This is your something blue."

She hands me the smaller bag. When I look in, I laugh loudly. Pulling out a blue garter belt with very tiny flowers all around it, I think it's perfect. Then Onyx pushes the larger bag toward me.

"Here's your something borrowed. Don't argue with me."

I lean over and look down to see a shoe box in the linen bag. And not any box but one that says Christian Louboutin. My mouth falls open as Bray giggles. Yeah giggles. That tells me her therapy sessions are helping her if she can let loose like that after what she went through.

"Brenna, I bought those a few years ago because they were so pretty and for some reason, they reminded me of you. I wore them once then put them in the back of my closet. I hope you like them."

Carefully, I pull the box out and lift the top. Removing the red ribbon off the box, I then pull two red bags out with a smaller red bag. Pulling the soft tissue paper apart, I gasp at what I see. Inside are the most beautiful heels I've ever seen. Thank God I've been practicing with the ones I bought, otherwise, I wouldn't be able to walk in these. I turn the box and see the name of the heels are Flora. I'm blown away then something pops in my mind.

"Oh my God, Onyx, I can't wear these. How much did they cost? And what are the red bags for?"

Onyx smiles then moves closer to me.

"First, Brenna, the two bags are dust bags for storage. The smaller red bag is heel replacement in case you need to replace them. Finally, don't worry about how much they cost. I'm not giving them to you, just lending, remember? Now let's get you ready so Ash's jaw drops when he sees you."

The rest of the morning is spent on all the beauty stuff that I guess every bride goes through. Since we are at our house, Gertie and Mom have been in charge of all the food and beverages. The mimosas were running freely and little Olivia had her own kiddy cocktail that she is enjoying thoroughly. The morning passes quickly with lots of laughs between us all. As the time gets closer the calmer I become. Mom and Gertie help me into my dress, which is perfect. It is well-fitted on the top, with subtle crystals on it that go down to the skirt that gently flares out. The skirt has an overlay of colored flowers, which I fell in love with. My mom not so much, but since that was the one I wanted, she didn't say much. Now after being zipped and buttoned in, I slowly turn with my hair down off to the side, curled with the accessories in it. When I look at Mom she is smiling and crying. Gertie too.

"Hey, none of that, I can't mess up this makeup, I'll look like Frankenstein. Now we need to get a move on, time's a wasting. Time for me to become Mrs. Ashton Sterling."

Both moms give me a brief hug then we make our way to the great room to see all the girls ready and waiting. I told everyone to pick whatever they wanted. I wanted it to look like a rainbow and it sure does. Everyone looks stunning then I look at Shadow and my mouth drops. She is in a simple, lemon-yellow A-line dress with a soft overlay of a shimmery rainbow fabric. Simple and beautiful. Her long hair is loosely braided, probably done by Panther, and soft curls are around her face. I know how hard that is for her so I hope my smile shows her how much it means to me.

We make our way outside to see the carriage with Warrior all cleaned up with his tail braided. Behind it is the huge wagon that has been cleaned. Since we are going to my field, we have to either go in golf carts—not —or take the carriage and wagons. This was my choice. My brothers and Ash are waiting to help us then they will jump in the golf carts. Once everyone is settled, we start on our way to the field of flowers.

As we get closer, there are battery operated candles all over with the fairy lights. It's perfect. I can see people sitting in the seats and the arch looks beyond gorgeous. When we finally arrive, I don't see Ash anywhere. Shadow comes up to me asking a few questions about the service then she goes up front. Everyone starts to take their places so I finally get down with Ollie's help. Well, he grabs me around the waist and lifts me out of the carriage as Orin and Bennett make sure my train stays up for the time being. I know having it out here in nature there might be some grass or mud on the train of the dress, but that's okay. I hear music so that tells me we are starting up. I'm far enough back I don't see the arch or Ash yet.

One by one, everyone in the wedding party makes their way down with their partners. That is, after first Joshua walks down with my little niece. Then Teddy and Olivia go down as junior bridesmaid and groomsman. Finally, it's just my dad and me. He's looking at me with such happiness on his face, I feel the emotions but push them down.

"You ready, Brenna? And, Daughter, you look beautiful. Thank Christ you got your mother's looks 'cause if you got this mug, it wouldn't look half as good with that gown. Now I think there's a young man who's probably going nuts. Ready to get this show on the road?"

Laughing, I nod. He offers his arm and I place mine in his. There are huge steppingstones so I don't have to worry about my fancy heels going into the mud. When we get ready to go down the aisle, everyone stands. Dad and I start to walk down the thick white runner when I look up and suddenly stop. Ash is at the end of the aisle looking beyond handsome. He's in a dark pinstripe gray tailored suit, with a crisp white dress shirt and a flowered tie. Yeah, flowered. And brand-new boots with his dress Stetson on his head. Damn, he is fine. Everyone is waiting when I lean into Dad and whisper. He starts chuckling as we begin fast walking toward the front. When we are almost there, I let Dad go, pick up my skirt with one hand, while hanging on to my bouquet in the other. Then I kind of jog-run down the aisle until I reach Ash, who immediately pulls me close. When he leans down, I raise my head so our lips touch. Right at this moment, I know this is the beginning of the rest of my life. And no matter what, as long as we are together, we can get through anything.

Well, that is until I hear that voice telling me we aren't supposed to kiss until she tells us to. *Leave it to Shadow,* I think to myself as Ash and I separate and turn so we can finally get married. Time to finally start the life we were always supposed to have. Just the two of us, together forever.

* * *

Want more Raven and Ash?
Go to https://dl.bookfunnel.com/pirmxw5gze *to download a bonus epilogue.*

* * *

Check out the sneak peek of Wildcat Book #8 on the next page.

WILDCAT, SNEAK PEEK

'WILDCAT'
Frankie

My God, my club sisters are dropping like flies. Never thought I'd see the women I admire and call my *chosen family* manage to find men who fit their personalities to a T.

These are the thoughts running through my mind as I've just watched Raven say her I dos to her high school sweetheart, Ash. Never would I have thought our hilarious technology nerd would have fallen for a Montana cowboy, though it makes sense. Raven grew up in Timber-Ghost and her entire family is now back here in town, well, all around it. Watching them exchange their vows and kiss, it brings back memories I've tried to keep at the back of my mind. Fuck, don't need that shit to surface now. Our club has had enough drama to last us all for the rest of our lives. Damn, between Tink,

Shadow, Taz, Vixen, Glory, and now Raven, we need a damn break.

Hearing everyone clapping, I put my hands together to join the crowd as we celebrate our friend's happy time. Looking around, can't believe how we've become such a close-knit community because, at one time, no one wanted the Devil's Handmaidens MC anywhere near Timber-Ghost. Over the years Tink and our club have proven ourselves to the townsfolk. As we all make our way to take a few pictures I feel someone plow into me from the back. When I turn around, our enforcer has a shit-eating grin on her face. And my God, to see her in a dress blows my mind.

"So you up next there, Wildcat? Let's see if you can live up to your club name. Some dude would be lucky to have you, sister."

Laughing, I ignore her comment. Little does she know been there, done that. Just that brief thought brings an overwhelming sadness to my heart. I can't change my decisions, even if I wanted too. Life goes on and, unfortunately for me, mine is moving along in Montana and not New York. I do reach out to my family occasionally, though they have no idea where I'm at. That can't be shared or I'll be bringing a shit ton of trouble to our neck of the woods. Both good and bad. Especially if my location gets out to Malcom, he'll lose his ever-loving mind. And I don't want to add to any more pain or sorrow to him, I've done enough.

* * *

Today has been a great day and also a day of difficult

to remember memories for me. Thank God I have one of the cabins behind Tink's huge ranch home because tonight I need some quiet and alone time. After I remove my colorful dress and shoes, I get in some comfortable lounge clothes. I grab a huge bottle of water since I did some drinking at the reception that was held here at the ranch. And got to say, Heartbreaker did a phenomenal job on getting it all together. It was beyond breathtaking with all the wildflowers Raven loves.

I walk to the bedroom, open the closet, and move stuff around to grab the Rubbermaid that holds my entire life before the Devil's Handmaidens. I drag it to the couch and sit down, pulling the lid off. The memories hit me so hard I have to lean back and take a few breaths. Damn, maybe tonight isn't the right time to go through all of this stuff. Last time I spoke to my mom she told me everyone was doing well and happy. That was all I ever wanted for everyone back home. Taking a deep breath, I lean forward and start to pull shit out and place it on the table in front of the couch. When everything is out, I push the bin over and start to go through it slowly. Pictures of my parents and siblings bring a few tears to my eyes. I gulp some water down as the pictures start to show me growing up, and at the first one with both Malcom and me in it, my eyes let loose. It was our freshman dance and the first one we'd ever gone to, but definitely not our last.

Looking at his handsome face never gets old. Even though he was young he was a big kid. By freshman year he was well over six-foot tall and would grow another couple of inches before he reached his adult height. His caramel skin was beyond gorgeous, especially with his multi-faceted eye color. They were a mixed of gray, green, and blue. Depending on what he wore, his eye color changed.

Moving stuff around, I see a couple of the pictures I want and grab them. Leaning back with the photos in one hand and my water bottle in the other, I drink more water before replacing the cap and putting it on the couch. I start to go through the small stack of pictures as memories flood my brain. My God, we were so young and naïve. Each dance photo shows how much we were growing up, but the look in both of our eyes never changed. Well, it did, we fell more and more in love. That love went from a kid's love to an adult one. When Malcom went down on a knee when I was in my first year of college, my entire family was in on it.

We were doing our usual morning routine of jogging through Central Park. As we turned to head back to our apartment, Malcom came to an abrupt stop by one of the waterfalls and grabbed my hands. Both of us sweating and kind of out of breath, I didn't know if something was wrong with him or not. Then I heard the music coming toward us. When I turned, both of our families were making their way to us, my baby brother with his iPad and speaker in his hands. The song "At Last" by Etta James was playing and it sent shivers down my spine. When I turned back to my man, he was on one knee in front of me, a jewelry box in his hand. My eyes literally popped outta my head. We talked about this and wanted to wait until I finished college with my Bachelor of Science in Criminal Justice Administration, and Malcom finished medical school and got into his residence program. His beautiful gray blue-green eyes were glittering as they looked right into my grayish-hazel eyes. This had been my dream since we first met and even though it was before I thought he'd ask, my heart was pounding as my mind started to dream of our future together.

When Malcom asked I didn't even let him finish. I jumped him as our families all laughed and cheered. The ring was perfect; it was a solitaire with our birthstones on either side. So on the left was an opal for my October birthday and on the right was a peridot to match Malcom's August birthday. The band was thick so none of the stones stood out. He thought of everything because he knew I'd never want to take the ring off, and if I became a cop I couldn't have a huge stone sticking out of the setting.

The next couple of months went by in a blur. I planned with my mom, sisters, Malcom's mom, aunt, and sister. Everything was so easy it just amazed all of us. In the meantime, I graduated summa cum laude from college with my degree and immediately was accepted into the police academy. Malcom was headed off to medical school, which meant our time was going to be very limited so we decided to take a short trip to Bear Mountain State Park, one of our favorite places. Both of our parents surprised us with a cabin rental. So off we went, naïve and stupid as fuck. Two young kids off for a short week away before their lives got crazy. Little did we know how that short trip would change our lives.

The cabin was quaint and rustic but gorgeous. It had everything we needed. One bedroom and bath, a small kitchenette, and a living room. Outside a front porch with a barbecue and farther out a firepit the view overlooking a body of water down the mountain from where we were staying. The next cabin was at least a half-acre or more away and not even sure it was rented at the time we were there. The first couple of days were beyond fabulous. We hiked, swam, and just spent quality time together. On the third or fourth morning as we were sitting on the front porch when two hikers approached, calling out.

Malcom immediately was his friendly self but something about the two men was off to me. I walked back into our cabin and grabbed the small handgun my dad always told me to carry, no matter what. This was an argument that Malcom and I had. He hated guns and didn't want me to carry, which was crazy I was going to be a cop, for God's sake. I also grabbed my mace, putting that in the pocket of my jacket, and the gun in the holster in the back of my jeans.

I made my way back outside and the two men were now sitting on the stairs of the front porch. Malcom looked my way and I could see his concern about these unexpected visitors. They started to ask some personal questions like if we were out there alone and if we had a few bucks we could loan them. Malcom came closer to me and told them our parents had run to get some groceries but would be back shortly, and we were expecting more of our family to arrive later in the day. They looked at each other before looking back at us. The look they gave to us was dangerous and we both felt it. I knew they were going to try and change the path our lives were on.

Malcom took a chance, pushing me back into the cabin, telling me to lock the door. I could hear the struggle outside as I grabbed for my cell phone and the satellite phone Malcom's dad insisted we bring with. The cell had no reception but the satellite immediately started up and I dialed 911. When the call connected, I calmly told the operator in a whisper our names and what was going on and where we were. She told me to stay on the line as she called the park's rangers. Also she put a call out to any available officers close to the park. Just as I started to give a description, I heard Malcom scream out in pain.

"Frankie, stay inside where you are safe. I know it's hard but going out there puts not only your fiancé in more danger but also yourself. Stay put."

"I can't. He's in a lot of pain and I can't just stand around. I'll put the satellite phone in the back of the bookcase so you can listen in as much as you can. Will leave the door open too. Thank you for all you do and for helping us."

"No, damn it, Frankie, don't, stay with me."

Once again in a whisper I thanked her and hid the phone. With the gun in my hand and the mace in my pocket, I made my way to the window first. What I saw I'll never forget. The two men were trying to hang Malcom off a tree by the edge of the mountain. He was fighting like crazy though he was already injured by the amount of blood on him. I took a breath and opened the door slowly.

"Get away from him now, you dicks. Let him go."

Both men turned and looked my way. That's when I heard the words that did change my life.

"No, Frankie, go back in. There's more than these two asswipes. Watch yourself."

I heard him before I saw him. Off to my right, I turned, aimed in that direction, and when a huge man appeared, I shot, hitting him center mass. He immediately fell backward hard, on to the ground off the deck. I could hear boots hitting the ground as I turned and before I could shoot, one of the men was right in front of me, hitting my gun hand. The gun went flying as he tackled me back through the cabin door. His weight sent me to the floor and I lost my breath. By the time I could think, since I banged my head on the wood floor, the other guy was also inside. He slammed the door as he came toward me.

"Bitch, you're gonna pay for what you just did to Buck. He's got kids, you whore."

The first punch took me by surprise but by the seventh or eighth I prayed I'd pass out before they took their party to the next level. Right before my mind went blank, I heard my clothes being ripped from my body.

Last thought before I lost consciousness, I prayed Malcom was okay.

Wiping my face, I reach for my water as I've had enough reminiscing. Finishing off the bottom, I push the photos to the side and stand up, going to the kitchen. I open the refrigerator and grab the open bottle of wine. Opening the cabinet off to the side, I pull a wine glass out and fill it. I sit at the kitchen table and suck back wine until my hand stops shaking. Not sure why, I pull my phone out and look up contacts. When I see his name, I hit the contact and wait. When the voicemail kicks in, I listen to his sexy deep voice

"Hi, you reached, Mal. I'm not available so at the beep leave your name, number, and whatcha want. I'll try to get back to you as soon as I can. And if this is Frankie, nothing has changed, please get in touch with me. Nothing was your fault. I miss your face beautiful."

The beep sounds and I look at my cell and hit disconnect. Then I finish my glass of wine, grab the bottle, and chug the rest of it, then I lose it, sobbing at the table like I lost my best friend, because I actually did. That life is gone forever.

ABOUT THE AUTHOR

USA Today Bestselling author, D. M. Earl creates authentic and genuine characters while spinning stories that feel so real and relatable that the readers plunge deep within the plot, begging for more. Complete with drama, angst, romance, and passion, the stories jump off the page.

When Earl, an avid reader since childhood, isn't at her keyboard pouring her heart into her work, you'll find her in Northwest Indiana snuggling up to her husband, the love of her life, with her seven fur babies nearby. Her other passions include gardening and shockingly cruising around town on the back of her 2004 Harley. She's a woman of many talents and interests. Earl appreciates each and every reader who has ever given her a chance--and hopes to connect on social media with all of her readers.

Contact D.M at DM@DMEARL.COM
Website: http://www.dmearl.com/

- facebook.com/DMEarlAuthorIndie
- x.com/dmearl
- instagram.com/dmearl14
- amazon.com/D-M-Earl/e/B00M2HB12U
- bookbub.com/authors/d-m-earl
- goodreads.com/dmearl
- pinterest.com/dauthor

ALSO BY D.M. EARL

DEVIL'S HANDMAIDENS MC SPINOFF

Running Wild

Running Alone

DEVIL'S HANDMAIDENS MC: TIMBER-GHOST, MONTANA CHAPTER

Tink (Book #1)

Shadow (Book #2)

Taz (Book #3)

Vixen (Book #4)

Glory (Book #5)

Raven (Book #6)

Wildcat (Book #7)

GRIMM WOLVES MC SERIES

Behemoth (Book 1)

Bottom of the Chains-Prospect (Book 2)

Santa...Nope The Grimm Wolves (Book 3)

Keeping Secrets-Prospect (Book 4)

A Tormented Man's Soul: Part One (Book 5)

Triad Resumption: Part Two (Book 6)

Fractured Hearts - Prospect (Book 7)

WHEELS & HOGS SERIES

Connelly's Horde (Book 1)

Cadence Reflection (Book 2)

Gabriel's Treasure (Book 3)

Holidays with the Horde (Book 4)

My Sugar (Book 5)

Daisy's Darkness (Book 6)

THE JOURNALS TRILOGY

Anguish (Book 1)

Vengeance (Book 2)

Awakening (Book 3)

Printed in Great Britain
by Amazon